BEN DOLNICK

Zoology

HARPER PERENNIAL

London, New York, Toronto, Sydney and New Delhi

Harper Perennial
An imprint of HarperCollins*Publishers*
77–85 Fulham Palace Road, Hammersmith, London W6 8JB

www.harperperennial.co.uk
Visit our authors' blog at www.fifthestate.co.uk

This Harper Perennial edition published 2008
1

First published in Great Britain by Harper*Press* in 2007

Copyright © Ben Dolnick 2007

PS Section copyright © Rose Gaete 2008, except 'Top Ten Favourite Books', 'A Day
in the Life of Ben Dolnick', 'How I Wrote *Zoology*' and 'Behind the Scenes'
by Ben Dolnick © Ben Dolnick 2008

PS™ is a trademark of HarperCollins*Publishers* Ltd

Ben Dolnick asserts the moral right
to be identified as the author of this work

A catalogue record for this book is available from the British Library

ISBN-13 978-0-00-725039-4

Set in Garamond and Cochin by Palimpsest Book Production Limited,
Grangemouth, Stirlingshire

Printed and bound in Great Britain by Clays Ltd, St Ives plc

Mixed Sources
Product group from well-managed
forests and other controlled sources
www.fsc.org Cert no. SW-COC-1806
© 1996 Forest Stewardship Council

FSC

FSC is a non-profit international organisation established to promote the
responsible management of the world's forests. Products carrying the FSC
label are independently certified to assure consumers that they come
from forests that are managed to meet the social, economic and
ecological needs of present and future generations.

Find out more about HarperCollins and the environment at
www.harpercollins.co.uk/green

*For my family
and
for Elyse*

Home

This book is about last summer. I'll start before David saved me, though, when I was still living at home. I should have been in school, or in an apartment of my own, or teaching English in a village somewhere with noisy outdoor markets and old women who walked bent under piles of horsehair blankets. Instead I was in Chevy Chase. I slept every night under the same green baseball sheets I'd been sleeping under my entire life, the furnace clanking and chugging behind its door, and woke up every morning to Olive whining to be let in.

I'd started a semester at American—just a twelve-minute drive from home—and I'd been getting three Ds and a C. I kept thinking that someone would warn me if I was really getting myself into trouble, and then they did. When I got home for Thanksgiving Mom handed me a skinny envelope with the AU stamp. There was a letter inside from Dean Popkin telling me to take some time off and come back as a freshman next fall. He'd signed it, *Have a restful year.*

"Henry," Mom said, reading over my shoulder, "is this a joke?" She sounded like it really might be.

Dad said, "Well, you know what? You may just not be a scholar. There's no shame in that—or else I should be ashamed myself. Fall comes around again, we'll see if you're ready to give it another go. But in the meantime, this is not just going to be time to loaf. Let's get you to work."

So every morning, for all those months at home, I walked with Dad the five minutes up Cumberland to Somerset, my old elementary school. It was like working in a Museum of Me. Here were these same yellow hallways with their same sour-mop smell, and the library with the hard orange carpet and wooden boxes of golf pencils, and the brown tile bathrooms with their squeaking sinks and empty paper towel machines.

And here was Principal Morrow with his pink head and wobbly walk. And mean, round Mrs. Kenner, who used to always say, "Do I come into your living room and put my feet up on the sofa?" (I used to picture her living in our classroom, reading *The Book of Knowledge* at her desk, making her dinner at the sink where we rinsed the paintbrushes.) And looking small and pale now, here was Mr. Lebby, who had lost half of his left ring finger in a woodshop accident as a kid. He was the only teacher I ever had who picked me out as a favorite—when I was in fifth grade we used to stand around by the coat hooks during recess and talk about the Bullets, my opinions all stolen from Dad and so more important to me than if they'd been mine. The first time he saw me back, standing by the water fountain on the second floor, we had a fumbly hug and then he stood there with wet eyes saying, "Well." But after that what could he really do? By January he and everyone else I used to know just nodded at me in the halls. I peed in the urinals that came up to my knees, and pledged allegiance along with thirty droning voices, and, in a trance of boredom between classes, I held a piece of paper over an air vent to make it float like a magic carpet.

I ate the cafeteria food for lunch. Holding a maroon ADMIT ONE ticket that could have come off the roll I kept in my desk in third grade, I'd wait in line, having to work not to feel like part of the nervous elementary school nuttiness around me. Seventy-pound boys would prowl, making tough faces, looking to butt or back-butt, and four-foot girls with headbands—they could have been the same girls I'd gone to school with—would either let them in, quiet lawbreakers, or else raise their hands for the lunchroom monitor.

When I was a student there, Mrs. Moore, the gray-toothed lunch lady, would Magic Marker a symbol on the back of one Styrofoam tray each holiday—a heart on Valentine's Day, a clover on St. Patrick's Day, a pumpkin on Halloween—and in the second before you turned your tray over your brain would go quiet. You got to go first in line the next day if you got the marked tray, I think, but the point was the feeling: The whole day turned into a lottery when you knew one of those trays was out there. But Mrs. Moore died of lung cancer when I was in eighth grade (Dad brought home a newsletter with a smiling picture of her on the back, over *1932–1997*), and the trays they used now were made of hard brown plastic.

I'd eat the chicken pot pies and tuna melts and square pizzas in the art room, looking out at the kids stampeding around the basketball court, feeling a combination of sleepiness and hopelessness and boredom as particular to school as the smell of uncapped markers. New teachers would sometimes come sit with me, hoping to talk about apartments or what college I'd gone to, but eventually word seemed to get out that I wasn't really one of them. I'd gotten lost in my life, I kept thinking, and now here—like someone lost in the woods—I'd walked right back to where I'd started.

Between classes, when I didn't want to sit with Dad in the teachers' lounge, I'd wander. That dark little staircase between Mrs. Rivini's room and the computer room, where I once saw Teddy Montel kiss Sarah Sylver, dipping her like they were dancing. The Sharing and Caring room, with its posters covered in crinkly plastic and its taped-up beanbag chairs and its boxes and boxes of tissues. I'd run into Mr. Bale, the black turtle-looking janitor who once was in a commercial for the D.C. Lottery, and every time he saw me, every single time, he'd laugh and shake his head.

Dad taught six classes a day, forty-four minutes each, and I was his assistant. The kids called me Mr. Henry, so we'd know they weren't talking to Dad, and it seems now like most of what I did for those five months was set up the xylophones. I can smell the spray we used to clean them if I picture pulling them out of the closet, the dark one the size of an oven, the little metal ones with corners that cut my hands, the long ones that made nice plunking sounds when the bars fell off. And all those classes of kids, Rachel and Lauren and Andy and Peter, with high voices and clean floppy hair and scrapes on their knees, always crying for reasons too painful for them to explain, and raising their hands to tell me their mallets didn't work, and lining up for bathroom breaks. And the foreign kids, Gabor and Amir and Evelina and Nico. Dad used a special slow voice when he talked to them, and usually they were the strangest, quietest kids in the room, full of bizarre stories and languages that came out, when their brothers or parents finally picked them up at the end of the day, like the babble of people who've been possessed. (But they're *all* foreign kids, I'd sometimes think—every one of them got to the world less than a decade ago.)

Dad seemed older when he was teaching than he did any other time, sitting on his tall stool with his elbows on his knees, treating every class like they ought to think about dropping out of school to concentrate full-time on their music. "If anybody wants to come in and play during recess, lunch, or after school, tell me and I'll stick around as long as you feel like staying. I see a lot of talent here, a scary amount of talent."

When I had him—when I was one of the little kids who loved shouting "Boo!" during the Halloween song—every music class was such a joy that all my weeks would aim straight for those Thursday mornings, the way other kids' weeks aimed for Friday afternoons. Having him was like being the son of an actor or a politician, but even more electric because I wasn't allowed to act like I was his son. I'd sit cross-legged on my mat, grinning, stuffed with secret power. At the end of the period I'd rush up to the front and stand there owning him while he packed away his music. From the piano bench now, though, I saw him the way the rest of the kids must have: an old man with huge glasses and gray hair and a loose belly who didn't seem to really listen to the questions people asked him.

Walking home in the afternoon, getting waved across Dorset by a crossing guard with a bright orange belt, he'd say, "You're a hell of a sport, listening to this rinky-dink stuff all day. You're going to put in some work, and people one day are going to be bragging you were their teacher."

Mom was less sure. Whenever Dad called me a musician, she looked down and starting paying angry attention to whatever she was doing. We sent little signals of hate and stubbornness to each other whenever she walked past me watching TV, or napping on the couch, or doing anything that wasn't pretending to plan on going back to college. Before she went up to bed to read each night, she'd put a hand on my shoulder, tired from all the quiet fighting, and almost say something but then not.

My leaving school was only the latest thing to disappoint her, the easiest thing to put a name to. She's always been dreamy, private, a little fed up with everyone she knows. She'll sometimes let bits of complaints slip—"How long has your father lived here and he still doesn't know where the can opener goes?" "If Uncle Walter doesn't want to be alone, then he should *do* something about it"—but they just feel like spoonfuls from a bath. She doesn't belong on the East Coast, she's not interested in the women in Chevy Chase, she feels cheated that she's fifty and all she's done is raise children (and furious when she senses someone thinking that all she's done is raise children). She has dark tea bags under her eyes, and for three, four hours a day she'll sit in her blue chair and read the *Post,* looking disappointed. When she's reading about politics she talks to the paper—"Unexpected by you, maybe," "Oh, ho, ho, you are an *idiot*"—but if you ask her what she means she doesn't answer. She clips her favorite "Doonesbury"'s and uses them as bookmarks.

When she was twenty-one she took a bus from San Francisco to D.C. for a protest. She got arrested and put in the Redskins stadium for the night with thousands of other people, and sitting next to her on the field were four loud-mouthed friends with beards and sweaters. They were in a jazz band, they told her, and the shortest, shyest one—the one who laughed like he had to think about it, who offered her his coat when she started to fall asleep—was Dad. She stayed in their house after they got out, and Dad convinced her to come on tour for a couple of months. She'd been looking for a reason not to go home.

She spent almost a year driving with them to clubs in Manhattan, Philadelphia, Delaware, even a few in Miami, only sleeping in the D.C. house a couple of nights a week. "I felt like an outlaw," she says now, "sitting around smoky bars at three in the morning. It was divine." But when the bassist quit to get married, Mom decided to go to nursing school. She loved doctors' offices, loved medicine, loved the idea of spending her days so busy and helpful and serious. But at the end of her first year she got pregnant with David, and that summer, after explaining to everyone she knew how women went through nursing school pregnant all the time, she dropped out. (She still has her medical books in a box downstairs, though, all of them heavy and covered in furry dust. When I was in fifth grade I used to sneak down to read the part in *Human Biology* on orgasms—". . . a series of involuntary muscular contractions followed by . . ."—and I'd go back up feeling as if I'd been downstairs with a prostitute.)

Dad had been managing a sheet music store in Georgetown while she was in school, and a few years after she dropped out he got a job teaching music to seventh graders in Gaithersburg. At night, instead of practicing, he'd stay up working on his lesson plans. "Those who can, do," he likes to say. "I don't kid myself about it." Sometimes he actually sounds sad when he says it, but usually he sounds like he's just trying to be modest, and hoping you'll realize he's just trying to be modest. Mom says—and you can see Dad wince whenever she says it—that she knew he'd teach for the rest of his life the minute he came home from his first day in the classroom. "You certainly don't do it as a get-rich-quick scheme," he says, but the truth is he doesn't need a get-rich-quick scheme. When he and Mom were in their thirties, just before I was born, they inherited a lot of money from Dad's parents. Mom, still good with a thermometer, still quick with cool washcloths, never got back to work.

In the pictures from when she was in her twenties she's smiling, sitting on a porch I don't recognize holding a cigarette, or standing in front of a mirror with Dad's sax around her neck, looking like a girl who might make me nervous. Her hair was still all brown then and her skin didn't hang and she liked to wear long, silvery earrings. Sometimes she sang with Dad's band. When I was little, before she was sad or maybe just before I realized she was sad, she used to sit on the edge of the rocking chair next to my bed and lean over me, singing in her whisperiest voice.

But now her happiest moments, or at least the ones she cared most about, came on Sunday nights when David would call from New York. She'd be ready with questions about a new show at the Whitney, or a new Spanish restaurant in Soho. "Will you get the phone?" she'd say, not moving. "Will you please get the phone? Someone *get . . . that . . . phone*! God *damn* it." On the *damn* she'd clap her hands and stand up. Once she'd convinced herself that at least one Elinsky had lived well that week, she'd hand me the phone, still hot from her ear. After a minute he'd say, "I'm beat, man, I've got to get to bed. I got up at five this morning, and then tonight we went twelve innings. Completely fucking braindead ump. My guys were getting reamed out there."

My brother, a resident in dermatology, lived with his girlfriend, Lucy, in her parents' apartment on Fifth Avenue. Her parents weren't there, though—they lived in a house with a fountain in Connecticut and only came to the city for birthdays and operas. Lucy has a doughy face that gets flushed after half a glass of wine or a few minutes without air-conditioning, and a long, pale body she likes to show off. She's a painter, but I don't think she's ever sold a painting to anyone who isn't related to her or a close friend. Her parents put together a show for her in their house once—David sent us the catalog—and the paintings all had names like *Never/Always* and *Music for Trilobites*. *Never/Always* is about September 11, David says, and it's just a long red line on an all-blue canvas. When David first started dating her he really was doing all the things Mom wished he was—on weekends he took cooking classes and went for walks through the Met—and he bought two of Lucy's paintings to hang above his bed. When my parents talked about her, before David moved into her apartment, Dad just called her "the artist." He said it teasingly, pretending not to have learned her name, and so Mom, for reasons having as much to do with Dad as with Lucy, started saying it respectfully, the way you'd say "the judge" or "the senator."

She and David came home this year for a weekend at the beginning of June, and that's when David invited me to come to New York. Lucy brought gifts for both of my parents and me—they were just cubes of wood, a little bigger than sugar cubes, each side painted a different color. When Dad unwrapped his cube he tilted his head back to look through the reading half of his lenses and said, "Wow," each time he turned it. She'd forgotten that Walter lived with us, so she rushed out to the car and came back with a blank cube, and while we talked on the front porch she sat there painting it with her "travel set," as careful as a Christmas elf.

OK, I've never liked her. And not just because she's

pretty enough to make my mouth dry or because David gets to have sex with her every night, but those things certainly don't help. I try not to think very much about how many girl-friends I've had, but: one. Two if you count Lisa Gabardine. David's life didn't used to be like this—sharing slices of cake after dinner, picking out necklaces for Valentine's Day, going to bed-and-breakfasts in Pennsylvania with hot tubs on the porch. On Friday nights when he was in high school he'd take me to the movies and we'd have to sit in the back of the theater so nobody in his grade would see him. He hid a stack of greasy *Penthouse*s underneath his rock collection. At night he closed his door and made radio shows on his stereo—I'd hear him through the wall trying to sound booming. He met Lucy at a gallery opening just after he moved to New York, and she was only his second serious girlfriend. She'd turned him into the kind of guy who owns shoes for every occa-sion. When he's eating she'll lean over and wipe the corner of his mouth, and he just keeps on talking.

During dinner out at the table on the patio she sat making a face like she was straining not to look at her watch. She only perked up when Dad asked about the paintings she'd been doing lately, forests full of trees with shiny black leaves. "I don't really know what they're 'about,'" she said, "in the sense of if I were writing a paper or something. I just want them to . . . well, capture what I saw, I guess. David and I were on the train up to Connecticut—did he tell you this already?—and we passed a graveyard behind some woods, and after that I just kept thinking about those dead people climbing up through the roots." Dad—who'd said, "Well, they aren't how I'd paint it," the first time he'd seen Lucy's catalog—turned to me now and thumped the table. "You see?" he said. "That's art. Taking life and turning it inside out. I love it." I'd put on too much bug spray before we went out, and besides my lips being numb, every bite I took had a dark green hint of poison.

After dinner Dad handed each of us a DoveBar (Olive barked and leaped up for Lucy's), and while Mom and Dad tried to get her inside, and while Walter stood by the fence and looked sad, David said to me, "Lucy and I have a proposition for you." He squeezed my shoulder. "Move in with us. Come live in our second bedroom for a little."

"Even just a month or two, we're thinking, could be really fun," Lucy said.

"I can't stand thinking of you here losing your mind." And then quietly, "Doesn't being here just depress you?"

My throat filled with tear-snot, my heart ached and seemed to lean out of my chest—it was as if David had yanked away a sheet and shown me, for the first time, the real wreck of my year.

"Could I come next week?"

"Of course," he said.

"Tomorrow?"

He laughed and said the job he had in mind for me—he knew someone at the Central Park Zoo—wouldn't be able to start for a few weeks. I said thank-you so many times that he finally said, "I get it. You're welcome. Shut up."

Now that I knew I wouldn't have to put up with them, the hundred little shames of home felt unbearable. Having to answer, again and again, "Oh, just taking some time off right now." And all the Sundays when the sun would set and I'd realize that I hadn't even put pants on. Or the lunches that summer when Uncle Walter and I would sit together not talking at the kitchen table and even he'd seem worried for me. Lately he'd been knocking on my door some evenings (did he wait for the sound of my bed creaking?) to ask if I felt like coming downstairs to talk. And when I said OK, when I pulled up my pants and gritted my teeth and stomped down to the living room, he wouldn't even have anything to say, he just liked having me around.

Walter has never gotten married, and he's never had a real job, so when I was ten he came to live in our basement bedroom. It was first going to be for a month, then for a year, and then we all stopped talking about it. He makes his bed every morning, drinks tea that tastes like hot water, keeps his five shirts folded and clean. His room looks like a hotel room between guests. He inherited just as much money as Dad did when my grandparents died, so even without a job he could live in a place of his own, but Walter alone is too depressing to think about. He's a balder, skinnier, sadder version of Dad—a failure who thinks, or pretends to think, that he's chosen this life, that he's living out some principled decision too obvious to explain. Being cheap is part of it. On the wall of his shower he keeps dried strings of dental floss, used and waiting to be used again. His clothes all smell sweet like cigars, even though he's never smoked, and he's got a permanent squint, Dad says because of how much he used to read. When I was home I'd go up into the office where he works, since it was right next to my room, and if it was eleven in the morning or four in the afternoon, he'd be snoring in his chair. "Quit sneaking up on me," he'd say. "I can't get anything done when you're always poking your head in."

Dad once said that when they were growing up, everyone thought Walter was going to be either a senator or a surgeon, but for three years now he's been writing a self-help book. "He'll be his own best customer," Mom likes to say. At least once a month Walter ends dinner in tears. He'll be talking, ordinary as can be, and then while he tries to get some word out his lip will start to shake. You hope at first it's just a twitch, but then he's looking down, and soon his eyes are red and full and he's gripping his fork too hard. Usually it's about being lonely, but just about anything can do it. How Olive never asks for anything from us, a sick kid he saw at Safeway, how lucky he is to be part of such an incredible family. The one topic that's always safe—the one topic guaranteed to cheer him up, even—is spine care. He's never had a mood so far gone that it can't be set right by someone saying, "See, even when I try standing with my head up like this, after a while my back starts hurting again right down here."

Within five seconds his eyes are dry and he's standing up slowly from the table, pushing you gently against the wall. "But of *course* your back hurts," he says. "You aren't changing how you hold your shoulders. Standing like that's an assault. Here. Now. Shoulders back. No, like this. Now try walking around like that." He'll sit down with a shy smile, and for a few minutes he'll be as proud as a kid after a talent show. When I was little he gave massages part-time at the Rockville Sport & Health Club. Even now, fifteen years after he gave his last professional massage, at any moment during the day he might appear behind me and start kneading my shoulders.

Before I'd finished my DoveBar, I'd already moved in with David. I'd keep my saxophone in the corner, and I'd practice every night, do theory exercises on the subway. Whenever I learned a new song, I'd come out and play it for David and Lucy and any neighbors who were over having cocktails. I'd knock packs of cigarettes against my palm outside of bars and get drunk on drinks with real mint in them. David and I would go for walks at night and we'd talk strategy for his team, whether they should maybe move this guy to cleanup and that guy out to center field. I'd start getting gigs and David would take the drums back up and someone, some fan or writer, years from now, would say, "And it never would have happened at all if Henry hadn't failed out of school."

* * *

When I told Dad that I was moving he took off his glasses and covered his eyes. You would have thought I'd told him Olive had died. But then he said, "You know what, that's great news. You're going to love New York. That's all I want, for my boys to be happy and together and for you to go give something an honest try. The kids'll miss you, but you're no music teacher, I know that. It's like making Larry Bird teach PE."

Mom hated the idea of me in New York, and for a few

days she just sulked whenever it came up. Finally, after Dad had been bugging her at dinner one night, she said, "If this was part of a plan for school then OK. But the fact that he flunks out and we *reward* him——"

"I'm not rewarding him," Dad said. "He's deciding to move, and we're not imprisoning him. Is that a *reward*?"

"Stop," she said. "You're being a shit and you know it." She turned to me, still carrying her anger at Dad. "We're not going to pay for you to have a year-round summer. That's not the deal."

"It *is* summer, for Christ's sake," Dad said, mostly to himself, and stood up from the table making more noise with his chair than he had to.

"Go to hell. Henry, promise me you're not blowing off school." So I promised, and I did the dishes while Mom looked mad at the TV and Dad and Walter finished their chess game from the night before. Olive stood wagging nervously next to me, sensing some change or just wondering if I'd hand her scraps.

The next morning I took my coin box to the bank and, while everyone behind me glanced at the clock and gave each other looks, I cashed it in for $143.56. With that I went shopping at the Banana Republic on Wisconsin—the air in the store is so fresh and leather-smelling that just walking in makes you feel more handsome. A pretty black saleswoman with a gap in her teeth came up to me at the mirror and said, "You look *good*. I think that shirt is *you*." So I got two of them, and I walked out feeling something I hadn't felt since I was about nine. It used to be that when I'd buy sneakers (at the Foot Locker in Mazza Gallerie, just across Western), I'd leave the store, laces tight, feeling strong and quick and full of new potential I couldn't quite get my mind around. On the walk home from Banana Republic I bobbled my shopping bag in one hand and gave happy little nods to every woman I passed.

That night Walter pulled me into the den and made me sit down on the couch next to him. It was after ten, and Mom and Dad were already in bed. He put his hot hand on top of mine. "Henry, you've been so unhappy for so long. Watching you's been very painful for me. I hope you understand the chance you're getting." He squeezed my hand. In certain moods his voice is much deeper than you'd expect it to be—a cello full of sad advice. "Don't take what your brother's offered lightly. Remember—for David's sake, but especially for Lucy's—that you've got to stay damn near invisible. If you throw a Q-tip out and miss, don't say, 'Oh, I'll pick it up tomorrow morning.' You've got to pick it up now, even if it's freezing cold and you're cozy in bed. And don't"—Were his eyebrows reaching out? Was his lower lip starting to shake? *Finish! Finish! Please finish!*—"don't let yourself get stuck in feeling blue. Just your expression lately, I was telling your father, it's felt like watching you give up." And now he'd infected me! To keep from crying I pretended to have just noticed Olive lying next to me. "We love you so, so much, kiddo. Your father wants for you to be happy more than he wants anything. I do too. I mean that." I stood up, feeling like I'd either been diagnosed with cancer or cured, and for a second, before I shook Walter off, he looked like he might kiss my hand.

* * *

Before I left I needed to break up with Wendy. It was something I'd known I had to do for months, but now I had a reason to do it. A reason better than not liking her. Wendy was the only person from high school that I still saw. She lived at home in Bethesda with her parents, just a ten-minute walk away, and—no matter how old we got, no matter how little encouragement I gave her—she'd always had a crush on me. Always since eighth grade, when she was a shy, pimply-foreheaded new girl from Long Island. She talked too loud and played with her toes in class. She asked me her very first week at school if I wanted to go see *Dr. Giggles* with her that Friday, and I lied that I couldn't because I had to go over to dinner at my grandfather's. I was lonely and embarrassed and I felt like she might be making fun of me in a way I wasn't following. But she wasn't. Later she found out I didn't have a grandfather, and for the rest of the year she followed me around saying that I had to make it up to her, teasing but serious.

I never made it up to her during high school, but in winter, after being home alone for a few months, I called her. The best part of my weeks at home, until then, would be going to pick up fajitas from Rio Grande, imagining while I waited for my food that it was an apartment full of friends I was going back to and not my parents and Walter. One Friday in December I'd gone to the bar in Adams Morgan where the kids from my dorm at American went, but I ended up standing by the bathroom the whole night talking to the little brother of a guy I didn't know, worrying that someone would ask me why I'd moved out. Suddenly Wendy—who I'd hugged at graduation and thought I might be saying good-bye to forever—seemed like my oldest friend.

And besides, I wasn't feeling especially choosy. I looked defeated and fat-faced to myself whenever I walked past a mirror, and the idea that Wendy might look at me and see someone completely different seemed too incredible not to test. I spent all of high school pretending to look through my bag when Wendy walked by, waiting for someone who looked like a girl from a music video to fall in love with me, and all I got out of it was a prom night with Abbey Budder asking if I'd mind having the limo drop her off at her friend's party. David says, and I think he's probably right, that girls are like boxing: You've got to stay in your weight class or you'll get flattened.

Wendy told me she was working part-time at a Starbucks downtown and the rest of the time she was acting, which meant taking acting classes at the Leland Rec Center. She'd deferred a year from the University of Wisconsin—she was hoping she'd have enough luck acting that she could stretch it into more than a year. I asked her when her next play was, and that was all it took. "You want to come? Seriously? It's kind of stupid, but I like my part. Sit in the front left so I can see you."

The play was about a jewel thief who falls in love with

one of the women he robs, just because of her jewels and the picture on her bedside table. The robber leaves her a note, and she falls in love with him too, just because of the note, and they start meeting up and breaking into people's houses together, and the woman's big, golf-loving husband never notices. At the end the jewel thief gets caught, and the woman can't stand to have her husband find out, so she testifies against the thief, but he still keeps writing her letters and sending her jewels even from jail. Wendy played one of the thief's last victims, and her only part was to come into her room, see that her things are gone, and say something to herself about how she bets her crook of a nephew did it.

I hadn't seen her act since *Chicago* in tenth grade, but based on this, and on her frizzy hair and (I'd forgotten) the twisted way she walked, I didn't think she was going to make it. Afterward I gave her a handful of flowers I'd chosen from the freezing fridge at the Giant next door. She hugged me so hard she knocked the wind out of me.

Once we'd been dating for a few weeks, she said, "Isn't it funny that we weren't even really friends in high school, and now *this*?" Another time, lying back on my chest, she said, "What if we moved to Las Vegas? Shut up! I'm serious! I could be the Vanna White in one of those magic shows, and you could do the music, write up all the different parts for everyone." I had to swallow when she said things like that, and pretty soon I'd stand up to get a glass of water. If you want to know how you really feel about someone, there aren't many quicker ways than having her lie on your chest and ask you to move to Las Vegas.

I decided I'd break up with her at her house. That way I'd be able to leave afterward and my parents wouldn't walk in and ask what all that crying was about. I went over for dinner and her dad met me at the front door with a bear hug. "Henry Elinsky." Just saying my name made Mr. Zlotnick smile. "Before we go in there, tell me what's new, what you've been doing."

"Oh, helping my dad. The same stuff. Just thinking what to do next."

"And what's it going to be? What's a young, talented guy do next? It's a great question. It's a question I wish I still got to ask myself. You spend every day thinking about what you're going to do, obsessing about what's going to come next, and pretty soon . . . well, you're fifty and you've got a daughter and a wife and a great guy coming over for dinner and that's that. It's a good life, though, a *great* life."

Sometimes I wondered if Wendy's dad had me confused with someone else. I'd give a halfway funny answer to a question and he'd laugh so hard, this high, terrifying yelp, that his wife would give him a look. Drunk at Wendy's cousin's wedding, he once asked me with a grin how long I was going to make him wait before I'd give his daughter one of these. He noogied my ribs until we'd both forgotten the question. He was rubbery, with curly black hair, and an older version of Wendy's pointy face.

We had turkey with potatoes for dinner. These potatoes were one more reason I was looking forward to being broken up with Wendy. The first time I ever ate dinner at the Zlotnicks', Sheila served them, and because I didn't know what to say and because I'd decided I wanted to lose my virginity to her daughter, I said, "These are great—I should tell my mom about them." Sheila jumped up and wrote the recipe on an index card in very careful handwriting, then put the card in an envelope and wrote, *For Carol—potatoes à la Moises* on the front. In the five months since, I'd never eaten a dinner there without those potatoes. And not only weren't they good to eat, but they actually *hurt* to eat. By the time I'd cleaned my plate, the back of my mouth would be stinging like I'd been sucking all night on pennies.

In front of her parents Wendy turned into a little girl, but she would always catch my eye and wink at me, or else put a hand on my leg under the table. "What did *you* do today, Mom? Is your knee feeling OK?" And then a big smile. And her mom, her scratchy-voiced, hairy-armed little mom, would say, "Thank you *so* much for asking! Well, my knee doesn't hurt as much. Not as much. It doesn't feel good, but I think these exercises may be starting to really work. Let's see what I did today. I went to physical therapy at ten, and that was hard, really excruciating today. And then I had to go to Sutton Place to talk to Carlos about the party on Sunday, and then . . . God, senior moment! Then I went over to Angie's and we had tea and talked about Susan's graduation—the most insane production I've ever seen in my life, and I have no idea how she's getting through it. And I think since then I've just been . . ." What kind of thrill does it give Wendy to rub my thigh while her mom goes on like this? Why? While her dad looks at Sheila hoping she'll shut up so I can start talking, and Sheila stares up at the ceiling trying to remember

what she did before she started cooking dinner, Wendy—
trying to remind me how wild she is, maybe?—teases me
about a hand job.

After dinner Wendy and I went to the basement. This was
what we always did after dinner, so we could make out and
watch TV. For the first few weeks we were together, I thought
this—watching David Letterman's monologue with Wendy
clinging to me in just her underwear—was a kind of simple,
animal happiness that might actually last. Slipping off her
shirt, unbuttoning her pants, even she could make my heart
speed up. Every once in a while her mom would open the
door at the top of the stairs ("Knock, knock!"), and we'd
have to jump under the blanket and stare at the screen. But
all this had started feeling like a trap sometime in May or
even April.

Before we sat down Wendy turned down the lights and
with one motion took off her shirt so she was only wearing
jeans and her blue bra. On the couch she started to kiss me,
but I turned my head.

"I want to talk," I said. "I don't know how happy I am
anymore."

"You're not happy?" She put a hand on my shoulder and
suddenly she really was the sweet girl she pretended to be
upstairs. I remembered her in tenth grade, turning red when
Mr. Vazquez made fun of her for not being able to roll
her Rs.

"I'm not happy with us," I said.

"Why not?"

"I don't know. I don't think it has anything to do with

you, but . . . I don't know, I just stopped wanting this. Something changed."

"When?"

"I don't know. A week? Two?"

"Two *weeks*?" I wasn't sure if she thought that was a lot or a little. "Let's talk about it," she said. "I want to figure out what's going on." There were goose bumps all over her chest.

"My brother asked me to move to New York, and I think I want to go. I told him I would. I think I want us to just be friends."

She was starting to cry a little, but less than I expected. "So just done. Like that. Your feelings just changed for no reason? Obviously there's something. What did I do?"

I didn't say anything, and suddenly I didn't know if I was going to make it out of this without crying too.

"What if I came with?" she said, and looked up. "To New York." The look on her face, wanting to believe in what she was saying, was terrible to see. "I could do the whole thing, wait tables during the day and act at night, or the opposite, or however they do it."

"I don't think I want you to go with me. I want to go and just get serious about music. By myself."

"You're not going to start practicing just because you're in someone else's apartment. What, do you think you're going to be out meeting girls at clubs, everybody crawling all over you?"

"No. I just want to stop living like I'm fourteen."

"OK, so why are you going to live like you're twelve, in

someone else's house, going to bed when they go to bed, not even working?"

"I'll be working. David knows somebody who can get me a job at the zoo, and at night I'm going to get gigs."

"You sound ridiculous. I can't believe you're doing this. I can't believe I'm crying." She stood up and didn't bother to put on her shirt.

"I think I'm going to leave."

"Why don't you give my dad a hug and tell him you'll write. He'll probably cry harder than I will."

"I'm going out through the back. Tell your parents thanks for dinner."

Sounding less like she cared and more like she was just annoyed, she said, "So am I going to see you again before you leave?"

"I think I want to leave this weekend, so I'm not sure."

She went into the bathroom and clicked the door locked. She blew her nose, and I could tell she wasn't coming out for a while. I stood up and went out into the backyard, my shoulders tingling. Passing the side of the house, I saw into the kitchen, where Mr. Zlotnick was standing in front of the family calendar and massaging his chin. I thought of the face he'd make when he found out, when in a few minutes Wendy came upstairs with smeared eye makeup, and for a minute, as I ran up Drummond and through the alley and onto Cumberland, I felt full of dizzy energy—something like the feeling of tearing off a scab. The rest of Wendy's summer would happen—the rest of her dull, complicated life would happen—and with fifteen minutes' work I'd cut myself free from it.

* * *

My last night at home I stayed up with Olive, lying at the foot of the stairs. Olive's always been fat, but now her legs were giving out and I wasn't sure I was going to see her again. Lying in the dark, with Olive the only other Elinsky awake, I started to feel like I might miss home a little bit. The grand-father clock ticking its tick I could feel in my teeth, and this same soft carpet I'd been lying on since I was four. I could hear Walter snoring downstairs. Mom, Dad, and Walter, each having a dream, tugging a sheet, twitching. Even a prisoner must feel whatever comes before being homesick when he knows he's seeing his cell for the last time.

I lay on my side facing Olive on her side, and we were like an old married couple in bed. The rug smelled very strongly of dust. She lifted her paw and put it down on my shoulder. "Take care of everybody for me, OK?" I said. "Mom needs it the most, probably, so just go over and sit with her some-times. And keep letting Dad take you on walks. Try to do it at least every other day." She *flmmphed* out her lip, breathing hot on me, and closed her eyes and fell asleep. I rubbed behind her ear and said, "Bye, girl. I love you very much. I'm going to bed."

But up in my room I couldn't fall asleep. A confused bird was six inches from my window singing his stupid song over and over. And every few minutes a car would drive by and I'd hear the car's music *quiet quiet quiet LOUD LOUD LOUD* at the stop sign, *quiet quiet quiet quiet.* Then silence. And then that goddamn bird would start up. I imagined leaning out the window with a tennis racket—the *thwack,* the puff of feathers. His song went: *Doe-ba-da-ba*-dee-*bo*? *Doe-ba-da-ba*-dee-*bo*?

Just when I was finally falling asleep the phone rang.

"Are you asleep?" It was Wendy.

"I don't know. I think so."

"How are you doing?"

"I'm OK. How are you?"

"I'm good."

"Why are we whispering?" I said.

"Because it's late at night."

"What time is it?"

"One thirty. If you hadn't broken up with me, you could be over here right now."

I didn't know what to say to that, so I didn't say anything. The room was completely dark except for the light from my alarm.

"I'm calling because I wanted to tell you that I'm not mad at you anymore. And I want to wish you luck in New York." She really didn't sound mad, but she did sound a little drunk.

"Thank you. I wish you luck too."

"And Henry? You aren't good enough to play professionally. Your tone's not very good. Sorry. I'm just trying to be honest with you, like you were."

"OK," I said, but a little hurt had jumped to the back of my eyes.

"Good-bye."

"Bye."

"We might not ever talk again, huh?" she said.

"I don't know."

"Too bad. Sleep well."

At nine o'clock Dad woke me up singing "New York, New York," and I got on the eleven-o'clock train.

New York

The sidewalk outside David's building isn't like most sidewalks. The squares are bigger, smoother, more like slabs. He's on the corner of Fifty-third and Fifth Avenue, and you go in through a golden revolving door pushed by a doorman who stands there frowning at the street, dressed to drive a carriage. No matter how hot it gets outside, if there are Italian ice stands on every corner and the horses in the park are sweating through their saddles, inside the lobby it's cold enough for you to see your breath. The lobby even *sounds* cold. (The building's depressing too, though, the way an empty hotel ballroom is depressing. Every hallway on every floor has the same purple carpet and 7-Eleven lights and yellow walls. Through the living room windows—and the walls there are really nothing but windows—the whole city sometimes seems as dead as a diorama in a glass case.)

A Greek guy named Georgi sits behind a marble desk during the day, running his hand over his silver hair, waiting for you to ask him where you can get good Thai food or a roll of stamps. Each of the elevators (polished as bright as mirrors) has a guy outside it who holds out his hand to guide you in. At first I always tried making conversation with the elevator men, to show that I didn't think I was better than them. I'd say it was a good day to be indoors, or if it wasn't, I'd say it sure was a long shift, huh? But most of the time they just stared straight ahead and kept their hands folded behind their backs and nodded at the rows of buttons. People who survive that kind of boredom, I think, ought to be celebrated like soldiers or astronauts.

But Sameer, from the first time I saw him, seemed not to be suffering at all. He turned around while we were riding in the elevator on one of my first days and said, "If you don't mind, what sort of opportunities bring you to the city?" He's even smaller than I am, and he has a mustache as dark and perfect as the one you put on a Mr. Potato Head. I told him about the zoo, and from then on every time I rode with him he gave me a tiny bit of his own zoo story. "In Karachi, I studied for over one year in the largest zoo in Pakistan, particularly I studied the behavior and mannerisms of a species of bat that is quite rare anywhere outside of Asia." For that first couple of weeks, whenever I didn't want to be in the apartment anymore, I'd go down to the lobby and ride with him up to forty-two and back down to the lobby.

Something was the matter between Lucy and David— they always seemed to be having some important, angry talk that they were careful to keep to themselves. This was for my sake, I guess, but Lucy would sometimes seem to forget that I was around. At dinner one of my first nights there, sitting around their glass table with plates of flank steak that could have been in a magazine, David said, "We should make this for the party Sunday, huh?" Lucy sipped her wine and stared straight ahead. The skin by her ears turned redder and redder. "All right," David said. "Henry, how'd you do today?" She threw back the last bit of her wine, stood up, and went into her room and closed the door behind her. David chewed a bite of steak longer than he had to, then said, "Look. She's . . . you know—this is something we're dealing with." And then, while we did the dishes later, he said, only half to me, "Well, this is just fucking great." She didn't come out until the next morning.

David's gone so much that it's hard to think how they build up enough stuff to fight about. Six days a week he's out of the apartment by six in the morning, and most nights he isn't back for dinner until at least eight thirty. He's been like that since he was at Somerset, finishing projects weeks before they were due, typing up ten-page study guides for quizzes that hardly counted, working in bed at night until Dad would come in and unplug his lamp. Especially compared to the hour or two Lucy spends up in her studio painting, it's a lot.

I shouldn't be so hard on Lucy, though—she's been through a terrible thing. Her first serious boyfriend, who she dated all through college, died just after they got engaged. This was in Brooklyn, about five years ago, three years before she met David. Her boyfriend, Alex, fell asleep reading one afternoon with a candle lit next to a curtain, and when Lucy came home from work her street was so busy with fire trucks and ambulances that she couldn't see, at first, which building had had the fire. Alex died from the smoke before the fire even touched him, David told me, and that word *touched*— the idea of fire tickling, then covering, then swallowing— left my heart pounding.

("How'd they know he fell asleep?" I asked, quietly enough to let David not answer me if he didn't want to, and he didn't.)

I stared at Lucy sometimes, when I first moved in, imagining her face when she walked onto her block, when she heard the roar, the second when she understood that the disaster everyone was watching was hers. But you could stare at her all day and not get any closer to understanding how that felt. This Lucy, the one who collects ceramic elephants and who talks on the phone to her mom twice a night, was someone who seemed never to have been through anything harder than a crowded subway ride. I froze, once, when she walked into the living room while I was watching *Backdraft,* but she just glanced at the TV, picked up her magazine, and walked out.

I got to spend less time sitting around the apartment once David gave me the number of Herbert Talliani, his patient who was on the board of the Central Park Zoo. "Just say some stuff about loving animals and everything. He says they're always looking for keepers. He's really a hell of a guy. Used to be an editor at *Newsweek*."

When he picked up, Mr. Talliani had a coughing fit and then said, "So you're the guy with the fever to pick up monkey shit, huh? Send my secretary your name and résumé and everything and I'll pass it on to Paul. Tell David my skin looks like hell, by the way." And then he laughed, which made him cough so hard that I had to hold the phone away from my ear.

My interview was at one o'clock, but I walked up to the zoo early to look around. I'd been there once, on a trip to New York with Dad when I was seven, but I didn't remember anything about the zoo except that it was raining then and that outside the gate a guy in a bright green suit kept wanting to wrap his python around my neck. I also remember Uncle Jacob, who we stayed with that week, telling me that the animals all looked "wretched." But today it was the sort of day when people talk about the weather without seeming like they have nothing to say, sunny with a few popcorn clouds, and even homeless people looking healthy, almost. The path into the park smelled like something sweet that could have been either pollen or pee.

In a tunnel past the ice-cream vendors, a bald Asian man sat with his legs crossed on a stool, playing a bendy-sounding instrument that only had one string. I stood listening for a minute, and there wasn't anything you'd walk away humming, but if you listened long enough, it started to sound like a lonely old woman singing. I put all the change I had in his case, and right away he stood up smiling and held out his instrument to me. Did he think I wanted to buy it? Borrow it? I was wearing one of my new shirts and David's gray pants, so he might have thought I was a banker looking for a hobby. He kept shaking the bow at me, grinning bigger and bigger each time, but he wouldn't say a word. "No, thanks," I said. "You sound really good, I'm going to go." And so I just walked away—feeling not much better than if I'd robbed him—while he stood there shaking his instrument at me and smiling.

A sleepy black guard let me into the zoo for free when I told him I was here for an interview, and just past the entrance was a tank and a sign that said, WATCH OUR SEA LIONS HAVE LUNCH! Kids were clustered around the glass, throwing popcorn in the water or struggling while their parents smeared suntan lotion on their faces. The sea lions—I could see four of them—had huge bright eyes, long whiskers, and skin like a wet suit. The tank smelled like fish and chemicals, and was as big as a swimming pool, shaped like a stop sign. In the middle was a tall island of brown rocks, and a couple of the sea lions lay there in the sun. There was just a short glass wall between me and the ones who were swimming. I could have dipped my hand in the water—with a little work I could have dipped my body in the water. Another sea lion was up there on a rock now, his skin still wet and dark, but if you stood watching for a minute you could see the light spread over his fur. A red-haired girl in a stroller next to me pointed at the water and said to her bored nanny, "Look! Look! Look!" Swimming sideways, a sea lion would shoot around the edges of the tank, one little flick of its flippers every time the tank's wall changed direction, its belly out to the crowd, the smoothest swimming I'd ever seen. It hardly even made a ripple. It would spin slowly while it swam, and a lip of water just above it would spill out onto the ground. Every now and then it would have to come up for a breath, but really it didn't look like it was any harder for the sea lion to swim than it was for me to stand there watching it.

One of the ones up on a rock, because he was too hot or maybe just because he saw how much fun his friend was having, decided to plop back in. He moved like a handicapped person who'd fallen out of his wheelchair—until he was in the water, where he could have been an Olympic swimmer. I hung around the tank for about forty-five minutes, sitting on a bench watching and trying to read a zoo brochure I'd picked up, but the sun was so bright that the pages kept looking blank.

Once I'd been sitting there for a while, a skinny zookeeper with thick glasses came up to the tank and rested her bucket of fish on the bench right next to me. She looked about forty years old, with straight brown hair and careful makeup—if it weren't for the fish and the uniform, she would have looked more like a lawyer than a zookeeper. "Hi," I said. "Do you work here? I've got an interview in a little bit to be a keeper. Is it a pretty good place to work?"

For a second she looked so confused, almost panicked, that I thought she might not speak English. But she was just considering her answer. "Oh, it's very rewarding. You have to really love animals, but if you do, you hardly even notice the other stuff." She gave a nervous smile, like she might have said too much, and walked off with her bucket toward the crowd.

The sun was just above us now, and I lowered my head to let it reach all over. A job like this might even beat playing music, I kept thinking. I'd put on a bathing suit in the mornings and jump in the tank, race the sea lions around the edge, hang on their flippers, then lie up on the rocks with my eyes shut while I dried off. A group of pretty girls would walk over to me (I imagined them visiting from somewhere like Tennessee, giggly and polite), and they'd ask how long it had taken to get the sea lions to trust me. I'd smile, sitting up, and ask if they wanted to come in. And even if the job was nothing like that at all, at least I'd be earning money that didn't feel like just another version of allowance. At least I wouldn't be measuring out my days in forty-four-minute chunks, listening to the same five songs fumbled in exactly the same places while Dad kept time on his leg.

Before I knew it I'd drifted off in the sweaty-faced way I sometimes do in the sun, and when a stroller wheeling against my foot woke me up, it was two minutes before one.

* * *

In a brown, empty office, a man with a fat neck nodded hi without shaking my hand and pointed me to a wobbly table. His name tag said PAUL. He couldn't have been older than twenty-five, but he acted like I was a student and he was a busy, disappointed principal. By the time we'd sat down,

I'd already decided—for whatever reasons we rush to this kind of feeling—that Paul was my enemy. He wore an outfit like a Jurassic Park ranger and stared past me with his forehead wrinkled. His clothes had the sour, bready smell of saltines. "So. Tell me why a job at the Central Park Zoo appeals to you."

I told him about all the pets I'd had growing up, about watching the keepers in the D.C. zoo wash an elephant. Everything I said just seemed to hang there, waiting for me to take it back. He played with his key chain while I told him, struggling to come up with the word *hidden,* about how I used to give Olive her pills stuck in a ball of cream cheese.

"All right. I'm going to tell you a little about the job, then you're going to ask me some questions." He hunched over and lowered his voice. "If we hire you, you'd be working in the Children's Zoo, and you wouldn't get moved to Main unless you stayed for probably over a year. We always start people in Children's so they get some offstage experience. It's not a nine-to-five, Monday-to-Friday thing. Your off days are scattered depending on the schedule, and if something needs to get done, you stay until it's finished. And there's not much glamour to it. I tell everyone who comes in, if you think it's going to be like the Discovery Channel, then you should walk out right now." I made a face like I thought it was funny that some people thought it was going to be like the Discovery Channel. "It's dirty work, and you've got to be out there all day if it's snowing, raining, a hundred degrees, thirty degrees, whatever. The animals always need to be taken care of. I've had too many people here who're good as long as the weather's nice, but it starts raining and suddenly I can't find anybody."

Together we walked over to the Children's Zoo, with Paul staying a few steps ahead of me, and when we passed the Asian man (who was sobbing with his instrument again) I kept my eyes down. Once we were through the gates, Paul said, "Children's is shaped like a doughnut, farm animals on the ring, aviary in the middle." His walkie-talkie kept buzzing while we walked, and he'd flip it out of its holster and say quick, military things to whoever was on the other end: "Children's one to base, fifteen thirty at animal Main. Over."

The first animal he introduced me to was Othello, the black bull. He smelled oily, and he lived alone in a pen that looked too small for him. When he saw us he grunted and walked up to the fence. You could see his muscles move under his skin. His nose was shiny with some clear goo, and his eyes, as big as pool balls, looked hungry and worn-out. To show how good I was with animals, I reached over and scratched him on the flat, bony place between his ears. He butted my hand away, and Paul said, "Othello's probably the rowdiest animal here—he doesn't know his own strength, and he gets jumpy with men sometimes. Don't ever turn your back on him."

Through a tunnel in a plastic tree came a group of little kids, all black, all wearing green T-shirts that said, SUMMER IS FOR LEARNING. None of the noise—the talking, the squealing, the laughing—seemed to come from any one kid.

"It'll be like this every day. Three to five camp groups at

once." In front of the sheep pen, a fat zookeeper with bushy eyebrows was saying, "No. No. *No*," to a group of Asian kids in pink shirts.

Paul moved like a cowboy-bear. Leading me around the ring, past the alpacas and the sheep, he said, "Here's Lily. Back there in the shed's Chili. They're potbellied pigs." The sight, at first, is like the kind of fat person you see on the subway who takes up three seats: You stare at them not quite believing they live entire lives in those bodies. Lily and Chili's stomachs scraped on the ground every time they took a step. Folds of fat covered their eyes and hung down from their cheeks. They looked miserable under all that, trapped. I reached over and petted Lily, and her hair, black against all that tough black skin, felt like the wires in a pot scrubber. "She's been overeating, so something you'd have to be very careful of is Lily eating Chili's food. She loves pushing him around." Lily grunted when I touched her, and it could have meant, "Help!" or it could have meant, "More!"

A purple thundercloud was hurrying toward us, and when it started to rain a minute later, big, slappy drops, I pretended not to notice the water on my glasses so Paul would know that I wasn't a complainer.

As we came through the screen door into where all the birds lived, it sounded like we were suddenly hundreds of miles from the city. The air felt thick from the mulch, and full of plant smell. "Right up there are the magpies. Those two are getting ready to mate, so we're trying to make sure they have everything they need." I couldn't see anything, but I made nodding noises. "We have three doves sitting on nests right now, so every afternoon you'll have to go around and count them and make sure everyone's here and the nests are OK. This is the chukar partridge, Chuck." A fat, striped bird waddled by, as uninterested in us as we were in the trees we walked past. "He's had a thing with his balance for the past few weeks, so we're trying him on a special diet, and he's spending every other day in the dispensary. You have to keep an eye on him and write down what he's doing every morning." On either side of the bridge we stood on was green water, and ducks with wild colors and paddling feet zoomed underneath us.

Finally, in the pen closest to the exit, I met the goats. There were seven. "That little one's Suzy. She's the mom. Her kids are Pearl, there, and Onyx, who's over there with the gray spot. Sparky's up on the stump, Spanky's this one— he's trouble—Scooter's asleep right there with the long beard, and that," he said, pointing to the tall white one, the only one without horns, "is Newman. He's a Nubian. Totally different species. He's a big goof. One of the security guards calls him Jar Jar, because of the ears." The goats looked smart and scrappy, a gang of cartoon grouches and goofballs. Their pupils went the wrong way, and they all looked up at me expecting something—they were the Bad News Bears and I was their new coach. Newman came right over, nibbled at my collar, then rested his head on my shoulder and took a loud breath. He had big pink nostrils and little square teeth. He smelled like dust and hay. His ears hung below his chin, and he looked—with his barrel of a body on top of those long, skinny legs—like a little kid's drawing of a horse. The

Summer Learners came around the bend with their hands full of food, and Newman scrambled to get in position, his front hooves in the mesh of the fence, his neck leaning way over, and his head bouncing from hand to hand.

"He's just a big kid, always hungry," Paul said, and that's when, with a quick bob, Newman lifted the glasses off my face. Paul jumped the fence and grabbed a handful of Newman's neck hair, then wiped my glasses on his shorts before he handed them back. "He's terrible sometimes. I'll make a note for him not to get Enrichment this afternoon. Usually, something like that happens, you've got to fill out a report. Last month he broke some woman's camera, we had to pay two hundred bucks."

I still haven't fixed the scratch on my glasses' left lens. He snuffled the food from a row of girls' hands, snuffled them again to make sure he hadn't missed anything, then lifted his head before bobbing off down the line.

* * *

When Paul called Monday afternoon to offer me the job, I decided to go for a celebration walk, and while I was looking for a place to get an egg-and-cheese sandwich, I realized I was right by David's hospital on Fifty-first. Long escalators led up to a busy lobby with a gift shop full of flowers and silvery balloons. A week before I would have felt uneasy in a place like that, suspicious that everyone who walked past was wondering why I wasn't at work. But I felt now like a businessman paying a visit to a friend, full of easy braggy charm.

In the elevator I only noticed that I was humming because of how the nurse was staring at me.

David's face—like mine but wider and flatter, like a cow's—can't hide anything, and he wasn't glad to see me. For some reason he shook my hand. "Good to see you. Just stopping by? What's up?"

"I can come back later."

"No, I'm sorry, it's just hectic here. I'm an hour behind on my afternoons and I've gotta get somebody's lecture notes for this morning. I'm about to see a nice kid now, though. You wanna come sit in? I'll tell her you're a first-year."

She walked into the office wearing shorts and carrying a folder, and she did seem nice, but to tell the truth I could hardly look at her. There wasn't a spot on her face that wasn't covered in acne, a Halloween mask she could never take off. David shook her hand without wincing, and she hopped up on the table, swinging her legs and crinkling the paper.

"Your chin's looking better," he said, "and it's a lot less angry up here around the temples and the hairline. How many milligrams do we have you taking now?"

"A hundred." It was strange to hear a little girl's voice come out of that face, like expecting milk and getting orange juice.

"I think we're going to step it up to one-twenty for the next two weeks. This is Henry; Henry, this is Joan. Henry here's at NYU, hoping to be a dermatologist himself." He stuffed his tongue in his top lip to keep from smiling.

"I want to be a doctor," she said, looking at me now.

"Either an open-heart surgeon or the person who helps with babies."

"She designed the entire Web site for her school. One of the most talented people I've seen," David said. "And within six months we're going to get her all cleared up and she's going to be one of the most beautiful people I've seen too."

She smiled and seemed so brave, so patient and gentle about living with her face, that I hated myself for being disgusted by her.

David has never had more than ten pimples in his life, but he's always been a fanatic about his skin. When we were growing up he was full of weird ideas: olive oil and sugar, Aqua Velva, ice water—his routine before he'd go to bed used to take half an hour, but I don't think he would have had any pimples if he'd wiped once with a wet rag and eaten nothing but chocolate cake. I wasn't so lucky. From the time I was in eighth grade until a couple of years ago, I didn't have a single day where I woke up and my face looked the way I wanted it to. Every night I'd smear on the creams and swallow the pills that Dr. Fordham, nutty in his toupee, would send me home with each month, but I may as well have prayed or done a skin dance. In the morning I'd stand in front of my bathroom mirror and with however many fingers it took I'd cover the biggest pimples of the day and think, *Like this you wouldn't look so bad at all.* On the worst days, Dad, who had bad acne when he was in high school and still has scooped-out-looking scars on his chin, would say, glancing over while he drove me to school, "You're a very handsome kid."

When the girl left, the office secretary, a fat woman with

braces and heavy makeup, said, "Stephen Takas just called and canceled, and Dr. Harrison's just come back in, so you've got about forty minutes if you want to take lunch. Now, is this your brother? Why haven't I been introduced?"

"Laura Ann, Henry; Henry, Laura Ann. This is the famous secretary who can balance her checkbook and do a month's schedules and talk to two people on the phone, all at once."

She blushed and looked down at her lap. Like he was already a big-shot doctor, David rapped his knuckles on her counter and said, "We're gonna go around the corner. What can I bring you back?"

"Nothing for me, I'm having cottage cheese," she said. "Here, Mona, come meet Dr. Elinsky's brother. Henry, this is my niece."

From a back room full of file cabinets stepped a girl who looked my age. Tan with blond hair pulled into a ponytail and a tight white T-shirt and a big smile. If I could get close enough I was sure she'd smell like warm laundry. "Hi there," she said.

"Can we bring you anything, Mona?" David said. There was something about the way he didn't quite look at her when he said it.

"No thanks." And something about the way she didn't look at him. "I was just about to leave for the day."

David took me into a pizza place on Fiftieth. He asked me about the zoo, what I'd be doing, how much I'd be getting paid, but all I could think about was Mona. The idea that girls like her lived in the same world as girls like the one with acne—that girls like her lived in the same world as me—filled me with bright, itchy panic, like there was something crucial I'd missed doing years ago.

A crumpled old man was working behind the counter, opening and closing the ovens. There was something wrong with his hands—arthritis, maybe. He held them and used them almost like they were paddles. "How you doing today, pops?" David said in a voice I'd never heard him use.

"I'm not dead, and if you can say that, how bad a day can it be?"

David laughed hard and patted the old man on the shoulder while he paid.

"This place is great, huh?" he said when we sat down, but my slice wasn't much better than the pizza I'd been getting at Somerset. "Silvio opened it when he was thirty-two, and he hasn't been gone for more than two days since. A doctor told me he ratted on his brother in Florence and sent him to jail. I keep meaning to ask him about it when it's not so crowded."

I couldn't figure out how to ask about Mona, but I had to know more about her. So I said, "Mona's pretty, huh?"

"Mona?" But he flared his nostrils and had to really work not to grin. "She is pretty. I guess I haven't thought about her like that."

"How could you not think about her like that? She's as pretty as a model."

"I just . . . I don't know—things in the office are a little strange."

"What things?"

"Nothing. Enough. Tell me more about work. When do you start?"

"Just tell me what's strange." I knew how I was acting, but I didn't care.

"Mona's one of these people who gets a lot of crushes. She's just young. How old are you now?"

"Eighteen."

"Jesus. I'm not talking about it anymore." The rest of my slice looked as good to eat as my stack of napkins.

"We don't have to talk about it, just tell me what you meant. Then I promise I'll stop."

"No." He put his big soft hand on my arm and looked right into my eyes like I was a mental patient. "No." Once he'd decided I got it, he said, "Listen, I'd been meaning to talk about something anyway. Really Lucy's been bugging me about it, just a couple of little things about staying with us—"

Had Mona seen David's facial hair? Since he was fourteen he'd had to shave twice a day, and still he had a five-o'clock shadow by two o'clock. I once walked in on him in the bathroom with shaving cream all over his shoulders.

In high school he was the manager of the JV baseball team, and he never went to a single school dance, not even after Mom said she'd ground him if he didn't ask someone. But while he worked in his room at night—when he was chubby and seventeen and I was chubbier and nine—I sat on the floor for as long as he'd let me, listening to his stories, mostly about the guys on the team.

"Seth and Pete screwed Carrie Feldman on the hood of

Seth's car, right in the parking lot. All three of them buck naked." My penis would almost tear through my pajamas. "Last weekend Jon went to a place on N Street, and for ten bucks a Korean girl let him rub her all over with hot oil." I'd throw tantrums when Mom would come in to make me go to bed. Just one more minute. Thirty more seconds. David sitting there muttering while he stapled packets at his desk was better than any TV show.

One night in his freshman year at Emory, when I was in fifth grade, he called home to talk to me. "I'm in trouble," he said, almost whispering. "Big, big trouble. I've seriously never felt this bad. Everybody said it was going to be so different. But it's not. It's the *exact same fucking thing.*"

I wouldn't have been any more terrified if he'd told me he had a brain tumor. I kept it secret from Mom and Dad, and I called him the next day, hiding in the bathroom with the portable phone crackling. After thirty seconds he said he had to run because his friends were leaving for a Braves game, and he never talked about feeling bad again. When we visited him that spring, he took me to a party at his frat, and I ended up playing Sonic the Hedgehog in the messiest bedroom I've ever seen with a guy with a yarmulke and a red beard.

While we dumped our crusts, he said, without looking at me, "What's happening with you and girls, by the way?"

"I had something at home, but, you know, just looking around." (*Mona, we could play barefoot Frisbee in the park.*)

"Nothing wrong with that," he said. (*I'd put suntan lotion on your shoulders, leave love notes on your side of the bed.*)

Out on the street he puffed out his cheeks, glanced down at his watch, and said, "Time to get back to it." He shook my hand again, squinting in the light, and said, "Look. Don't worry too much about Lucy. Bottom line: I'm enjoying having you live with us, and it's my place as much as it's hers."

I n the elevator after one of my first days at work, Sameer asked me, sounding shy, if I liked to play Ping-Pong. He and Janek, the tall doorman from Slovakia, played every day on the seventh floor, next to the laundry room, with broken paddles and a baggy net and only one ball that wasn't cracked. In middle school, before one of David's friends jumped on our basement table and snapped two of the legs, I used to play most afternoons with Dad. We didn't keep score—Dad said, smiling, that he didn't like the idea of beating me. I kept score myself, though, and by eighth grade I beat him at least as often as he beat me. But now I couldn't seem to remember how I used to grip the paddle, and my backhand wouldn't stay on the table.

"Yesterday," Sameer said, while we rallied, "I read a fascinating article in a magazine in the doctor's office. In Elizabeth, New Jersey, there is a man who funds his life and his exorbitant family merely by the sale of his own hair." The sounds of the game were as steady as a metronome. Janek sat in a chair by the door, picking at the rubber skin on his paddle. "This man has been blessed with the most lustrous and healthful hair that doctors have ever seen, and when he sells a full head of it—a head of hair more beautiful than Daryl Hannah's—he earns for it upward of twenty thousand dollars, and this is hair he produces simply by the existence of his head."

"Sameer, I am thinking that you read too much," Janek said. "Every minute spent in a book is a minute spent not in a woman." He laughed, and a speck of the foam that was always in the corners of his mouth flew onto the floor. Janek looked, every time I saw him, like he hadn't shaved in three days, and there was something damaged-seeming about his body. He was at least a foot taller than me and Sameer, but he stood with a tilt that reminded me of Frankenstein cartoons—once when he pulled his left pant leg up I thought I saw a rubber foot.

"I will admit I read to the point of sheerest infirmity," Sameer said, not looking away from the table. "When you one day pay me a visit, Henry, you may say that you have never seen so many books in your life. They are piled from the floor as well as on top of every surface, and all of them are both old and extremely well-read, first by me but also by my son, who is turning out to be a first-rate mind, albeit one without a sense of dedication. Even in the oven and in the cabinets there are stacks and stacks of books at all angles."

"I don't like to read any more than two things," Janek said, still grinning, still foaming. "I read the instructions on how to cook food, and I read the instructions on how to cook women." He held his arm out to give me five and spread his eyes wide, hoping we'd collapse against each other like teammates at the end of a game.

"As much is evident," Sameer said. "Because otherwise you would be too distraught for foolishness by the news that there has been still another suicide bombing in Israel, in which seventeen different people have passed away. Every time an Israeli takes his place on a bus or in a café, he is risking the end of his life, and these are even the citizens who have no military association whatsoever. It is no better what Israelis are doing with the Palestinians. For our unfortunate friend Janek I already know the answer, but are you a religious man, if I may ask?"

"Not really," I said. "I'm Jewish, but I don't go to temple or anything."

A little ripple of shock ran over his face. "You are a Jew? Oh, the Jewish people are a most fascinating people to me. I will tell you a horrifying secret. I have been studying the Jewish people for many years, and for the past year I have even been taking lessons from a dear friend in the art of reading Hebrew. Janek can verify as much. I do not read with much speed, but each night I practice my characters for one hour sharply, and I find improvement in myself every day. Oh, it is so wonderful that you are a Jew. Are you an Orthodox Jew, a Conservative Jew, or a Reformed Jew, if I may ask?"

"You had better click the lock on your door when you sleep," Janek said. "Sameer loves a Jew even more than he loves a blond woman."

Most of their fighting seemed like just a show for me, but now Sameer looked truly embarrassed. With his lips pulled back and his teeth gritted, he fired his next shot as hard as he could into Janek's chest. It couldn't have hurt more than a pinch, but it was enough to make Janek stop smiling. Sameer turned back to me, served a cracked ball from his pocket, and said, "The Jews have, in my opinion, played one of the most instrumental roles in every matter of human development. They have studied medicine, literature, music, and many other fields in which they have made great strides for all of humankind. I am honored and I am pleased." For the first time since I'd met him, Sameer, leaning over the table, shook my hand. "I would be deeply honored if on a free occasion of your choosing you allowed me to accompany you to temple for prayer. I do not wish to impose, but it would be as utterly fascinating an event for me as I could conceive."

"I don't really go to temple."

"Right, right." This was something he said a lot, usually when he wanted a conversation to be over, and he used it to mean something like, "Well, we don't have to worry about such small matters now." He laid his paddle on the ball, still careful not to look at Janek, and, before he walked out of the room, he shook my hand again. "I will look forward to your invitation, and may I say in departure, 'Shalom.'"

* * *

I spent my first few weeks at the zoo wondering if I'd been there long enough to quit. I came home each day too tired to practice, daydreaming about skipping work the next morning, hurting in my kneecaps and wrists and the right side of my neck (never the left, for some reason). And each morning, still so tired that I'd feel my mind wobble every time I blinked, I'd stand downstairs in the freezing zoo kitchen and chop yams and zucchini and carrots with a knife that could have chopped off a horse's leg. Taped all over the room were angry messages from Paul, disguised as jokes: *Animals Don't Have Forks and Knives! Cut Veggies Small!* The radio on the shelf could hardly get reception through the floor, so I'd listen to talk radio with gospel and oldies buzzing underneath. No matter how fast I chopped, by the time I was stacking the bowls to bring upstairs, Paul would show up in the doorway. "Hungry animals upstairs," he'd say, "hungry animals. Let's go."

By the ten-thirty break, the idea of still having a full day ahead of me seemed like an emergency, something I couldn't possibly be expected to bear. Zookeeping wasn't hard work the way I imagine house building would be, where by the end you'd feel like tearing off your shirt and diving into a lake. It was hard work like making a hole in a concrete wall with your fingernails. Until I'd been there for a week, I had no idea how *small* the Children's Zoo was. I'd walk circles and circles past Cow, Sheep, Pig, Goats, Cow, Sheep, Pig, Goats, and the only thing worse than walking those slow circles was when I had to stop and actually do something.

Cleaning Pig was the easiest job, because they lived on a hard floor—I'd shovel up their poop, soft apples that barely smelled, and then hose the whole pen down. The hosing was sometimes even fun, tilting my thumb over the hole, trying to make the water curve in a perfect sheet up over Lily. But when Paul would assign me to do Sheep or Cow, my legs would suddenly feel like they couldn't hold me up. Such stupid, embarrassing work—raking and scraping and shoveling for animals that only wonder, while you grunt under another load, why you haven't fed them yet. At first I'd make friendly, tired faces at the families standing looking in, but eventually I realized that they weren't looking at the keepers any more than they were looking at the water bowls. We were stagehands in a play starring Dudley and Frankie and Kramer.

Cleaning Othello's pen, even though he had more personality than the sheep, was the worst. He covered his square of dirt with heavy black Frisbees of poop, and the smell—sharp, sour, eggy—made me have to breathe through my mouth. But gnats were everywhere in his pen, and if you held your mouth open for too long one would fly in, tickling your lips or choking you. Every afternoon when Othello's hay needed changing, we all fought to be the one who could hide out in the bathroom.

Cleaning Goat was almost as bad, at first—raking up all those piles of hair and hay and thousands and thousands of coffee beans of poop—but the Nubian goat, Newman, wouldn't stand for sulking. While I leaned on my rake, he'd walk up next to me, like a dog, and nudge his head against my arm until I petted him. The rest of the goats made noises when they wanted something—they'd open their mouths, standing perfectly still, and force out a hard, angry *myaaaaaaaa*. Newman, though, was completely silent. In the afternoons, when I'd be squishing sweat with every step in my boots, I'd sit on the stump and he would try to crawl onto my lap. Fat, clumsy, and with elbows as hard as hooves, he'd stare up at me with his yellow eyes, wondering why he couldn't fit.

The zoo disappoints most people who come, I think— the rats swimming in the duck ponds, the food machines that give you almost nothing for fifty cents, the animals that are too hot and tired of having their ears pulled to let you pet them—but that first sight of Newman makes almost everyone smile. He stands tall and white with his horse neck way out over the fence, and kids, coming around the corner, let go of their babysitters' hands and start running.

After dinner once, David asked me if I'd mind taking a walk so he and Lucy could talk. I walked up Fifth to the zoo, not really thinking about it, and the Cuban security guard, Ramon, let me in without any fuss at all. First I walked a slow lap of the whole zoo, feeling gentle toward all these sleeping animals, embarrassed at how much hate I worked up for them during the day. Only the dim orange security lights were on. When I came around to Goat I was surprised—and, I realized, happy—to see Newman standing awake at the fence. His eyes followed me around the pen, and when I got close enough, he nibbled lightly on my sleeve—not to eat, I don't think, but to check on me, to say hello. I scratched his head and he shut his eyes and pressed against my hand. I rubbed the smooth places where his horns would be, if he had them. You don't really know how lonely you are, I don't think, until you get some relief from it. I climbed into the pen, followed Newman back to the corner where he slept, and sat down feeling quietly and perfectly understood. Within a few minutes his huge white side was lifting, falling, lifting, falling. His head was against my leg. The ground in the shed was not quite wet, not quite dry, and almost the same temperature as Newman's body. I scratched along his spine and talked to him—about living in the apartment, about being surprised to miss home—and whenever I'd stop for a minute, he'd tilt his head up so I could rub behind his ear.

When I was still living at home, I'd watched a show on the Discovery Channel one night about an African tribe called the Masai. I hadn't even watched all of it, but for some reason now, in the dark, in the shed, I couldn't stop thinking about it. The idea that right then there were people walking in red robes with herds of animals, under a brighter sun than I would ever see, gave me goose bumps along my arms—it seemed like a challenge to change my life. To love an animal, to walk with a spear and a goat past loping giraffes, to sleep in a hut protected by thorns—sitting there with Newman it all seemed so admirable and, even stranger, possible.

As I was leaving, I said something to Ramon about Newman, how different he sometimes seemed from the rest of the animals, and Ramon said, "These goats, man, they're like my seven other children. I get in a shitty mood sometimes, working overnight, I just walk over there and check out Newman, check out Suzie—five minutes and I'm good to go for the rest of the day, I mean seriously."

Ramon worked some day shifts during the summer, too, and from then on he was the person at the zoo I talked to the most. Every day, no matter how hot it was, he wore his blue jacket with his name stitched on the chest. Besides security, he was in charge of rat control, and about this and everything else he talked like tomorrow he was taking a vow of silence.

"All my life I've been hating rats. As long as I could remember I been wondering, Whose life would it make even the littlest bit worse if you killed all the rats? People don't think in those kinds of terms often enough. Whose life would it make worse if you killed all the mosquitoes? I'll tell you: the birds'. And people don't have birds, then the rest of the bugs get out of control and you'll think the times before with the mosquitoes were a picnic. That's honest thinking. But not with rats. All rats fucking do since Adam and Eve is give people diseases, bite people, scare people, ruin lives that were going along just fine till those sick gray fuckers showed up."

He'd walk up anytime I didn't look busy, and once he did I might be stuck for the entire afternoon.

"My father, have I told you about my father's restaurant? The only good Cuban food you could find in the entire New York area. Seriously, unless you're in my grandmother's house, the only place in all of New York where you're going to find halfway decent *vaca frita*, or if you want the real sweet *maduros*, the only place you're going to find it's in my dad's restaurant. Right on the main drag in Washington Heights, one of the most popular restaurants in the Cuban community, probably on the whole East Coast. Oh yeah. Closed up by the city, though, and my dad died before we could raise the money to open it back up. One of the major regrets of my life. No, *the* major regret of my life. And you know why that happened? Rats. You get bathroom pipes coming up from the sewers and everybody thinks it only goes one way, but really rats are climbing right up those pipes, and man, you'd come into the bathroom and there would be rats just crawling right out of the toilet. My old man—man, you should have seen my old man—he's in there with a broomstick he sharpened up like this so it's just like a spear, and he's stabbing those fuckers in the toilet, and man, it's like a war zone in there. And me and my big sister are standing outside the door telling customers someone's in there working on the pipes. This went on for like two years, rats in the kitchen, rats in the bathroom, one fucking rat even ran right through the restaurant under people's legs one time, and I think that's what did it, I think somebody went and told the health inspector to come bust our ass. One of the biggest tragedies ever to happen for all of New York."

Ramon had a son in the army, and I tried sometimes to steer the conversation toward him, because on the slowest, hottest afternoons I liked to daydream about being in the Middle East, riding around in a tank with a gun against my shoulder and the desert blowing around outside.

"My son, third infantry, stormed right into Baghdad on March twenty looking for Saddam. Oh yeah. Stormed right in there with guns drawn ready to kick ass. Last Saturday of every month he calls up on the phone and you know what the first thing he says is, every time?" I've heard the first thing his son says about ten times more than his son has ever said it, but I always raise my eyebrows. "He says, 'How are the Mets? How's Piazza?' Every time, that crazy fucking kid, from the middle of the desert, and all he cares about is how are the Mets, this from a kid who stormed right into Baghdad looking for the worst guy since Hitler.

"You know, I meet people who are against the war, people you see going around with the handouts and chants and everything, and I tell you what—I respect everything they say, I listen to it, I nod my head. But I don't care whether you're a Republican or a Democrat or a goddamn Martian, when our country's at war you gotta support our boys. My son didn't decide we should start a war, but as soon as it got going, he made sure he was on the first plane over there, and you know what I call that, no matter whether I think George Bush is a great president or not? I call that courage."

Sometimes I imagined Ramon with a faucet on the top of his head, and when he'd been talking too long I could just reach up and twist it to off.

* * *

I decided to start swimming for twenty minutes every afternoon, first thing after I got back to the apartment. It would be as good as a shower, and maybe I'd burn off my stomach. Being on my feet all day I felt like I might be losing weight, but I was putting it all back on each day at lunch. On Fifty-sixth there was a place with Reubens, and every night, in bed, I promised myself I wouldn't get one the next day, and every lunchtime I decided I'd worked enough that morning to deserve one. My high school PE teacher, Mr. Delia, told me when I was a senior that if I swam ten laps three times a week for the whole year he guaranteed I'd lose fifteen pounds. I stopped after two weeks, though, and ended the year five pounds heavier than I'd started. This time I promised myself I'd be disciplined.

Pool locker rooms smell just like pool locker rooms, even in a place as fancy as David and Lucy's building: bleach and mold and person. When I was a kid I used to go to the Somerset pool all summer. Fifteen minutes out of every hour were adult swim, and I'd sit on the steps shivering while Dad and Walter played water H-O-R-S-E. Mom never swam, she just liked to sun. Even on cool days, when she had to drape a towel over her back, she'd wave her hand to get me out of her light. I hated it, having my wrinkly mom lying belly-up on a beach chair with pubic hairs crawling down her thighs. I had a crush on the lifeguard, a high school girl with brown hair and a tattoo of a dolphin above her anklebone. Abby. Once, during the worst of my crush, I saw her at United Artists in the popcorn line with her friends, and she smiled at me, but like an idiot I rushed into the bathroom and stood in front of the sink until I knew she'd be gone.

This pool was simpler. It was indoors, on the eighth floor, and, the first time I went, it was totally empty except for one old man swimming laps and wheezing in the far lane. A matchstick of an old man who I'd seen before in the elevator, always headed out for a run. A sign said, SWIMMERS ARE UNSUPERVISED AND RESPONSIBLE FOR OWN SAFETY. Four big windows looked out from one wall way above Fifty-third Street. Lucy swam first thing every morning, before she went up to her studio. I thought about her peeling off her bathing suit and running hot water over her boobs, and to stop myself I dove in. It wasn't much of a dive, but it wasn't a belly flop either, it was more like a tumble. The water felt cold for a second, and I let myself sink down so my feet tapped the tile, and, blowing bubbles, I rose back up and gave a big *"Aaaaaaahhh,"* because aside from the skinny old man there was no one there to hear me.

I started to swim, and the water felt chunky. Which sounds gross, but no, it was wonderful, it was chunky the way Jell-O's chunky if you take it out of the fridge too soon, like every time I swept my arms big, solid pieces of water were being pushed back and I was shooting through empty space. I love looking at my body underwater. Every little arm hair waving and the three freckles in a line along my left wrist, my hands looking so huge and weird, every nick and dry-skin flake like it's under a magnifying glass. What an amazing thing to be, a pink ape underwater! I love thinking in the water. For some reason it feels like I shouldn't be able to do it, but I'll putter along the bottom, my belly just barely clearing the tiles, and over and over I'll think: *I'm thinking! I'm thinking! Here I am thinking!*

It only took two laps for me to start to get tired, and to start to wonder if ten minutes a day might be a better plan than twenty. I decided I'd rest for a little, then swim a couple more laps and see how I was feeling. I was holding on to the edge when a tall girl about my age walked in holding the hand of a skinny black-haired boy, six or seven years old. OK, I was peeing. The girl had thick brown hair, and it wasn't that she was fat (but she wasn't skinny), it was just that she was *big,* much taller than me, maybe heavier. If a lumberjack had a beautiful daughter, I thought, this could be her. She wore a blue T-shirt over her bathing suit and no shorts.

In case the water turned cloudy I had to start swimming again. Breaststroke is easiest for me, so that's what I did. I can usually go the whole length of the pool with only three breaths, but after a few strokes the top of my chest was starting to burn.

I was resting again on the edge, pretending not to look at them. She was sitting on a pool chair reading a book while the boy jumped in and climbed out and jumped in and climbed out again and again and again. She had her left leg crossed over her right, and she looked like she was waiting for someone to fit a slipper onto her little curved foot. Her hair looked like it would weigh five pounds by itself. When she talked I thought she was going to tell me to stop looking at her, but instead she said, "Would it be all right if you watched him for a minute?" There was some little something in her accent—I thought she might be from Minnesota.

"No! No, I can watch him for a year if you want!"

She laughed loud and bright and went into the locker room, and I climbed out and went and sat in her chair. I started to open her book—it was purple with a crumbling cover—but my fingers left dark spots, so I turned it over and left it alone. The old man climbed out, shook off like a dog, and left. The kid didn't seem to have noticed that I was watching him now. "That's not bad jumping," I said.

"I'm the best in my group. My dad says I'm the best jumper he might have ever seen for my age."

He'd stand on the edge, gather himself for a few seconds, then jump in and move his arms and legs like he was being electrocuted before he hit the water. "Do you want me to show you the knee bounce?" he said. On the edge of the pool he got down on his knees and he hopped in and seemed to smack his chest, because when he came up he had a red splotch. "Do you want me to show you the flying kick?" For this one he jumped and stuck one leg out and gave a karate yell. "Do you want me to show you the double twister?" He bent his knees, jumped the highest I'd seen him, spun around, and on the way down smashed his face so hard on the edge of the pool that I screamed.

There was blood in the water. An instant, terrifying cloud. He came up and it looked like his whole mouth was full of blood, and he was howling. I reached over and pulled him up by his skinny arms, and I didn't know what to do, so I took off my towel and sat him on the chair and tried to wipe off his mouth. *"Noooooooooo!"* That made sense, not to touch his mouth, and now blood was all over his chin too and dripping on his bathing suit. This was very, very bad. "I'm going to go get someone," I said, but before I could get up the girl came back, and that made him start howling louder.

"What happened?" she said. "Oh, shit, what *happened*? What happened what happened what happened? Are you OK? Fuck. Are you OK? Is he OK?"

I told her about the jump and the spin and the side of the pool, and she went over and looked in at the bloody water, and she just kept saying, "Fuck. Fuck. Fuck. Fuck."

"Can you walk?" she said, but he just kept crying, rising and falling like a siren, so she scooped under his legs and under his neck like he was a baby, a baby with wet black hair and dark blood still pouring out of his mouth, and she carried him out fast through the girls' locker room, flip-flops clacking.

I was the only person in the entire pool area now. If part of the pool weren't still dark, and if there weren't a trail of bright drops leading to the locker room, it might never have happened.

The strangest part of terrible things is how fast they're over. For the first minute or two afterward, like when Tucker, my old golden retriever, got hit by a car, I always think about how simple it would be—we could just go back a few seconds, a time close enough to touch, and it would never have happened. My mind would rush to the thought—a happy, grasping feeling—then bump against common sense, then rush to it again, then bump.

I didn't know what to do, so I went over and looked down into the bloody part of the pool. There was a pink cloud now and a few darker drops floating up on top. For some reason I leaned down and with both hands scooped up some of the water and just looked at these drops of blood, a pair of dark little fish. My heart was pounding like someone was chasing me.

* * *

Sameer didn't know about a little boy and a tall girl, so I came back again after the shift change and asked Richie. Richie was the oldest doorman, and he took the job more seriously than anyone else. If you walked in with a suitcase, he practically tackled you to get it out of your hands. Whenever he saw me he gave a hard, short nod and said, "Sir."

"Do you know if there's a little black-haired boy who lives in the building with a tall girl with brown hair?"

He nodded, not taking his hands from behind his back. "You're looking for Matthew Marsen in twelve-F, I believe. And the young lady—whose name, unfortunately, slips my mind—is the Marsens' goddaughter. Just here for the summer."

That night David and Lucy were out to dinner with friends, and when they came home David was a little drunk. He laughs a lot when he's drunk, and his cheeks get splotchy. He sat down with me on the couch, smelling like alcohol and cologne.

"How are you, buddy?"

I heard Lucy get in the shower.

"Something bad happened today," I said, and I told him the whole story. Listening was such work for him right then that his mouth fell open.

"This happened to you today?" he said. "What I'd do, I'd write up a nice note, something about how you're so sorry and you think the kid's so great, and I'd put it under their door. That's rough." And then he stood up to leave, probably to get in the shower with Lucy, but he got distracted by the Mets game and stood there behind the couch with his shirt unbuttoned. "They've been down the whole time?" he said. I nodded. "They really stink, don't they?" Then he looked at me, and I thought he was going to add some warm, wise touch to his advice before he said, "They actually, totally stink."

In a drawer in the kitchen I found a card, still in its plastic sleeve, with a picture of a puppy running through a bed of sunflowers. Inside I wrote:

Dear Matthew and family,

I'm writing to tell you how bad I feel about what happened with Matthew at the pool, and I wanted to wish him the best of luck in feeling better. I also wanted to be sure you knew that everything that happened was my fault, and not at all your goddaughter's. She seems to care about him very much, and I was the one watching when the accident happened—I should have been more careful.

Again, I'm sorry, and if there's anything I can do, whether it's bringing ice cream or anything else, please let me know.

Very sincerely,
Henry Elinsky, 23B

On the envelope I wrote again, *Matthew and family,* and before

I sealed it I decided to add one of the hotel chocolates that David keeps next to the cereal. Before I went to bed, I took the elevator downstairs, my heart pounding like a thief, and slipped the envelope under the door at 12F.

* * *

The next night I was lying on David and Lucy's bed watching Emeril make jambalaya when David came in and handed me an envelope with HENRY written in small capital letters. On a folded sheet of lined paper I read:

Henry,

I'm not going to show your letter to the Marsens. I'm sure you'd agree that it doesn't add much to a babysitter's credibility to have left a child in the care of a complete stranger—especially when the stranger let the child chip two teeth and split his lip.
The chocolate was delicious.

Yours,
Margaret

"Who's writing you letters?" David said, and because he sounded a little insulting, I ignored him. I liked her handwriting, small and sharp. Yours. Mine. Delicious delicious delicious. In my memory she was suddenly beautiful. I imagined her eating the chocolate while she wrote. She must be lonely, I thought. She was probably desperate for someone to talk to other than this weird little kid.

That night I was too happy to keep it to myself, so while

Lucy cooked dinner I said, "I got a letter today from a girl downstairs."

"Oh?" she said, but she didn't turn around. She was barefoot in her shiny purple bathrobe, chopping a cutting board full of mushrooms. She never touched cookbooks or measuring spoons—she made satisfied noises when she tested her sauces, and dropped in pinches of spices from jars that didn't have labels. Usually I tried to act like I didn't notice that her food was particularly good, or even that she was the one who'd made it, but tonight, with her chicken and onions and soy sauce sizzling, I said, "That really smells great."

She softened the way she was standing a little, and while she slid the mushrooms into the pan, I told her about the pool and the boy and the notes. From her cheekbones I could tell she was smiling.

"You should invite her to the zoo," she said. "Tell her you'll get her and the kid both in for free. She'll love it, I promise you."

All during dinner I spun out fantasies of the visit. I'd lift Matthew into Goat, give him a handful of hay to feed Newman, teach him all their names. Margaret would like the birds best—on the love notes I'd eventually write her, I'd draw a Mandarin duck instead of signing my name. Matthew could climb on the metal turtle if it wasn't too hot, and afterward we'd walk into the park and I'd buy them ice cream. Standing under that row of tall trees, laughing at the silly wonderfulness of meeting each other, I'd kiss her. Would I have to stand on my toes? She could bend down. Matthew would be away picking flowers or watching a juggler, and Margaret, with her lips damp, would lean back against a tree and . . . I could hardly stay sitting at the table.

I took a shower and brushed my teeth and put on more cologne than I meant to, and wearing one of David's polo shirts I went down to the Marsens' at eight thirty. It seemed like a time of night when Margaret might be sitting in front of the TV in her pajamas. For some reason I thought of her wearing glasses, sipping tea.

It was so long before anyone came to the door that, just before Dr. Marsen appeared, I had turned back toward the elevator. He had a pink, scrubbed face and gold glasses, and he was holding a cloth dinner napkin—he looked rich and happy and ready to be entertained by whatever I wanted. "For Margaret, yes, yes, right this way," he said, and led me through the apartment, past the wide staircase, into the dining room.

"Because that doesn't make any sense!" I heard Margaret saying, sounding delighted, before I even saw her face.

"Well of course it doesn't make *sense*," Mrs. Marsen said, and she and Margaret both leaned back in their chairs and gave in to laughter so pleasant that they had to close their eyes.

Drowsy classical music played quietly, and the lights were set just low enough to make everything wooden in the room glow. At the center of the table was an almost empty bottle of red wine and a tray of what was left of a salmon. "I present . . ." Dr. Marsen said, displaying me like a game-show prize.

"Henry," I said.

"Henry!" Mrs. Marsen and Margaret called out together, dissolving again in laughter that didn't have anything to do with me. The way Margaret looked at me, once she'd stopped laughing, was friendly but somehow not at all inviting. It was the look she would have given a dessert she didn't want. I considered apologizing and rushing out of the apartment before anyone could tell me to wait, but Dr. Marsen pointed me toward the chair closest to Margaret.

"So do you live in the building, Henry?" Mrs. Marsen said. She was thin enough that her collarbones seemed to push out of her skin, and she wore a complicated brown wrap pulled tight over her shoulders. "Get him a glass, Steven. Excuse me. Would you like something to drink? Margaret says we always push alcohol on everyone."

At the first sip of wine I felt my lips turn purple. "I live on twenty-three, with my brother and his girlfriend," I explained—I could talk so long as I kept my eyes on Mrs. Marsen. "Margaret and I met at the pool."

"And what does your brother do?"

While I explained, sipping whenever I needed to pause, I started to risk taking looks at Margaret, and I decided that she wasn't unwelcoming after all, she'd just had a few glasses of wine. Dr. Marsen had started to gather the dirty plates, but Mrs. Marsen and Margaret both leaned on the table and watched me with sleepy, gentle interest, as if they'd half known I'd come downstairs even before it had occurred to me.

"My dermatologist at home," Margaret said, "once tried

to convince my mom that she needed Botox. He wanted to give her a shot right between her eyes."

"*No,*" said Mrs. Marsen. "*Your* mother? How could anyone think she needed that? I don't believe it."

And that was how conversation worked, like a card game just complicated enough to keep you busy but simple enough that you didn't need to pay complete attention. We talked for what felt like half an hour—Margaret would describe for me whoever they were talking about, and Mrs. Marsen would jump in, smiling, to add more—and by the bottom of my glass of wine I felt practically like we'd already been on the date, and asking to see Margaret again would be as easy as smiling at one of her stories.

But when Matthew appeared in the doorway, wearing pajamas and smelling like a shower, I felt my easiness start to evaporate. "Mom?" he said. "Can you come look at something?" He turned toward me, and I thought he was going to ask what I was doing here, but all he said was, "I got seven stitches."

"He managed to bash himself swimming the other day," Mrs. Marsen said. "I'm sure Henry couldn't be any more impressed."

"Bravest patient I ever saw," Dr. Marsen called, walking in from the kitchen.

"Look," Matthew said, stepping close, and pulled his upper lip away from his face to show me the inside—it looked like he'd had a purple marble sewn just under the skin.

For some reason I stood up—he seemed to want to push

his lip in my face—and while everyone was watching me I said, "I actually had a question about inviting you and Margaret somewhere." I realized that I shouldn't just be talking to Matthew, so I looked at Margaret, who seemed to be trying not to smile. I wasn't sure how long ago the music had stopped. "I was thinking you guys might want to come to the zoo for a free visit."

"Ooooh," said Mrs. Marsen.

"Do you feed the polar bears?" Matthew said. On some words he sounded like his mouth was full of bread, and it took me a second to understand him.

"We don't have polar bears in Children's. We can go see them in the main zoo, though."

"I'm a vegetarian," he said.

I opened my mouth but didn't know what to say, and Margaret laughed then and I decided that if for the rest of my life the only thing I did was make her laugh that would be enough.

"If you came tomorrow," I said, "you could help me feed the crocodile."

"Well, that sounds like terrific fun," Mrs. Marsen said. "And I think *I*"—she tapped out a few beats on the table—"had better go look at whatever Matthew needs to show me, and then I'm off to bed. It was very nice to meet you, Henry from the twenty-third floor."

"Very nice to meet you too."

Matthew rushed upstairs ahead of his mom, and in the second before Margaret stood up too and started the slow-motion walk toward the front door, I let myself think that

Margaret and I might be left in the dining room alone together. But she did stand alone with me, holding the door open, and for a few seconds she was close enough—and the lights from the hall were bright enough—for me to see that the fuzz above her upper lip was stained red.

"Hope to see you tomorrow?" she said.

"I'll be there."

"Then I will too," she said, letting the door close. She practically whispered it.

The next morning Paul asked me to start with Pig. The sun was up, but still low enough that it was just an orange light behind the trees, and the fences and mulch were covered with dew.

Chili hadn't eaten in a week. He wouldn't stand up from his bed, wouldn't look up when you'd wave a slice of apple in front of him, wouldn't even move when you nudged him with your toe. When I'd reach around him with the rake to pull out the old straw, he'd show me his teeth and grumble. I'd feel the way I always do when an animal doesn't seem to like me, like he'd insulted some important secret part of me.

His stomach looked like a sagging beach ball. I'd throw

new straw on either side of him, and he'd grunt and fall back asleep—or back to whatever miserable, quiet place he spent his days now. He smelled like he was rotting. Every day Paul would say, "Any luck?" and every day I'd say, "Nope," feeling proud to be depended on for news. We were mixing a table-spoon of castor oil in with his food, in case he was just con-stipated, but he never pooped and he never ate.

Meanwhile Lily was as healthy and as busy as ever—maybe even busier, the same way one kid acts his best when his brother's in trouble. I wouldn't put her food down right away, because I had to deal with Chili first, so while I woke Chili up and slid his bowl in front of him, she'd snuffle on my boots. When I did put her food down, she'd snort it up in less than a minute and then, once she'd knocked her bowl upside down, she'd come back and rub her fat, bristly side against my legs. Janice—the keeper I met out by the sea lions before my interview—told me once that when Lily's having her period she gets very friendly with men. I didn't know pigs got their periods, but the idea—tampon strings and tough black folds—made me want to never touch Lily again. To make her leave me alone, all I had to do was throw a handful of pellets to the other side of the pen. Hairy and solid as she is, you can somehow still tell that she's a girl—her little tap-ping hooves are like a fat woman's high heels.

I tried practicing the surprised smile I'd make when I first saw Margaret and Matthew—the face I came up with didn't have anything more to do with happiness, though, than with sadness or worry or anything else. I imagined holding her hips and staring at her in the wet dark behind the catfish tank. I imagined leaning over the aviary bridge with her, dropping bread crumbs for the ducks.

Across the path and the fences between us, I nodded at Newman. He was standing watching me, his head tilted like he was trying to remember what he'd walked out here for. But he just had an itch—he shook his head and his ears made three loud claps. "Good morning," I said. "How'd you sleep?" Each morning when he first came out, his legs still stiff and his eyes even smaller than usual, I felt for a minute the weight of all the thousands of days he'd spent here. The day I moved into the dorm at American, falling asleep that first night on my new sheets with the new traffic sounds outside, Newman was in his pen. High school graduation, while I sat itching in my robe, not remembering which hand takes the diploma, he was in his pen. The Thanksgiving in tenth grade when Walter dropped the turkey taking it out of the oven. Every time you're waiting in line at the pharmacy. Every time you wake up in the middle of the night and can't decide whether to get out of bed to pee. How does he survive it? Is he miserable or just empty? Or is he happy—is he like a prisoner who discovers religion and turns gentle and stops noticing the bars?

During morning break, while I sat on a step stool eating one of Lucy's PowerBars, Paul came in and told us to listen up. He clasped his hands behind his back. "Garret, come take a seat." Garret's only sixteen—two years younger than keepers are supposed to be—but his dad raises money for the park. He's giggly and spoiled and fat the way that babies in paintings are fat, with soft boobs and a wide back and no chin. But somehow—with his blond hair and red cheeks—he manages to be handsome. I heard Clarissa, the keeper who reads thousand-page fantasy books at lunch, once say that Garret's cute, and then one break a few weeks later they were choosing a movie together out of the back pages of the newspaper. Right then he was poking at Frodo, the fourteen-year-old ferret, with the metal end of a pencil.

"Chili's gone down to the vet," Paul said, "and they're going to hopefully figure out the deal. He'll probably be there the rest of the day. Henry, how about you go hose out in there. Everybody else, check the board. Me, back to trying to get this damn computer hooked up."

While I raked out the old straw, Lily kept eating patches of the garbage bag. My rake—like all but one of the zoo's rakes—had a broken wrist, so the claws sounded loose against the concrete.

"Sorry, but are there any other animals here?" A woman with jean shorts and too much lipstick was standing at the fence.

"Other than what?"

"Well, there's the cow, and there's the sheep, and there's the goats, and there's the pigs, and there's the birds. . . ." She was sweating, and her T-shirt was yellow in the armpits. She looked like someone who might be in an episode of *COPS,* the worried mom watching through the window while her son gets dragged away.

"The main zoo's down there," I said, but she'd stopped paying attention.

"Listen. Do you know anywhere I could get rid of a rabbit?"

"What do you mean?"

"I have this beautiful lop, gray, one and a half years old, and I'm moving to Tampa and I need to find a place for him. Do people leave animals here ever?"

"Somebody left the crocodile," I said, because someone did.

"You serious? Gandalf's beautiful. Most lops, you reach in their cage, they'll nip you. But he doesn't at all, he just sniffs a little bit, you know? You know about rabbits, all the problems with vegetables? I gave him this ball, like one of those exercise balls, and he uses it to roll on, like stretching out his stomach, and he's good to go, you know?"

"That's neat," I said, and picked up the hose.

"Girlfriend of mine invented it, but yeah, it's pretty cool." She went silent, staring at nothing, then said, "So I can leave him?"

"You probably shouldn't."

"Would you guys kill him, or is it the kind of thing where you'd be like, 'She shouldn't have done that, but now that she did I guess we'll take care of it and all 'cause we're a zoo'?"

"I'm not the one who decides. I wouldn't kill it."

"Thank you. I'm serious. You meet the biggest"—she looked both ways—"*ass*holes, and then you meet somebody who's not and it's just, like, the nicest thing."

She walked away, and something—the conversation with this nervous woman, the work of waiting all day for Margaret—had left me feeling like I needed to sit down.

Maybe it would be better if Margaret didn't come in at all. I could ask Paul for a job indoors, something I could stretch out for hours—scrubbing behind the cages or cleaning out the fridge. If I saw her back in the apartment I'd look confused for a second, then say that I must have been on break when she came. I'd stay away from the pool for the rest of the summer. The challenges of avoiding her suddenly seemed as important as the challenges of seeing her had seemed an hour ago.

And all because this woman was moving to Tampa! Worrying always turns me into someone who believes in horoscopes, but whose horoscope could be hiding in the weather, the stock market, a complete stranger.

I decided to stay outside. Margaret would come in and I'd be standing there, every possible clumsy conversation already burned off by worry, and I'd talk as easily as I do in dreams, sometimes, never turning quiet, never adjusting my glasses. I'd show her how to feed the animals, flex my forearms while I tore off a garbage bag—I'd make her laugh until her chest hurt.

After lunch Paul put me on Change. The change pouch is made of red canvas and has three pockets: dollars folded on the left, small coins and new rolls in the middle, quarters on the right. Wearing it always made me feel like a hot-dog vendor. After an hour or two on duty I'd start itching for people to ask me for change—I'd go up to groups and shake my quarters, say things like, "I'll be right here if you guys need anything," and "Everybody all set?"

I'd been jingling the quarters, and I'd just sniffed my

metal-stinking hand when Margaret and Matthew came around the bend from Othello. "Hey Henry," she said, in a voice like we were acting something out, like coming here was a joke we'd both agreed to be in on.

She looked even prettier than she had in the Marsens' apartment—she wore sunglasses back on her head and had her hair pulled back in a loose ponytail. She was taller than I'd remembered, too. She was wearing a long white skirt and sneakers, and when she smiled only one corner of her mouth went up. She looked like she might not have slept. "The cow back there's beautiful," she said. "Is he a Dexter?"

"You know cows?"

"I worked on a farm a couple of summers ago. We had two Dexters, but their coats weren't nearly that nice—he's *gorgeous*. Who's this?" she said, and she put a hand on Newman's neck.

I imagined us on her farm riding horses together, clopping over a creek in a forest. We'd gallop when we came into a field, and then together at the end of the day we'd fall onto our bed in our cabin and I'd kiss her and pull pine needles out of her hair.

She waved Matthew over to Newman, who was standing with his front hooves in the fence. Matthew held out a handful of pellets, a foot too far for Newman to reach—Newman wobbled his lower lip. When Margaret nudged Matthew forward, he shuddered. "You don't have to be scared of him," she said. "He won't bite. Right?"

"He doesn't even really have teeth," I said, and as soon as I said it I realized that it wasn't true. But he doesn't have teeth in front, or at least not on top. I reached up and let him nibble on the tips of my fingers. It felt like being bitten by an old person, warm and gummy.

"I know he won't *bite,* but he's disgusting," Matthew said.

Margaret looked at me with her tired, happy eyes, and the work of controlling my face seemed like too much for me, all of a sudden—my cheeks sagged and my lips felt made of clay.

A girl with glasses and long, sharp fingernails came up for the tenth time that afternoon and asked if I could give her two quarters for the machine, *please* could I give her two quarters for the machine, she promises me that her brother will come pay me back later today, he'll pay me *double* if I'll just give her two quarters for the machine.

I'd been telling her no for an hour, but now I fished out two quarters for her. "I've got to do Enrichment now, if you guys want to watch," I said.

"I've got nowhere to be," Margaret said.

When I came back out a few minutes later holding Newman's trash can, I felt like I'd managed to stir up a kind of street-fair energy in myself. Newman and I were going to put on a show.

"Where's the other pig?" Matthew said. He stood on his toes in front of Lily and Chili's pen with his hands on the fence.

"He's at the doctor. He hasn't been eating."

"Why hasn't he been eating?" he said, but before I could answer, the camp group ran at me to see what I was doing with the trash can. The long-nailed girl kept pushing her way closer to me, saying, "What's in there? Do you eat that? Who eats that, mister? Can I take some of that and feed it to them?"

"Watch," I said. "Take a step back." At Somerset I'd been too embarrassed ever to really boss the kids around—I'd felt too much like a kid myself—but here I'd tell them to stop jumping on the bridge or not to feed trash to the sheep, and they'd get the same scared, shy look as if any adult had yelled at them. It was a flimsy sort of power, but I enjoyed it. I held the trash can out in front of Newman—I'd smeared the insides with peanut butter—and he plunged in his head. This, or giving him a plastic ball to bump around, or dangling a set of keys from the end of a bamboo pole, was what we called Enrichment. These things are enriching, I guess, the way a honking truck might be enriching for a driver falling asleep on the highway. When Sparky and Spanky rushed over to join in, Newman shoved them away with his stump-tailed butt. When he finally came up to breathe, after a minute of such frantic eating that he'd almost knocked the trash can out of my arms, the fur on his nose and above his eyes was smeared with orange.

"He's *incredible*!" Margaret said. "I love him. You're amazing," she said, not to me but to him. "What are these floppy things under his neck? I've never seen a goat with these before."

"They're wattles," I said, "for fat storage." This is what I heard Paul explain once, but in the old Nubian goat book on the break room shelf there isn't a word about wattles. They're too pretty to be mistakes, but I don't know what else they could be. I held one up to show Margaret how soft they are—they feel like strips of velvet—and he laid his head on my shoulder, rubbing peanut butter on my cheek. He sneaked out his tongue to lick the peanut butter back off my face, and I saw, suddenly, that Margaret was glad to be here, that I was making a kind of progress. Spanky and Pearl were jumping up to be included now too, so I took off my glasses and lowered my head so they could lick my face and nibble my ears. It's hard to explain exactly what I hoped to tell her, carrying on with them like this, but I counted on these goats somehow—with their strange eyes and twisted horns and long stretches of quiet—to give a truer, more complicated account of me than any person could have.

Sparky or Scooter butted the top of my head with his horn then, and for a second every thought I'd ever had was replaced by a long steel spike. My eyes filled up with tears, so I kept my head down and sucked the insides of my cheeks.

My head was still down when Paul came out, walking with Garret. "Did you just give the goats an extra Enrichment?" Paul said.

I felt like I'd pass out. "I just gave Newman a little peanut butter, because he didn't really eat breakfast."

"We don't *ever* want an animal getting two Enrichments, especially not Newman. Quit showing off." He walked off like he'd slapped me with a glove.

The long-nailed girl and Garret both said, "Uhhhhhhhhh-hhhh," in that rising way I hadn't heard since Somerset. Margaret, to spare me, pretended to have been watching Lily. Oh, I hated Paul. With his goatee that never grew and his lumpy face and his tiny, terrible zoo. He sits in the air-conditioning all day reading car Web sites, slurping and sucking his Diet Sprites. He's got the soul of an elementary school tattletale. I don't think he remembers what it's like to carry garbage bags full of sheep poop in the pouring rain when you're wearing rubber boots to your knees. How the bag keeps ripping on the sharp pieces of the fence, which makes a stream of poop and hay fall out behind you while you walk, which means you have to get down on your knees (which sting in a gravel-pressed, scraped-red way), and with your bare hands you have to pick up the pieces of poop and hay and shove them all with the old bag into a new bag, which is now even heavier and which you've got to carry all the way down and then heave up into the blue Dumpster because Antonia can't lift them anymore with her bad back.

I'd worked myself into such a sulk that I shoved my change belt at Garret ("What'd I do?") and led Margaret and Matthew over to Nessie's tank, right past Paul's window. Nessie is the zoo's three-and-a-half foot crocodile, a yellow-green, smiling muscle. Most of the week she just sleeps in the water—kids rush by her without a look—but on Tuesdays and Thursdays she wakes up to eat a mouse. You're supposed to wait to feed her until after the zoo's closed, but I didn't think Paul would come out again for a while. The front of Nessie's tank faces out onto the path that leads into the zoo, but to feed her you come to the tank from behind and above. If you throw the mouse too far to one side, so it lands on the rock or gets caught up in the reeds, Nessie usually won't even notice it. But if you manage to plop it into the water, she comes to life—you see the quiet monster she could have been in a swamp somewhere—and in a few bites she gulps it down.

The mice come from a shoe box in the freezer, where they're heaped as messily as ice cubes in a cooler. First thing every Tuesday and Thursday morning the person who does Aviary brings two upstairs in a Ziploc bag and lays them on top of the rise of dirt behind Nessie's tank to thaw. They lie there damp and gray and cold, paws up, yellow teeth out, eyes as dead as pebbles. The first few times I fed her, I felt, after I'd tossed the mouse (you can feel the ridges on its tail through your glove), like I couldn't wash the imprint away. I got over the feeling soon enough, though—anything other than raking eventually became a prize job. I'd even come up with a kind of prayer—"I'm sorry, and I promise you won't feel a thing"—that I'd mutter to myself just before each throw.

I could see Matthew and Margaret through the glass from where I was crouching above the panel. Margaret's head almost came up to the plastic billy goat, and Matthew stood next to her, half-distracted by the kids his age who were streaming by behind them. I lifted off the panel, dangled the mouse over the water (it looked like it had died trying to hang onto the edge of a table), and threw a little too hard. The mouse bounced off the front glass—one hard knock, like from a knuckle—and Matthew jumped back. When Nessie snatched it and started tipping it down her throat, I saw Matthew grab Margaret's arm.

As soon as I walked around to the front of the tank, Matthew slipped off to the bathroom, and I realized that I hadn't planned past this moment. I stared at Nessie's yellow eyes as if she were the one I couldn't figure out how to talk to. "I hope we didn't get you in trouble," Margaret finally said, and I exhaled for the first time in a minute. I told her she hadn't, she asked me how long I'd been in the city, she told me she was here for the summer from Montana. "On Fridays," she said, "all the guys from my high school get drunk and race down the creek road." She said *creek* like *crick,* and she laughed when I asked her to repeat it. Every answer I gave was like a little paper airplane I'd folded and creased before sending out. I made jokes but not too many, I kept eye contact but tried not to stare. It had only been two minutes, but I'd spent more energy already than I had in all those months at home.

"Are you in school somewhere?" she said.

"No. I'm taking a little break. I started college last year, but I decided I wanted to do something else for a while."

"I know exactly what you mean." (My chest filled with *yes yes yes.*) "I've done two years of school now, and it's like I've never *done* anything, you know?"

"I'm actually a musician. I play saxophone, so I figured New York's a good place to hear people and get gigs and everything."

"Seriously? My dad's the *biggest* jazz fan. Louis Armstrong and Benny Goodman were like the sound track when I was growing up. I haven't been to any music here yet—I'm trying to see one new place every day. We should go to a jazz club. Where do you go?"

But before I could tell her where I went (or didn't),

Matthew came back. He took Margaret's hand and I looked at his mouth, thanking him without saying anything. *If it wasn't for that jump* . . . But then I didn't want to finish the thought, because I didn't want to put a limit on what Margaret might eventually mean to me.

"We're gonna go do some shopping," Margaret said. "He's got a camp trip Monday."

"Have you ever gone rock climbing?" Matthew said. He'd pulled a blue rubber ball out of his pocket and was dropping it and snatching it, dropping it and snatching it.

"No. You can teach me." And I looked up fast so I could see Margaret smile. Seeing it almost made me make a noise. When she pulled her sunglasses down over her eyes and turned for a second to face the sun, I realized that she was the sort of girl that people stare at on subways, across restaurants. She was, with no makeup at all, as pretty—as smooth and as bright and as unlikely—as any of the yellow tulips planted along the path behind her.

"I'm serious about hanging out sometime," she called, as they walked down the path and around to the gate. "Jazz club or not."

I nodded until my face jiggled.

And even though I had to strip Sheep when I went back in, and even though Milo had thrown up yellow furry stuff in his water bowl, and even though Paul made a point that afternoon of not inviting me to the zoo banquet, the whole rest of the day I was somewhere else.

* * *

The next night, still drunk on all this new hope, I went down to the Marsens' to ask Margaret if she wanted to get ice cream. She answered the door in a hooded sweatshirt and shorts, holding the same book she'd been reading at the pool, but just when I thought she'd say, "Sorry, but I'm staying in for the night," she said, "That sounds great. Let me go tell them." And two minutes later we were out on the street.

We walked up Fifth—a wide, bright river of fanciness, churches tucked between stores with glass walls and billboards of women's mouths—and then all the way to Second, the streets getting emptier and emptier as we went east. We were looking for a place that Lucy had told me about: they served nothing but dessert, and had one sundae with sugarcoated rose petals. Margaret was a fast, distracted walker, jaywalking without seeming to notice that she was doing it, and with every step we took I felt more and more certain that this place I was taking her was a mistake. When we finally found it on the corner of Fifty-ninth, a long wooden room with golden lights and low sofas, I was relieved to find the door locked.

"Not a problem," Margaret said. "We've had a lovely walk." She said "lovely walk" in a jokey half-English accent. I bought ice-cream sandwiches for us at CVS, and we sat down on a stoop on Fifty-third. The bread part kept sticking to my fingers, and the ice cream was soft enough that if you pressed the sandwich it puffed out smooth as a marshmallow.

For a few seconds, again, we didn't talk, both just looking out at the street, but then I asked, "What's the happiest you've ever been?" It was, I realized as soon as I'd said it, the kind of question Dad asked on birthdays or New Year's Eves, nights when he'd had a few drinks and felt like taking the long view.

"Ever?" She was almost laughing. She had a dot of chocolate under her lower lip. "Let me hear yours."

I could have said, *Sitting next to you with a mouthful of ice-cream sandwich,* and it didn't feel right then like it would have been a lie. Other happinesses, old ones, suddenly looked quaint. But I tried to think of something else—of course, it wasn't a true answer I was digging for so much as an appealing one. "I think mine was a couple of Thanksgivings ago," I said. "It was me, my parents, my brother, my uncle, and his librarian friend, Dora. We finished dinner and we were doing the dishes and David—that's my brother—brought down the yellow boom box from his room. He wouldn't let anybody see what CD he was putting on, but everyone was in a good mood from dinner, especially my uncle. And I don't know where David got it, but the CD was the Fine Young Cannibals— you know them? They sing, 'She Drives Me Crazy'?" For a second it turned hard to talk. "It was really loud, so you could hear it even with the sink on. And all of us knew all the words, and we started dancing a little, even Mom. Dad stood behind her waving her arms for her, and Walter and Dora were sort of slow-dancing in front of the oven, and David was by himself snapping and smiling. This was right before he met Lucy. I remember looking around at everyone and thinking that this was probably the happiest I'd ever get. It's hard to explain why, but every note sounded completely perfect. I don't think I've listened to it since, because I don't want to ruin it." I couldn't look at Margaret. I felt like I'd just proposed to her.

"I think mine was last summer," she said, "when I was visiting my cousins in Pennsylvania. I usually go for a few weeks every August. There's this bookstore I go to at night about a mile from their house, Tommy's, and they have couches where you can just sit and read or talk or whatever. I biked there one night and I started talking to a girl who works there, and by the time I left it was totally dark out. The way I go is down this path instead of on the street, except the path doesn't have any lights and it's totally lined with trees. I started out, and it was the darkest dark I've ever seen. I thought my eyes would adjust once I'd started off, but I got about fifty feet into the trail, far enough not to be able to see back to the street, and it was still like being in a closet. I couldn't see my bike, I couldn't see the path, I couldn't see if there were people walking. But for some reason I kept going, I didn't even really slow down. And all of a sudden these fireflies started lighting up. Hundreds and hundreds of them, flashing in all these different places, high and low, right up in front of me and ten feet back. I just biked right into it. It felt like such a gift, you know? I'd seen them before, but only like little flickers in my cousins' yard a few times. It made me feel so lucky to be alive—which I almost never feel."

"That's much better than mine."

"No," she said. "Yours is about other people. Other people are important."

We started walking again—neither of us had to say,

"Should we get going?"—and she asked about David, so I told her about how much older he is, what he does, about Lucy and about her parents' apartment. "You sound like you really love him," she said, and right away I did: I was ready to believe anything about myself, so long as she was the one seeing it. I wanted more than anything to take her hand, one terrifying motion, but instead I stuffed my hands in my pockets.

She told me about her little brother, Damien, how smart he is but what a terrible time he has in school, and the night was going so well that I almost said, "I can't wait to meet him." When we were crossing Fifth again, a cab couldn't decide whether to speed in front of us or slow down and wait for us, and Margaret hooked her arm inside mine to pull me ahead. She didn't take her arm away (and I wasn't holding her there—I wasn't at all), even once we'd crossed the street. I would have walked like that all the way to Maryland, mile after mile after mile, if she hadn't steered us back to the apartment.

* * *

After work a few days later, I went to David's Fourth of July softball game. He manages a team for a league of New York med schools, and keeps a notebook in his bag full of roster ideas and statistics. There's a type of guy who manages teams—it's the same type who volunteers to take notes for a group, or who rushes to hold open doors—and David has always been it. The field, just a ten-minute walk from the zoo, was empty when I showed up, except for a happy young dad hitting grounders to his son, so I sat down under a tree and read. That morning I'd asked David to pick something out for me—Margaret told me she would give up dessert years before she'd give up reading—and he gave me *The Hunt for Red October*. "You won't put it down for a week," he said. "When I finished, I really felt like you could put me in a sub and I'd be fine."

David had said that if any of his guys didn't show up, I could play instead, so I waited for almost an hour, smelling dog shit every time the wind blew, trying to get into my book. There were lots of place names and submarine names and Russian army jobs that didn't mean anything to me, and I was thinking that I'd ask David for something else when Ramius, the Russian sub commander, kicked Putin's feet out from under him and snapped his neck against the edge of a table. My shoulders prickled. Ramius wanted to take the *Red October* to America, and Putin, the political officer, had figured him out. I knew, by five thirty, that David wasn't going to show up, but I stayed to finish the chapter where Ramius, pretending to cry, tells his men that Putin slipped in a puddle of tea but that they'll have to maintain perfect radio silence.

When I got home, David said, "It wasn't at that field. Why the hell would you think it was there?"

I didn't feel like watching the fireworks from the window with him and Lucy, and I didn't want to risk bothering Margaret, so I went out alone and got a shish kebab at the stand on Sixth where all the cabdrivers ate. The kebab came in tinfoil and smelled smoky and buttery—white juice kept running onto my hands and my book. It was the sort of food Mom tells me that I need to forget if I'm serious about ever losing weight. I ate by the fountain outside Citibank, trying to imagine that the fireworks I could hear way off were bombs. But imagining war didn't transport me the way it did a few days ago—or not unless I imagined lying on my bunk, opening letters and packages from Margaret.

Sixth Avenue is uglier than Fifth—all the buildings are the same color as the sidewalk, and you have to look straight up to see the sky—but I felt more comfortable there, less like I was in everyone's way. I thought of riding bikes with Margaret in Montana. Side by side on a silent path in the dark—mountains in the distance and the moon like a spot of Elmer's glue—and then sleeping in her bed, surrounded by her rug and bookshelves and windows.

An old black man in a baseball hat sat down next to me, and I could tell, as he looked out at the street, that he was gathering himself to say something.

"I'm looking for a place to find a calendar," he finally said. "Calendar from last year, two thousand two. I do a little legal work, you understand, and you just got to keep up, you know, any little thing wrong can slip you up."

Strangers in Chevy Chase never talked to me the way strangers here did. Most of the fun—and it was fun for me—was in figuring out what story the person was actually working around to telling.

"I went to my friend's copy shop right down on Forty-ninth," he said, "and my friend thought he had one, but he went down to the basement and he couldn't find it. I need an old one, you understand? Two thousand two, so I can keep my facts straight."

"Did you try the Barnes and Noble on Fifth?"

"Not a new calendar. An old one. This is for just a little legal work I do, you understand. You go in there and make any mistakes, they'll be all over you. I had a stroke in, let's see, 'ninety-six. So that's seven years ago August, and since then I've been studying the law. I had to teach myself to write again, read again, all of it. My granddaughter had her schoolbooks, so I just went through it with her, letter by letter. Before that I worked for twenty-two years for the coast guard. Retired in 'ninety-one. Before that I worked security." He pulled out a plastic-looking gold badge on a chain.

We both looked out at the street for a couple of minutes, families with guidebooks looking for the subway, cabs with their lights off, a pair of white horses, and then he stood up. He took off his hat and rubbed the little hair he had left. "Good luck," I said.

He broke into a big grin. "You *all right*," he said, and he shook my hand. "You *all . . . right*."

Back at the apartment, feeling full and slow and all right, I stopped to talk to Georgi. "You are doing well this evening, Mr. Elinsky? I see you are reading a book?" He was standing at his desk, staring out at the street as blankly as Olive does at home.

"I'm doing very well," I said. "How're things tonight?"

"Well, they are extremely boring. I should be at a picnic,

but I'm working twelve hours today, and already I have written two songs, read a magazine, used the Internet—nothing
is left for me. Everyone is going away for summer vacations."

"You write songs?"

He stood back. I'd never noticed before how much gel he
wore. "I am a singer. You didn't know? Oh yes, I've been
singing for almost twenty, thirty years. Standards, originals,
whatever people like to hear. Every Tuesday night, at the
Oasis on Seventy-seventh Street and Lexington Avenue—
have you been to it? Every Tuesday my band and I, we go
and we play, no big deal, just for fun." I'd never seen him
look happier—I'd never seen him look happy. "Mr. Elinsky.
Why don't you stay with me and have a drink? If someone
who would mind comes in, hand it to me and I will put it
under the desk. It's no problem. A Fourth of July toast." He
pulled out a square bottle of yellow liquor and two short
glasses. "Please," he said.

"I'm a musician too," I said, wincing at the first sip. "I
play sax."

"Then you will have to come and play! Tuesday nights at
ten thirty, open microphone, no tryouts. You're twenty-one?"

"Eighteen."

"Say you know me, it's no problem."

"This Tuesday?"

"Every Tuesday, all year round. And after you perform,
you can see me sing, you can tell me what you think. If you
think we're very good, you can come hear us anytime. Some
people have said we are better than almost anything you can

hear on the radio. It is me, my friend Alex, my friend Nik, and a young man named James. We call ourself One Percent, because I usually say ninety-nine percent of popular music in America is, excuse me, *shit*. Britney Spears, Janet Jackson, Mighty Mighty Bosstones—they sell millions of CDs, but they don't make you feel anything, so when it comes on the radio, I go *pop,* turn it off."

Leaning on his counter, we stayed up drinking until eleven, but Georgi only emptied his glass once. I could feel myself getting lighter and lighter, less and less attached to the things I said. It was the first time I'd been drunk since my last week at American, when I already wondered if I'd be coming back, when I threw up strawberry margarita all over the yellow flowers behind Tenley Mini-Mart.

"Georgi," I kept saying, feeling like there was something very important I had to tell him, if only I could think for a minute. A few people came in while we drank, and each time Georgi would move the glasses behind the orchids on his desk and say, "Hell-o, how are you?" in his Georgi voice.

"Georgi," I said. "You get a feeling about a person sometimes, where even if you don't know them for that long, you just have this feeling like . . ." But whenever I would get to the part where I wanted to gush about Margaret—where he'd tell me how right this sounded, how much like love— my thoughts would scatter like pigeons from a stomp.

After my third glass, he put his hand on my shoulder and said, "Tomorrow we can talk, but tonight, as we say, I think you have had your fill. I have loved to find someone to talk with about music. We will play anytime."

I climbed into bed in my clothes, not bothering with the sheets, and slept so hard that my face sweated. For what seemed like hours I dreamed that I was in my bed at home but underwater, speeding but safe, chugging along at the black bottom of the ocean.

I pretended to be as surprised as everyone else when Paul, before giving us morning assignments that Sunday, said that a gray lop had been left in a cage by the front gate. "None of you guys know anything about this?" I shook my head in a way that I hoped would look bored. "Nobody? Not anybody who's"—Paul unfolded a piece of notepaper from his pocket—"'Short, glasses, really a cool guy'? You didn't tell anybody they could leave a rabbit here?" He was feeling so pleased with how well his trap had worked that he kept rising up on his toes while he talked.

"A person . . . someone asked the other day, but I told her she couldn't."

"When I ask you guys something," Paul said, looking only

at me, "you've got to tell me the truth. If you can't do that, you don't have any place here."

"I wasn't—"

"Case closed. Everybody fucks up, it's a question of whether you learn. But we don't have space for another rabbit. Call the Bronx during lunch today and see if they'll take him. Or figure something else out. For now, go clean out the rabbit cages. Janice can come help when she finishes Pig." He turned toward his desk, and when I kept standing there, expecting some further chance to explain myself, he looked back and said, "Hey—I'm over it if you are."

Hardly anyone came in that morning—even the animals did their best to stay in bed. The rabbit cages, crusted with months of hard patches, had a bitter stink that I kept having to resmell to believe. My hands were sweating and sore in my yellow cleaning-lady gloves.

At lunch I called the Bronx, sitting at Paul's desk while he and Maurice from Polar ate cheeseburgers on the break table. Maurice is tall and black and wears a hunting knife strapped to his leg, and around him you see Paul at his most naked: eager, pushy, laughing too hard.

"Bronx Zoo, this is Ellen speaking."

I explained why I was calling, and she listened as quietly and thoughtfully as if I'd been talking about a baby in a basket. "Does he have any distinctive markings? Any spots or colorations or anything like that. Is he comfortable around humans? Other rabbits?" Finally, after a long *hmmmm,* she said, "Well, I hate to tell you this, Henry, but I don't think we're going to be taking him. So tell you what I'd do: Hold on to him, either at your house, if you can, or at the zoo, and then I'd just put up flyers everywhere, see if somebody wants him. Sound like a plan?"

So I carried Gandalf back to the apartment that afternoon. He huddled in the corner of his cage looking sick and terrified of wherever he was being taken, and Richie politely acted like he didn't notice him. Once I had him in my room, I closed the door in case anyone was home. His fur was completely gray except for a white circle around one eye, and his ears looked like a hat he'd pulled too far down on his head, trying to disappear. I reached in to pet him and he started to shake. "You're OK. See?" I held one of his food pellets out for him, and he pressed against the cage's back wall. He suffered so much doing even the most ordinary things that when I was with him they stopped seeming ordinary—every step was like a step on the moon. "Where's your exercise ball? How are you supposed to eat vegetables with no ball?" I filled up his water bottle, and while he rattled at it he finally, with a shudder, let me touch him. His ribs felt as thin as fish bones. His fur was soft enough to remind me, for the first time in years, of the fur coat that Mom's cousin Rachel used to wear. She'd come for dinner some Sunday nights when she lived near us—she was a tall, loud-voiced woman, and she always told stories about the soap opera she'd once been on. I'd wait until she and my parents were smiling over coffee so I could go to the closet and bury my face in her long brown coat, the acres and acres of it. "Somebody'll take you," I told Gandalf. "Maybe a kid. Maybe somebody with a yard so you can run around." For twenty minutes he sat watching me, his head pulled back into his body, his eyes ticking after me around the room.

For most of the night, once he'd let me lift him out of his cage, I played with him on the floor. It may not have been play for him. I'd put him on my shoulder and he'd scramble with his rice-grain nails down my shirt. I'd throw a pillow-case over him and he'd immediately curl up and go still, probably grateful for the dark. I didn't put him away until Lucy and David were in bed, so I didn't get to do any of the practicing I'd meant to do, and then all day Monday, Lucy was in bed with a migraine. On my way out Tuesday morning, when Georgi said, "You are coming tonight?" it wasn't until I was in the revolving door that I remembered what he was talking about.

But at ten o'clock that night I met Margaret in the lobby and we took the six train up to Seventy-seventh, my saxophone case tucked under the seat. This was a vision of myself I'd wanted, the New York musician riding to his first gig, but now that it was happening it felt wrong and clumsy and small. A homeless man with a rumbling voice and a duffel bag full of sandwiches crashed onto the train. "TONIGHT THERE ARE THOUSANDS OF PEOPLE WITH NO-WHERE TO EAT, NOWHERE TO SLEEP." We all got very interested in the posters on the other side of the car. My entire torso felt full of razor blades of gas, and I wondered if I should tell Margaret that I was sick and couldn't play. "IF YOU OR SOMEONE YOU KNOW IS HOME-LESS, PLEASE . . ." I leaked a few seconds of burning poison and prayed, even while I saw Margaret's nose wrinkle, that it wouldn't smell. My body, my enemy. Dad used to get sick before his biggest gigs—maybe this meant I'd play well, that my body was getting out all of its failure and mess before it turned into a light, beautiful success machine.

"I can't wait to hear you," Margaret said. "I'm so incredibly unmusical—they always used to ask me to just pretend to play during band concerts. Do you know who you're playing with?"

"Georgi says it's just an open mic. It probably won't be very good."

"Do something when you're up onstage. Wink at me."

"THANK YOU AND I HOPE YOU HAVE A BLESSED EVENING," the man said, and crashed into the next car.

It looked like Georgi had stood me up. Oasis was cramped and dirty, a restaurant with its lights turned low, and in the corner a skinny guy in a tank top had his head down on the table. A man in a jacket stood in front of the bar watching baseball, seeming like he wished someone were watching with him. The windows back onto the street were covered in curtains as thick as bath towels.

"Charlie Parker!" someone said, clapping a hand on my back, and when I turned, prickly with nerves, there was Georgi. It's no wonder I hadn't recognized him. He was wearing a white T-shirt with a V-neck and a gold chain buried in his chest hair. He looked, out of his doorman suit, like Georgi's shabby cousin.

"You missed us! We played once already, and it was one of the greatest sets we've ever played." Grabbing the hostess, a pretty, big-eyed woman, he said, "Tell my friend Parker how our performance was tonight."

"It was really good."

"It was better than really good. It was *really fucking great*!" Aside from the passed-out guy, the only people at the tables in front of the stage were a family of four trying to eat dinner. The little daughter kept sliding off her chair, and the mom kept picking her up and slamming her into place, harder each time she did it.

"You're up at ten forty-five if you want to play," Georgi said. "Tory—my friend Henry could get on at ten forty-five? He is a very good friend."

"Anybody with a drink receipt can get on," she said.

"It's open microphone. No rules at all. Just improvise. One of my favorite clubs in New York City, and you can play lead saxophone." Georgi blew me a kiss, then pulled out a cigarette and headed outside.

I bought a Jack and Coke ("Hope you didn't pay too much for this thing," the bartender said, tilting my ID in the light), the hostess pointed me toward a door next to the stage, and there in a white back hallway was my band. A middle-aged guy sat melted on a stool, holding an alto, sucking on a reed with loud, bubbly sounds. He had curly hair that covered his neck.

He popped the reed out of his mouth and said, "Help you with something?"

"Hmm? I play too." I held up my case. "I'm Henry."

He nodded. Then he looked down the hall at a waitress in black pants who was counting a stack of bills on a card table.

He was older than I'd thought at first, maybe even as old as my parents, and his front teeth crossed like the alpacas'. His nose looked like he'd been punched straight in the face with a heavy glove, over and over and over.

"What kind of stuff are we playing?" I said, while I slid in the neck and twisted on my mouthpiece. The smell in my case hadn't changed in all these months: mint, from the cork grease, and a metal tang from the places where the bell was rusting.

"We'll play whatever the spirit moves, bud. Can you blow?" He looked at me. "You still in high school?"

"I'm in college. About to finish college." My neck strap felt thicker and more uncomfortable than I'd remembered it.

"Where at?"

"It's a music school. In D.C."

He put his hand on my arm and said, "Guy? Just get out there and blow." And then he looked back at the girl's ass across the room like he was going back to a conversation.

Onstage, the only chair for me was a footstool. But I just sat down—my sax could have rested on the floor. The only sound in the room was the bartender's blender. I was so thirsty that I could feel the bumps in my throat when I swallowed, but my drink, when I took a sip, only made me thirstier.

It was me, the alto, a stiff older man in a suit at the piano, a happy red-haired drummer, and a guitarist with black fingernails who kept darting out his tongue. Margaret sat in a booth against the wall next to Georgi, drinking a Corona with a lime in the neck. She smiled at me and raised her eyebrows, but when I looked right at her I felt like I might not be able to play at all.

"All right, warm up with 'Satin Doll' in A," Alpaca Teeth called out. "Ah-one, ah-two, ah-one . . . two . . . three . . . four."

It took me a few seconds to flip to it in my *Real Book*. Everyone else seemed to have had the page dog-eared. Alpaca Teeth made a face when he played like he was trying to suck sour milk from a cow, but his tone, I realized, reminded me quite a lot of Dad's. That same warm polish, that easy bounce that always somehow embarrassed me, as if playing were giving Dad more pleasure than someone ought to feel in public.

I hadn't played on a stage since the spring concert senior year, and that had been just two loud songs with a band big enough to disappear in. *I'm onstage in a New York club,* I thought as I started to play. *I'm enjoying this. I am.* I looked at Margaret, but trying to smile around my mouthpiece made my tone bend, so instead I looked straight ahead at the round window over the door. A few more people came in while we were playing the head—a group of women who looked set on acting like they were having a great time, a middle-aged man with a face like a walrus—and now it felt more like a real club.

My tone was raspy at first, a strain to get out. I could feel my lungs starting to open up by the second chorus, though, each note like someone shrugging a jacket into place. But just when I was starting to get it, Alpaca Teeth cut us off and made hand signs to each of us. To the drummer he pushed the air forward to say, *Hold back, hold back*. To the guitarist he wobbled his hand and made a face like he couldn't decide between two things on a counter. To me he just bit his lip and shook his head. "All right, 'Maiden Voyage.' Let's do it in G. Ready? Music school, you take the high part." I sat up and honked out the first note, but the sound was full of spit.

Oh, playing music is awful sometimes. When you don't play, you imagine laying down a book in the evening, picking up a cello, and shutting your eyes while you ease out a warm, simple solo. But it's really all squeaks and finger cramps and tuning. And when you're part of a group that's playing badly, music seems, suddenly, like a crazy thing to force on people, an hour-long slide show of a rash. One problem, I think, was that Alpaca Teeth and I weren't in tune. I might have been sharp from the cold in the hallway. But the bigger problem was that "Maiden Voyage" is just a terrible song. There's nothing to it but those two damn notes that you have to hold until your ribs burn, and if anyone in the group misses either one by the littlest bit then the whole room turns sour.

Once we'd been through the melody, the piano player kept putting down chords like napkins on a table, and Alpaca Teeth stood up to take the first solo. He wobbled around, he stomped, he turned red—the audience loved it. One of the women at the bar yelled out, "Hurt me now!" and everyone laughed and whistled. The piano was going to solo next, and then me. I wanted so much to be off the stage that I thought about pretending to faint. I've never understood soloing, not once in the five years and five hundred lessons people have spent trying to explain it to me. I've spent hours nodding my head and making thoughtful noises, I've told Dad at least ten times that *now* I really get the key cycle, but soloing—and the whole business of chords and scales and keys—has always stayed in that out-of-focus part of my brain with sine graphs and mitosis and the subjunctive.

Dad had given me the same speech that launched all of his other students happily into improv. "You know those ads for the *Post*?" he said. "Think about the jingle: 'If you don't get it, you don't get it.' Now, what does that mean?"

"I don't know," I said, defeated already.

"Yes you do—it means if you don't get the paper, you don't understand the world. 'Get it' means those two *completely* different things. Halfway through, just like that, the meaning changes under the words, and 'get it' stops meaning newspapers and starts meaning the world. You got me?"

"Mm-hmm."

"I'm not convinced. You follow?"

"I *get* it."

On the important words he'd pull his lips back and raise his eyebrows and pronounce every syllable. Dad gave his lessons in the basement, on the old piano bench facing his heavy black music stand in the corner. Olive liked to sleep in front of our feet, and Dad would kick her and tell her to get out of here whenever I was screwing up an exercise.

"Now, soloing's the same deal. No different at all. The *meaning* changes under whatever *sentence* your saxophone is saying. The note F over a G-seven *means* a different thing than it *means* over an A Dorian."

I didn't take the trouble to find out what he was talking about then, so I didn't know now, standing up from my stool in front of these fifteen drunk people and Margaret. I had the same plan that I'd had before every high school concert: I'd play fast enough and messily enough that I might seem to be carrying an enormous pot of brilliance and only spilling a few unimportant mistakes. My legs were asleep as I started— they might as well have belonged to someone else. I was trying to find a note to hang from, but the more notes I tried, the more wrong each one seemed. Time felt like a rubber ball bouncing in too small a room. I heard Margaret whistle, and finally I found B-flat. I stuck on it, noodling up and down, even jumping an octave once, but I always came back to my one right note. Maybe an E would be right too? I dipped my toe in: It was! And (this is probably too much to ask) an F? Yes! With three notes I could make loops, I could spin, I could dance. Getting louder and louder, I whooped and I squawked and finally, for a grand finale, I flapped my right hand fast over the keys at the bottom, which makes the sax stutter, fast as a fly buzzing. I felt, for that minute when I was racing between my three notes, like I was singing in the shower with no one home.

But the crowd was quieter than they should have been. I peeked one eyelid open and saw Margaret nodding while Georgi whispered to her. I'd just closed my eyes again when I felt a wet knock on my forehead. My first thought, weirdly, was that there must be a leak in the ceiling, but then I tasted cherry on my top lip. The man with the walrus face was smirking and looking into his drink.

I wasn't sure the crowd had seen—I wasn't even sure what had happened—so I tried to finish the solo. There was a sticky cherry-tear in my eyebrow now, but I played a low, curvy bend with my F and B-flat, and then, when it worked, I did it again. The room filled with applause—I had a happy swell in my chest until I saw that the guitarist had stepped forward. I sat down, out of breath and light-headed. Alpaca Teeth patted the back of his head, so I closed my eyes and we went back to the head. Soloing—or maybe the shock of the cherry—had loosened me up, and for the first time we were sounding something like a real band.

Alpaca Teeth held up four fingers when we got to the end, so we played the last four again. And then he held them up again, so we played them again, and then one last time he held them up real high, and I knew that this was it, so I sat up on my stool and puffed out my chest. And then—just when I'd meant to finish with such a loud, solid blast that the walrus would melt—it happened. My sax decided it had played enough—I might as well have been blowing on an eggplant. Except the eggplant wouldn't have squeaked like this around all my hot huffing, worse and worse as I blew harder and harder. Oh, this was awful. Was the reed cracked? Did the mouthpiece slip? Could I kill myself without opening my eyes?

We finished and I laid my saxophone down in my lap. I didn't look up even after the piano's last chord had faded. Alpaca Teeth walked over, put his hand on my shoulder, and, leaning down, he said right into my ear, "Why don't you sit out a tune, just listen." Someone at the bar hooted. Staring at the floor, I walked down the stairs, offstage, and into the back hallway. Spit splashed on my hand when I pulled off my mouthpiece. A sign on the door said, ALARM WILL SOUND IF OPENED, but I wasn't going to go back out past Margaret. I pushed the door open and the alarm didn't sound.

Out on the street, though, there she was, standing by the wooden palm tree, looking at the menu in the window. "Hey," she said. "Well, that was all right." I shook my head. "You did what you wanted to do. You OK?" She put her hand on my arm, and looked so full of real worry that I wanted, all of a sudden, to tell her I was fine and to mean it. "Let's go watch *Emeril*," she said. Maybe I didn't want her to stop worrying completely: I didn't say a word.

If Dad had been watching—and thank God he wasn't— he would have said, "Well, we'll chalk this up to the growth column, huh?" Missing a penalty kick, managing not to get invited to a dance, losing the election for class treasurer— for Dad I was like one of those vines in the Amazon that grows three feet in an afternoon.

Two black girls were standing on the subway platform, and I heard one of them say, "Because when you're getting fucked, that *is* it! That's *all* it is right now!" Margaret laughed but stopped herself. "I told the guy who threw the cherry I hope he goes to hell," she said. She was playful, a little crazy—the kind of girl, I realized, who would have sneaked vodka on to a field trip, who you'd want on your side in a fight. Miserable as I felt, some deep part of me was glowing at being with her.

"My reed was bad," I finally said, while we sat down.

She nodded seriously.

But I suddenly knew, as clearly as I knew my height or my face, that I didn't have any talent. There it was, as simple as an ax blow. I felt dizzy and a little giddy: I was awful! I was ordinary! I was (and if I knew it, how could Dad not know it?) never going to be even a semigood saxophonist, no more than I'd be a dancer or a movie star. I'd never see Oasis again. In the mood now to do something drastic, I decided I'd take my saxophone downtown the next afternoon and look for a place to sell it. It was still in good shape—my mouthpiece alone must have been worth fifty dollars.

Margaret rested her head on my shoulder (she had to scoot away from me to do it—her hair smelled like apples), and I looked at our reflection in the window and flashed myself a smile. I could feel my bold mood getting away from me, but before it left completely I put my hand on her arm, just enough so she had to know that it was on purpose. She didn't move, and when I started to get up at our stop, she pretended—by jolting upright, shaking her head, looking around—to have been falling asleep.

* * *

"Romance," Sameer said, serving, "can inspire happiness to an extent that I find most horribly humbling. I have been blessed with one love, and even though it has proved to be merely a strong affinity, that is more than one could ever truly ask."

"I just can't believe how this feels. I seriously think about her all day. It's weird when I'm doing something and I realize I *haven't* thought about her for a few minutes."

"In youth particularly romance can be richly sustaining, even romance that is between people who know each other very little. In later years, one turns to scholarship, one turns to certain other matters. I call my religious study a kind of romance. There I am known completely. Have you, if I could ask, been seeking out a religious aspect to your happiness since we spoke?" Sameer's jacket was folded on a chair, and he was playing with the top two buttons of his shirt undone. His chest was as thin as a little boy's.

"No," I said, and then because he looked so disappointed: "Not really. I think I'll probably get into it when I'm older."

"My son is less than half of your age, and every day he sets aside time for prayer and for reading. Every single evening. If you were to read every day from a scholarly book on Judaic history that I would give you, you would find yourself like a man who stumbles into a cave of great treasure. There are large forces concerned for your being here. What are your favorite books, if I may ask?"

"Favorite?"

"Your favorite books."

"I'm reading a pretty good one now."

"Entitled?"

"*The Hunt for Red October*. Have you read it? It's about a submarine that goes missing."

He hit the ball into the net twice in a row. "My only advice to you is that you seek very early to understand what are the things composing a happy life. I spent many, many years not understanding these things."

"What are they?"

He laid his paddle down on the ball so he could count with his fingers. "They are spirit. Love of family. Love of a person who is *not* your family. Good food. Bodily cleanliness. And work that feels as if you must do it without choice."

"Margaret says she's known she's going to be a writer since she was six."

"And what have you known since you were six? I can say with all certainty that my passion for medicine dates precisely to a long illness when I was nine. Are animals your great passion?"

"I hope not. I'd always rather stay home than go to work."

"A vocation is a blessing that far too few of us receive. I studied medicine for many years, until the point that I became a fascinating doctor, and when I received my diploma I remember embracing my father and telling him that this was the proudest moment of my life. I felt something very, very hard to describe, that I was doing something very right. Perhaps your music gives you that feeling?"

"No. I don't think so. Margaret says when she writes it's the only time in the day she really feels awake."

Sameer smiled and picked his paddle back up. "Your Margaret seems to have imprisoned your heart and buried the key under miles and miles of sand," he said.

"She really has. And I think"—I felt nervous even saying it to him—"I might have imprisoned her heart too."

"That would indeed be the desirous circumstance." He

served a slow, loopy backhand, and I knocked a lucky shot off the edge of the table. "Fully and utterly desirous."

* * *

On Tuesday afternoon, I was sitting on the bench in front of Goat when Paul walked out looking like he might yell at me. His hands were in his jacket pockets, and his scowl—usually aimed at the computer screen or at his clipboard—was pointing right at me. I made sure I wouldn't be surprised: I hadn't put the covers on the food machines even though it was starting to rain, I'd done a sloppy job stripping Sheep that morning, I'd forgotten to cut the grapes in half for the catfish.

"I'm going around telling everybody some bad news," he said. "Chili died this afternoon. They put him under to operate, and he didn't wake up. Ruptured bladder."

"Seriously? All along?"

"We don't know how long."

"What should we tell people when they ask about him?"

"Tell them he had a good long life, and Lily's going to have a new friend soon."

Ramon, who'd started unfolding the covers for the food machines, said, "That Chili never gave off a real lust for life. With Lily, with Newman, you feel like every day they get up and think to themselves, 'Thank Jesus for another day,' but Chili, that guy I felt like he was hanging on by a thread ever since we got him."

"What happens to him now?" I said.

"Heaven," Paul said, and walked off to tell Janice and Garret.

What I meant (and I knew Paul understood me) was, *What happens to his body?* Do zoo animals get buried? In cemeteries? In Central Park? Or would we just treat him like one of the rats we catch, put him in a trash bag in the freezer and then send him away to get burned up? Who would erase his name from the roster sheet in the break room? Who would take his greasy bottle of castor oil out of the fridge?

Ramon was singing to himself— "If you ever see a sick pig . . ."—and I wondered if he could really know a song for just this occasion or if he was making it up.

There were still eleven minutes left in my break, so I walked out the gate and down to the infirmary building. The door was propped open with an old block of wood.

The floor in most of the zoo's buildings is brown and dirty—pieces of straw and food pellets are piled up against the walls, and the hallways all smell like rotting fruit—but the infirmary seems always to have just been sprayed and mopped. In a bright room to the right was the metal autopsy table, and on the floor next to it was a gray plastic crate. "Is Chili in there?" I said to Tony. He had a gray ponytail and mad-scientist glasses, and Garret once told me that he'd been married and divorced to the same woman four times.

"He's in there. We just got finished. I'm sorry—were you close?"

"I work over in Children's, so—"

"I'm sorry," he said, and he started spraying the table. "We're about to take his body over to the parking lot so they can take him to the Bronx—do you want to come?"

So with Tony and a bitter-looking woman from Otter,

I lifted Chili's coffin onto the flatbed of one of the zoo carts. He was heavy enough that we each grunted when we lifted him.

There were round holes along the side of the crate, and I wanted to look inside—or at least it seemed like the sort of thing I'd always wonder about if I didn't. So I tried to peek, without letting the woman from Otter see me, but all I could see was a dark lump and a flash of something wet. Every few steps I'd get a whiff of rubbing alcohol and something sweet and terrible underneath.

A van was waiting with its back doors open in the parking lot, and while we lifted Chili in, I thought, *This pain in my forearms is from lifting Chili's body. These red creases on my hands are from carrying Chili's body.* I wondered, for the first time, where Chili's parents were, if they still knew each other, whether they lived on a farm or in a zoo, if they'd even noticed when Chili moved away. I imagined them living in my grandparents' farm in Virginia in the empty horse shed. They were standing by the river on a pile of dirt where their son was buried, and tears were running off the mom-pig's snout while the dad-pig, quiet like Chili, just looked out at all this grass and rock and river and shook his head.

I slammed the back doors harder than I'd meant to, and the van pulled out through the exit and into traffic, where it could, for all anyone knew, have been carrying air conditioners or two-by-fours.

That Saturday morning, I went with Margaret, Sameer, and Sameer's son, Nishant, to temple. On an afternoon that she'd played Ping-Pong with us, Margaret had made me promise that we would go. I'd pretended to need convincing.

"To see a Saturday-morning service would be more dear to me than I could convey," Sameer said, and at eight thirty on his day off he was waiting in the lobby in a striped suit. "Margaret, Henry. Please meet my son, Nishant." Sameer's son, wearing a suit of his own, nodded and seemed to study the carpet. He was eight years old, as frail and as wary as a squirrel. "It will one day seem to him a symptom of divine grace that he should have had the opportunity to attend a Jewish service so early in his life."

Sameer had started to tell me, in the weeks before we went to temple, how he'd come to be interested in Jews. He told the story in a voice much warmer than I'd ever heard him use before, cupping my shoulder at his favorite parts. Each day when he decided that he'd talked enough, he would say, "And for the next installment, you will have to tune in tomorrow."

When he first came to America, he hadn't been able to find a job for six months. He lived in his cousin's house in Edison, New Jersey, sleeping on a short couch in front of the TV. Each day he'd take the bus to a different shopping complex and go from store to store, telling whoever would listen about his education and asking if they wanted to hire him. He didn't have a mustache yet, and he wore his cousin's clothes, which were small even for him. He was turned down by Chinese restaurants, by hardware stores, by florists. One night, when he'd fallen asleep on the bus and woken up in a part of the city he didn't know, he walked into a bookstore that seemed to carry only torn books with coffee stains. The store had no customers, the shelves were spilling over, and Sameer, unsure how to get back to Edison, went to sit down on a stool in the back. "I was as near to declaring life intolerable as I have ever become," Sameer said. "I even let out a moan of anguish." The old man who owned the store, who'd been unpacking a new box of books, heard Sameer and came to see what was the matter. "We talked for the loveliest hours I had known since leaving home, about medicine and religion and history and everything else in our minds. He was a very scholarly man, very formidable, may he rest in peace forever." The old man, who I imagine in a loose, dirty sweater, with one gray wing of hair standing up on the side of his head, hired him on the spot. The store turned out to be only a fifteen-minute bus ride from his cousin's, and Sameer worked organizing the shelves until the old man died two years later. "Without the warmth of a Jewish spirit, my start in this country might never have occurred." Sameer brought me a birthday note the old man had once written him (*For a scholar and a pal . . .*), and he held it like a copy of the Declaration of Independence.

We had to walk slowly up to the temple, not much faster than if we'd been looking for a lost ring on the sidewalk, because Margaret was tottering and stumbling in her high heels.

"What do Jewish people think happens after you die?" Nishant asked.

"Nothing, I don't think," I said, when I realized that Sameer was waiting for me to answer. "They just think you die."

"It is in fact both a fascinating and a thorned issue," Sameer said. "The belief in an afterlife seemed, when I was beginning, so vital to the religious way of life that to be fully honest I could hardly fathom the Jewish practice." While Sameer spoke he kept glancing over at Nishant, who really did seem now to be looking for something on the sidewalk. "There is a terrifying lack of comfort in the absence of either heaven or reincarnation."

"I think there's something kind of nice about just dying and having that be it," Margaret said. "You wouldn't have to worry so much—it would just all be over, no matter what."

"Once you are my age you will never again say anything so foolish."

"I don't think it's foolish," Nishant said, almost to himself.

Sameer stopped and leaned down, and in the middle of the sidewalk, either not noticing or not caring about the crowds that rushed around him, he held Nishant's upper arm and scolded him too quietly for us to hear.

When he stood up he tried to leap right back into the conversation, the way someone does who's fallen asleep for a second in class. "There are so many wonderful stories to the Jewish religion. The Passover legend is one that I've cherished for years and years," he said. "You have enjoyed many seder meals with your family?"

"Not for the past couple of years. My uncle's an atheist, so we always have to kind of fight to do it."

"I confess that to hear about possessors of such rich history treating their heritage lightly plays against my heart. Your bar mitzvah was no doubt a meaningful occasion for everyone concerned?"

"Honestly, it was a little bit bigger deal than a birthday. It meant a lot to my mom."

"And what, may I ask, was the subject of your Torah portion?"

"It was . . . the Tower of Babel. I had to learn every word of it in Hebrew, and it's weird, but it's completely gone."

On the steps outside the temple, Sameer took my hand

for a second and said, "Today I hope you won't mind if I will consider this in a degree to be my own bar mitzvah."

He would have to share it. At the door we picked up yarmulkes and color-printed guides to the service: ADAM GERTNER'S BAR MITZVAH, JULY 12, 2003. Adam was small and blond, in a suit with boxy shoulders, and he sat in a throne of a chair onstage between his goofy parents. The temple was much fancier than Temple Shalom—the seats were padded and the floor sloped toward the front like in a movie theater. While we all found seats, an organ buzzed in a way that went right to my stomach, making me have to pee. Sameer's yarmulke kept sliding off, so he pinned it to his head with two fingers.

"Shabbat shalom," said the rabbi. He looked like a hobbit.

"Shabbat shalom," said the two hundred people around us.

It didn't take more than a minute for me to remember why I'd stopped going to temple. Each time I got comfortable in my seat, or got anywhere in a daydream, the rabbi would tell us to stand up, and Adam's guide to the service—full of curly Print Shop letters and color drawings of trees—didn't seem to have anything to do with what was happening onstage. Could the rabbi even be enjoying this? Could all this standing and singing and waiting and staring actually mean something to anyone in the room other than that another Saturday morning was gone?

I remembered all the hours I'd lost to this feeling. Sunday school, Hebrew school, temple on Fridays, lessons with Cantor Milus on Mondays: The actual business of being Jewish didn't have anything more to do with God than piano lessons did, or being on the soccer team. What did Mr. Levitz, with his sleepy voice and huge ears, know about God? He drove a crappy little yellow car, and, when we were on our retreat to the Chesapeake Bay, he stomped into our cabin in just his tighty-whities and told us to shut the fuck up.

"It's boredom as a tool of suppression," Walter once told me. "What other excuse could there be for speaking a language nobody understands? Try sitting home some Friday night with me and we'll read any English book off the shelf, and see if you don't get more out of it than you do at temple."

But when I'd take this argument to Mom, she'd look at me like I'd brought her a ball of used tissues. "We don't ask *anything* of you," she'd say. "You can do this for us. I don't want to hear another word." So I'd stop, but the arguments she didn't want to hear would curdle in me all through temple. *What stupid, selfish, delusional . . .*

Adam Gertner had come to the bima now. "Today I'm going to read from the story of Abraham and Isaac. Please follow along in your guidebooks to the service on page eight." It wasn't as boring to listen to him as to the rabbi—he had a little kid's fluty singing voice, and he was so nervous that even the fifty or so kids from his school were suddenly quiet. His left leg was going like chattering teeth—he'd get it under control and take a deep breath, but then when he missed a note or had to say a word twice, *thumpthumpthump,* it would start up again. *You won't remember this in three years,* I silently beamed toward him. *It'll be a photo album on your parents' coffee table and you'll never think about it again.*

When I was getting ready for my bar mitzvah, Rabbi Tillman said, "I'm going to shake every ounce of nerves out of you before that Saturday." He was completely bald, with red eyes that looked like he was being choked. At services he always spoke like he was angry at everyone for coming. For those two months before my bar mitzvah I'd meet him on Thursdays at six for practice, and we'd walk right past all the empty rows of seats and up to the bima. He'd lift out the practice Torah, the one that wasn't rescued from the Holocaust, and I'd run my metal pointer over the tiny letters while I sang. He'd sit alone in the front row—it was hard to believe an adult this important could be so concerned with me—and say to no one, "Psssst! Psssst, Kimmy! Kimmy, did you hear what Rachel said about Henry? Did you? I couldn't believe it." If that didn't screw me up, he'd crumple pieces of paper into balls and throw them at me. "He isn't polished," Mom would say in the car after lessons, "but you really will be grateful, I think."

Adam unfolded his personal statement. His friends were the most bored people there, but they were the ones who were making him so nervous—his hands were shaking now too. "It may seem to you," he started, in a voice that could have come out of a girl, "that the story of Abraham and Isaac is far removed from our lives here today. After all, it describes a land many miles away, and many years in the past. But in fact, if we read the story closely, we will see that it has a lot to teach us about the world of America at the beginning of the twenty-first century.

"Today, as we all know, we live in very dangerous times. On September the eleventh, two thousand and one, America had a feeling that it had not felt for many years. That feeling was fear. I know that I personally was afraid, because my cousin Isaac works just five blocks away from the World Trade Center." He held out his shaking arm to point at Isaac, who waved. "He was extremely lucky to survive, but before my father was able to get in touch with him, my parents and I felt extremely worried.

"And also for the first time in many years, the United States is involved in a war. Someone my age might be asking himself: 'Is the whole world falling apart? Are all the good times over? Maybe I shouldn't even believe in God anymore, if such terrible things are happening.'"

Someone near the front giggled.

"The story of Abraham and Isaac teaches us that we must continue to believe. Even when things seem to be going very bad, and even when we can't believe what we're being asked . . ." The second he looked up I knew that he wasn't going to finish. His leg was going so fast now that he could hardly stand, and the cords in his throat were standing out. "Even when . . ." he said again. He looked back at his parents. His friends were sitting up now. Sameer's eyebrows were raised. Margaret whispered, "Oh, *no.*" Even Nishant was watching.

Adam refolded his pages and tucked them back into his suit pocket. "Thank you," he said, and then he went back to his seat and burst into quiet tears.

The sturdy little rabbi came up to Adam's place and said, "On a day as important as today, it's little wonder that one might have a case of nerves." He looked back and smiled at

Adam and his parents, but they were busy coping with their disaster. "Myself and Adam's teachers worked for many months helping Adam to develop his speech, and I don't think it would be fair to deprive all of you who have come today of the wisdom that he has drawn from this story. I will try to give my own sense of what he might have told you, and Adam, if you feel that you would like to join in or to correct me, please do so."

An old woman in the row ahead of us whispered to her husband, "I think he's enjoying this."

"God appeared to Abram and told him that he was to be the 'father of a multitude of nations,'" the rabbi started. "To consecrate this change, he would now be called Abraham, and his wife, Serai, would now be known as Sarah. Surely this is familiar to many of us, but it is a story that we could do well to hear repeated. God granted Abraham and Sarah a child—this despite Sarah's old age—and He told them that the child's name would be Isaac. Sarah did indeed give birth to Isaac, and when Isaac was just a boy, God appeared again to Abraham and presented him with a test. 'Take your son,' God said, 'and go to the land of Moriah, and once there, offer him as a sacrifice.'"

The rabbi had a gentle voice, and while he went on I felt my eyelids getting heavy. But it wasn't really sleep I was going toward. It was that almost-sleep, like during movies you start watching too late at night, where every thought you have turns right away into a dream.

"Isaac was Abraham's only son, his beloved son, and yet when morning came Abraham woke early and set off for

Moriah with Isaac and a load of wood to carry out the offering. A group of young men accompanied them to carry supplies, for it would be a three-day journey. When something difficult has to be done—a shot administered, a bit of bad news received—it is common that we should wish it to be over with quickly. There is no need to prolong the suffering, we say; simply deliver the pain and leave us to recover. So I would like for all of us here today to imagine what those three days must have felt like, seventy-two hours of walking and waiting during which Abraham's mind could focus on nothing but the gruesome task that awaited him at his journey's end."

I half dreamed myself onto a mountain, where I was wading through bushes and looking for Dad. We'd been playing a game, but now he'd turned himself into a tree, and if I found him I was going to explain that he'd gone too far. I tried running my hand over the barks of trees as they passed—they slid by, as if they were on moving walkways—but certain ones, when I reached out, would draw back, or shrink, and the sun was getting so strong now that I knew Dad was going to need water. Newman was with me, I suddenly noticed, and he was trying to help me look, but his hooves kept getting tangled in vines and I thought that I might have to leave him. "I'm sorry," I heard Dad's voice say, but just before I could turn to see which tree he was, I shot forward in my seat feeling like everyone in the temple was staring at me. But Nishant was the only one.

The rabbi was still going. "This story, then, as Adam would have gone on to tell you, is about more than mere faith, if faith can ever be described as 'mere.' It is also about being alone, about being without protection. It is about realizing that the world can be a profoundly cruel place, one in which any day could bring horrors on a scale that we have never even thought to imagine. And yet we must go on. We may take comfort in one another—indeed, we *must* take comfort in one another—but we must also realize that our lives could be stripped to nothing in less time than I have been speaking here today. It is a grim truth, but it is one that we would do well to remember, for it turns our eyes to God with an urgency that a pleasant day, and may He grant us a lifetime of those, simply does not provide. God is not one in a constellation of comforts—He is *One,* and this we must never forget.

"When, in a few minutes, we exit into our Sabbath, I would like for each one of us to take a moment and to inhabit the mind of Isaac as, with his new understanding, he descends from the mountaintop at Moriah. We will feel grateful for the gift of life; we will feel newly aware of our own solitude—we will feel hushed."

And the whole temple was hushed. He took a long sip of water and we all listened to it *glug* down his throat.

"Please rise and join me on page seventy-three of your prayer books for the Shema."

Out on the street it took a few minutes, until we were back on Fifth, for the temple silence to lift. It was barely starting to rain, more like leaking, and we all looked down while we walked. "May I offer you my most humble gratitude for sharing your service," Sameer said. "The Jewish practice contains beauties I would not have known even to suspect. And the rabbi I found to be very knowledgeable, very intelligent."

Because of the dream, or maybe just because I was finally up and outside, I felt the quiet sort of roominess that temple—and I'd forgotten this—could sometimes give me. Like exercise, I think that religion is never so appealing as just after you've finished with it for the day. Maybe Margaret and I could go to temple together some Friday nights, then out for a nice dinner, where we'd both lean forward with our hands around the candle. I wasn't sure it was what temple was supposed to give me, but I felt, walking slowly down Fifth's wide sidewalk in my jacket, a little flare of love for my life, a wandering, curious, clearheaded feeling.

Margaret hardly talked at all while we walked, and I thought that she must have been feeling the same thing. But I looked over, ready to say something thoughtful, and she was nibbling a flap of skin on the edge of her finger. "I keep thinking about him with his parents now," she said when I asked her what was wrong, and it took me a second to figure out who she was talking about. We came to a stop while Nishant, frowning and kneeling, tied his shoe. "Were you watching?" she said. "He didn't lift his face up once."

*   *   *

The rain that started while we were in temple kept on falling for days—every night the weatherman on NY1 would say, "I've got bad news, guys," and the anchors, at their desk, would smile and sigh. Hardly anyone came into the zoo. None of the animals would even leave their sheds, except when we cleaned, and then they'd stand outside looking like hotel guests when someone's pulled the fire alarm at three in the morning. But on Wednesday afternoon, while I was on Change, the sun poked a gold bar through the clouds, and I decided it was time to bring Margaret in after closing. You haven't really been to the zoo until you've been at night, I told her that afternoon. During the day you can't really understand what it means that this is where all these animals live.

"What happens if we get caught?" she said. But I'd told Ramon to expect us, and when we walked in a few minutes after nine, he nodded at us from his night-guard hut without even opening his eyes. First we walked into the main zoo. The sea lions, sleeping, looked like part of the rocks they were on. But when the clouds blew away from the moon after a minute, I could see their wrinkles, their flippers. They were so still they could have been dead, and we didn't make a noise. I kept looking over to see if Margaret was bored, but she was smiling and her eyes were wide.

I jumped when Ramon put a hand on my shoulder. "You want to see something real nice?" he said, quieter than I'd ever heard him talk. "Man, you're going to love this."

He swung open the heavy black gate into Polar. There were no lights in the tunnel, and it smelled like wet rocks and moss—right away the cold made my arm hairs prickle. Behind the glass wall in front of us was Penguin, and when we moved right up close to it I could see them sleeping, pressed together on the fake shore. I put my hand on Margaret's arm, and she was covered in goose bumps too. Ramon led us farther in, to the bears' tank. The glass could have been painted black. "Now check this out here," Ramon said, and he turned a dial on the wall. The tunnel stayed black, but the water in the tank started to glow blue. Margaret put a hand over her mouth. A polar bear, fluid and enormous, drifted by the glass a foot from our faces. I felt my pulse tick in my temples. The bear held his front paws against his body, and even his ears seemed to be pressed back flat—he'd turned himself into a slippery missile. He drifted back and forth, his millions of white hairs flowing, gulping air once each lap (and turning back into a bear for that instant when he was above the surface). He couldn't have weighed any less than eight hundred pounds, and if the glass had disappeared he would have crushed my skull, but in the water he looked as gentle as a mermaid. His nose was long and black, and the fur around his ears was yellow. During one lap he turned his face toward Ramon for a second, and all three of us laughed. Margaret held my arm now.

"He does this every night, you could set your clock to it. He doesn't move the whole day, people always asking if there's something wrong with him, is he depressed, but at night he goes like this for hours. I thought of it and I said to myself, 'They're gonna love this.'"

"It's incredible," Margaret said. "Thank you so much."

"I thought, 'This is something anybody who likes animals has gotta see.'"

Back out by the sea lions, Ramon winked at me and said, "Now I got to go look out for bad guys. Henry, you can get into Children's?"

Children's, after Polar, felt as cozy as a sweatshirt. "Isn't it weird being here with the birds silent?" I said, but Margaret didn't answer. I could hear Lily snoring. Margaret hopped the fence into Goat with that one-hand-on-the-pole jump that keepers do, and I hopped after her, but I banged my kneecap against the pole hard enough that I felt it for a minute in the bottom of my stomach.

"Look at Newman," she said. "I can't believe how mellow he is." He was asleep in the back left corner of the shed, and Margaret had to duck to get over to him. "Look. He's letting me play with his hooves." I think he would have let her take out his liver. His nostrils were whistling.

I squeezed in on the other side of him, and it wasn't a date over rose-petal sundaes, sitting with seven goats and all this dust and dirty hay, but I knew, listening to all of them breathing, that this was when I should kiss her. Both of us had an arm on Newman's side. For what seemed like a long time we just sat there facing the wall of the shed, listening to the traffic.

"My dad called today," she said. "This is just such a hard summer for him." Was she asking me not to kiss her, or was she just nervous? Or was she really just thinking about her dad right then? He was a photographer for a newspaper in Montana, and he'd gotten mixed up in some kind of scandal that I could never quite follow. The paper thought he'd charged them for trips that weren't for work, but there was something else to it too, something to do with Great Falls politics—she talked about it like I already knew the basics.

"He's thinking he might just quit and do a book of Yellowstone pictures he's been talking about. I think he should.

He has all these amazing pictures from when he was growing up next to pictures from now, and he'd write little essays about them and everything."

I made a friendly noise, but I thought anything I said would only take us farther from the moment where we'd been. For a few seconds, then for almost a minute, we just watched the silence stretch out. My heart sped up, my hand started edging across Newman's body to hers, my shoulder tilted toward her. Just the very edges of our hands were touching, and then my palm was on the back of her hand, and then, before I'd had time to think about it, we were holding hands. She'd turned her palm over to meet mine, and our fingers—sweaty, a little sticky, but what could matter less?—were curled together.

"Henry," she said, and I knew, even before she drew her hand away, that it was going to be bad. "I've got a boyfriend." I could only see the outline of her face. "I kept wanting to tell you, but at first I thought you knew, and then I didn't know a good way to do it. I'm so sorry. We've been together for almost three years. I really didn't want to make this any big dramatic thing. I'm sorry. You promise we'll keep being the same way we are with each other? I thought you knew. That's who always calls."

I nodded, and my whole body started to shake. I kept my eyes focused on Newman, and I only realized how hard I was petting him when he lifted his head and sneezed.

"I completely understand if you're mad at me."

"I'm not mad."

"Thank you. But if you don't want to talk to me for a few

days, or if you want to see me less, I promise I won't be mad. I'll be sad, but I'll totally understand."

I shook my head, and my lower lip tugged into a frown.

"Let's go back," she said. "I shouldn't have said anything tonight. Thanks for bringing me here."

We walked back to the apartment a few steps apart, not talking, and in the elevator I couldn't look at her. "Good night," she said, with the doors open on twelve. I didn't say anything. "Good night," she said again, and I still didn't say anything. And then she left.

Margaret's boyfriend was named Drew. She'd grown up just streets away from him—for their entire childhoods they'd been staying for dinner at each other's houses on school nights, spending vacations together at a cabin in the mountains, getting yelled at by each other's parents. When they started dating at the beginning of junior year, it felt so natural, to their families and to everyone at school, that it took work to remember that they hadn't been together all along.

In a photo that she kept in a drawer at the bottom of her dresser, he's sitting on a hill in front of a brick wall wearing shorts and a baseball jersey, floppy brown hair tucked behind his ears, squinting at the camera. He's a shaggy, monkeyish sort of handsome ("He needed a haircut! He doesn't usually look like that!"), and he's smiling like whoever's taking the picture has just made a joke he's heard before. He was back in Montana for the summer, working with his older brother as a forest ranger in Yellowstone.

"Have you had sex with him?" I asked. We were eating pressed sandwiches on a bench just outside the zoo. Kids sat near us, sulking in strollers, and men with easels leaned forward, drawing bright cartoons of women who sat up very straight, hands in their laps, mouths puckered.

"Why would you want to know?"

"So I'll know how serious it is. If I should give up."

"You should give up, but you should still be my friend."

"I don't want to be your friend."

"That's very sad."

"Have you had sex with him?"

"Henry. Stop."

"I want to know. You don't have to answer if you don't want to."

"I said I don't want to."

"OK, you do have to. Have you? Just tell me."

"I don't understand why you'd want to hear about that."

"So you have?"

"We have."

"I'm not hungry anymore."

"Then you shouldn't have asked!"

"Have you told him about me?"

"What about you?"

"About being friends with me. How we go for walks, how you put your head on my shoulder. How I almost kissed you."

"You didn't almost kiss me. Yes, I've told him about you. He's glad I'm making friends."

"He's not worried?"

"About what?"

"About me."

"What would he be worried about? He doesn't really get jealous. It wouldn't even occur to him."

It occurred to me. I looked at her hands now and saw them on his back, I watched her talk and saw this mouth, these lips, around his penis—there wasn't a part of her I could look at anymore without it dropping a little fizzing pill of hate in my stomach. What I wanted, it suddenly seemed to me, was for her to have no body, and no past, at all. The thousand little things we agree to forget when we think about each other, the lying, the shitting, the hair, the mess—suddenly I couldn't do it. I'd sometimes catch myself watching her the same hateful, fascinated way you watch a stranger pick at pimples on his neck.

But I still saw her every night—still called her the minute I left work—and a few times each week she would come to meet me for lunch. Matthew was at day camp, so I may have seen her even more now than I had when seeing her had had a point. And even when I wasn't with her, when I was raking Goat or picking up rat traps with Ramon or just waking up in the morning, I was gnawing away at the thought of her. Or the thought of her was gnawing away at me. Sometimes, with no warning, my body would turn light and I'd suddenly know—not think, but know—that Margaret and I were eventually going to be together. This might happen just after lunch, or when I'd be walking home down Fifth at five thirty in the slow crowd, all those heads packed in and bobbing like in a New York movie. But then there would be times (sitting alone at the kitchen counter with my cereal in the morning, tossing out fish-smelling pellets for the turtles in the afternoon) when I'd feel so hopeless that just living, standing and speaking and climbing stairs, would seem beyond me. But even during the miserable stretches I couldn't keep myself from going through everything I heard, everything I saw, everything I remembered, for things I'd like to tell her. Things that she might write about.

She had a notebook with her that she'd been writing in every night for two years—descriptions of sex with Drew, first impressions of me, pages of plans she was too superstitious to talk about—and there it was, on her bedside table. The cover was blue, and she'd written *Margaret Payson* in black marker along the bottom edge. When she was in the bathroom, once, I flipped it open to a middle page and read, *With a simultaneous expansion and narrowing of my affection, I admitted to myself that I'd cared for them at least as much they'd cared for me. . . .* But I never learned who "they" were. The toilet flushed, I slammed the notebook, and, to keep myself from having to lie to her one day, I made myself promise that I'd never read it again. The next day I asked her, casually, if she ever let Drew read it. She said no. I asked her, even more casually, if she'd ever let me read it. She told me to stop it.

I'd gotten into the habit of asking, whenever she'd just told a story, if she'd also told it to Drew. Just a tic, the way you might say, "Is that so?" or, "Isn't that funny?" Finally— we were walking by the Reservoir one day just after a storm— she swore to God that if I asked her one more time she'd never tell me anything else. She might as well have threatened to slit my throat. I loved listening to her stories the way I once loved listening to David's—I'd laugh out loud at things that she didn't even mean to be funny, just because for a second my joy in being included in her life would bubble over. "My eighth-grade science teacher got fired for sodomy with a student," she told me once, when we were lying in her room on top of the made bed. She always looked cheery when she was telling her stories, no matter what they were about. "I'm serious. He was totally cool, he always let us have class outside, and he didn't care if we smoked around him. Mr. Page. He was this stumpy little guy, the sweatiest person I've ever seen. He always had a towel over his shoulder. We called him 'Willow.'

"All this stuff was such a mess when it came out, they made us all see the counselor and everything. My father just about killed our principal. It was this kid in my class, Keith Bladser, this quiet guy with glasses and a hearing aid. He was an amazing painter. We knew Mr. Page took him to hockey games and got him presents and stuff, but we just thought he liked him. It was so bizarre. They didn't send him to jail, for some reason, and he ended up working at the Kinko's five minutes from my house, so you'd see him whenever you went in to Xerox a presentation or anything. Some parents wanted to make him move out of Great Falls, but I think he couldn't, because of his probation."

I asked her to tell me about every teacher she'd ever had, in order. The names of her pets. Her phone number at home (which I dialed one night while she was out to dinner—I couldn't believe how easy it was to hear her dad's voice). I made her draw her room for me. I wanted more and more and more—a map of her life exactly the size of her life, one I could walk around in and study until I knew every staircase and nightmare and cousin.

But then at night, I'd be lying there listening to car alarms, replaying whatever she'd told me that day, and suddenly a vision of Drew would assault me, clearer than if I'd actually been looking at him. I'd see him sleeping folded in her long arms, or crouching to kiss the inside of her thigh just by the elastic of her underwear, or whispering, "I love you," in the back of her head first thing in the morning. And for the hour afterward, whatever nutty fever made me need to know what sort of cars her parents drove would break. I'd remember that she didn't know my birthday.

One night when I was feeling too awful to fall asleep, I heard David and Lucy start having sex. Lucy had decided to move their bed against the wall, trying to make the room "open up," and their heads were now a couple of feet from mine. Their TV was on, and I heard Jay Leno say, "He's still thinking, 'Where can *I* get one of those?'" Lucy started making a high-pitched question-mark noise, a sound from porn, and my penis started to lift its head. Then I heard David groan and say something short, and shame ran all through me to my toes. And worked up like that, who could fall asleep? Who wouldn't go to the bathroom and jerk off standing in front of the mirror just to get it out of his system? (And then who wouldn't stand at the window in the dark looking down at traffic for a while, wondering how different a real wish to jump felt from this shaky, quiet tug?)

Lying there with everything smelling like Vaseline lotion, I said to myself, with a weird touch of pride, *This is it, this is as bad as I've ever felt.* I turned on my lamp and opened my new notebook (I'd lied to Margaret that I wrote sometimes), and at the top of the first page I wrote: *I don't understand why I feel so much about so little and so little about so much.* I couldn't think of anything else to write, and the sentence looked ridiculous alone like that, so I closed the book. I turned on SportsTalk 570, turned off the light, pulled the sheet and blanket up so only my face was poking out, and I imagined a Zamboni coming to clear out all the mess in my brain. This was an idea I'd been using for years. The Zamboni driver was old and quiet and very proud of his work. He made slow laps around the rink until the ice was so clean that it glowed—no thought, about Margaret or anything else, could stick to the surface. With my new clean brain I heard only the radio.

"The question isn't who's going to take over his stats, 'cause there are any number of guys on the team who can do that. Arroyo might even improve on points and rebounds. But you get to talking about who can replace the trust he's built with Sloan for the past fifteen years, and you're talking about something different."

In elementary school I wouldn't go to sleep unless I had

my radio against my head with the volume turned so low that I could barely hear it. I'd listen for hours to Don and Steve arguing about the Capitols' play-off chances, the thinking behind the Orioles' pitching changes, whether the Bullets' guards were overpaid. But the real reason I kept the radio on—the thing that made me feel the happiest, when I'd wake up and hear a snippet—was the commercials. The Bill Clinton impersonator in the ones for Jerry's Subs. The blizzard sounds in the ones for Park Auto Insurance. The Motel 6 man, Tom something, so honest and gentle and old-fashioned. Such amazingly unchanging friends, and all as cheery at three in the morning as they were in the middle of the afternoon. For some reason, Dad couldn't stand that I slept this way. Every night after he figured that I was asleep, he'd sneak in and turn the radio off and move it away from my head. "Now, that's better, isn't it?" he'd whisper, and I'd make sure to keep my breathing slow and loud.

"Let's go to the phones on this. Rob in Manhattan, you're on SportsTalk 570. Do the Jazz get better or worse when Stockton goes?"

"What's up? Thanks for having me on. You guys rule. I think they get worse. I think they have to get worse, because if you look at what Stockton's done, he's unquestionably one of the best point guards ever to play, and I'm sorry, but Arroyo—"

"That's one vote for worse. Let's go to Elvin in Jackson Heights."

"I just have a question to ask you. How can we be sitting here talking about John Stockton when the greatest power forward in the history of the NBA, probably the greatest athlete in any sport, is going to the Lakers and—"

I was asleep before Elvin finished his question.

* * *

If Margaret was lying awake at night wondering what would happen between us, she was good at hiding it. She just kept on showing up at the zoo to chat while I shoveled, or calling at night to ask if I felt like watching a movie, or ringing the doorbell to see if she could come play with Gandalf for a few minutes. Gandalf, to my semihorror, had become our main topic of conversation. If I felt, at eleven some night, like I needed to call her but had no reason to, I'd just invent something cute for Gandalf to have done and she'd insist on coming up to see him. Every time she walked into my room she'd fall down on her knees and rub her hair against him, cooing and burbling. She'd make a hammock with her T-shirt and let him fall asleep in it. She'd lift one of his long ears and whisper to him, then pretend that the noises he made—nervous squeaking, mostly—were an answer. She bought him a pack of green chew sticks from PETCO (she wanted to train him to live free in my room), but he sniffed one and never touched it. Instead, while I was sleeping, when Margaret said that he had to be left alone to practice being out of his cage, he chewed two places bare in the rug, he chewed a hole in the toe of one of my work sneakers, and he chewed through a lamp cord (unplugged). One night while Margaret was setting up an obstacle course with a shoe-box lid and carrot sticks, David walked in to tell me about Dad.

"What the hell is that?" he said.

"A rabbit."

"I got that part. Let me be clearer: What the hell's it doing in my apartment?" Margaret was holding Gandalf in her lap, but David didn't even say hi to her.

"They couldn't take it at work. Paul asked if I'd take it until they found somebody who wanted it."

"But you kept it a secret?"

"It was only supposed to be a couple of days."

"How long has it been?"

"A week. A little bit more than a week."

"If Lucy sees it . . . Is that piss? Find somewhere else for it."

"I will."

"Good. I just got off the phone with Dad. He's coming to New York to visit Uncle Jacob. He gets in tomorrow at four."

"Why's he visiting Uncle Jacob?"

"I have no idea. Ask somebody at the zoo tomorrow how you can give away a rabbit. Maybe you can just let it go in the park. We're meeting at Jacob's at seven o'clock to go to dinner."

When he left, Margaret had to press her hand over her mouth to keep from laughing. "He's so *serious,*" she whispered. "My God. Think about Gandalf loose in the park!" If it wouldn't have made her furious, I would have loved to turn him loose—I would have been fine just setting him down on Fifty-third Street. He'd stained the crotch of my best jeans with pee, twice he'd bitten my hand so hard that I bled, and he was the reason that I spent sixty percent of my time with Margaret talking about rabbits.

David's telling me about Dad unsettled me more than his

finding out about Gandalf did, though. I hadn't thought once about Uncle Jacob since I'd moved to New York, and now that I was going to see him I felt a flush of guilt. Jacob—who's actually my great-uncle—had been ancient for my entire life, thin and slow and silent except for the occasional complaint. His cheeks hang down like a bulldog's, and his scalp is covered in brown dots that look somewhere between moles and scabs. His wife Sadie's funeral was during finals my sophomore year of high school, so I didn't go—that might have been part of the guilt—and Dad didn't really talk about it when he got back (except once when he said to Mom, while they were unpacking groceries, "*Completely* alone. Not another soul left," and I knew somehow who he meant).

After work I took the B to Brooklyn and found Jacob's street looking exactly as it had ten years ago, even though I wouldn't have thought that I remembered it at all. The sidewalk squares were cracked and loose in places, and all of the houses were pushed back from the street by steep brown staircases. An old black woman sat on her stoop petting a ratty dog. A little boy rode his scooter in the street. Jacob lived in one of the only wooden houses on the block—it had been there before any of the others, I remembered him telling us, but now it looked like a house that you'd find falling down on a beach.

Dad opened the door when I knocked and made his joke-surprise face with the open mouth. He looked a little gray. "*God,* it's good to see you. How's work? How's life? I've got a million questions. You boys are going to have to catch me up all night." He had to shout for me to hear him—it sounded like an airplane was about to take off somewhere inside. David was standing with a glass of water in the kitchen, wearing his work clothes, and Jacob (it took me a second to see him) was deep in a chair in the living room. And there was what was making all the noise: A tube under his nose ran to a chugging, clanking, brown machine. He could have been a hundred and twenty.

"Hi Jacob!" I yelled. I wasn't sure that he could survive a hug.

He looked up at me with eyes that had started to turn milky, and without smiling he said something I couldn't hear.

The stairs were covered in boxes and old magazines, but the first floor—which must have been the only part of the house that Jacob used anymore—was as tidy and depressing as a waiting room. Pencils were lined up next to each other on the stand by the couch, mail was stacked up on the coffee table, no dishes were out in the kitchen. My whole body itched from the heat. Jacob wore a sweater and jacket.

Once I'd poured my own glass of water—water I didn't want at all, but something told me to put off the talking part of the visit—I sat down on a hard chair in the living room, where (and maybe a glimpse of this is what had told me to keep busy in the kitchen) Dad and Jacob and David sat silently looking at the center of the room. Jacob turned his machine off as soon as I sat down.

"So, Jacob," Dad said. "Tell the boys and me how life's been treating you. We haven't all been together in, my God ... forever."

"Not good."

"Health? You're a real trooper, just getting up, feeling the way you must feel."

"I barely . . . get out of bed."

He talked so slowly that by the time he'd said anything, we all had to spend about a minute nodding and making interested sounds.

"Well, boys. Why not give your uncle a sense of what you're up to? Did you even know they were living together in the city? Isn't it neat?"

"You could stay with . . . them."

"*Ha!* No, I couldn't slow them down. Just wait till you hear what Henry does all day."

After everything anyone said was a silence long enough that the conversation seemed in danger of being called off altogether.

"What if we forget going out to dinner?" Dad said. "How's Chinese by everyone? Is there a place in the neighborhood?" David, Dad, and I all jumped up at the same time. Twice, while we were waiting for the food, making conversation like a person with kidney stones makes pee, I went into the front hall and grimaced in the mirror. David and I turned setting the table for dinner into about twenty minutes' work.

While we ate—greasy piles of noodles and slimy beef and pale vegetables—Dad studied the back of one of the paper menus. "Who knows what Chinese year it is?" he said, seeming to know that he wouldn't get an answer.

Then David said almost his first words of the night. "What are you doing here again, Dad?"

"Fair question." Looking at Dad, while he refolded the menu and chased a squirming dumpling with his chopsticks, I kept thinking for some reason about the word *drowning*. "Oh, your mother . . . I'm right there underfoot in the summers, I think. And besides, I figured I'd see you guys, see Jacob. I don't like going so long between visits."

"It's been eight . . . years."

We'd started treating Jacob like a bird in the corner of the room. He ate white rice and rested between every bite.

"My plan," Dad said, "is to stay up here about a week, if you guys can stand having me around. Don't go rescheduling your lives for me, I'll just be a fly on the wall. And there's a bunch of old clubs I'd love to check out, if I have some time to kill. We used to come up here just about every month."

At nine, after we'd thrown out the soggy cartons and helped make Dad's bed in Jacob's guest room (the pillows were stained yellow and the windows were stuck shut), we finally left. If I'd been alone I would have whooped. Instead I said, "Lucy's doing something tonight?"

"I didn't want to drag her to Brooklyn." He talked without looking at me. "Do you think Dad's lying about something?"

"Like what?"

"What he's doing here. I mean . . . Jacob?" David had sweat stains under his arms, and when he walked under a streetlight, I noticed (happily, miserably) that the front of his hair was thinning. He hailed a long black car that he said was the closest we were going to get to a cab around here, and then he spent the whole ride home tapping on his

BlackBerry, even as we went over the bridge. Somewhere near Fourteenth Street we passed a man riding a unicycle, and I almost said something but decided not to. I remembered, for the first time in years, the tantrums David used to throw, and how when he was in eighth grade Mom made him see a doctor, who sent him home with a special pillow to punch.

At the apartment he sighed and said, "Fuck," before he went into his and Lucy's room, but he wasn't talking to me. While I read *Hunt for Red October* (Jack Ryan made a presentation to the president about the *Red October*'s silent engine, and another Russian sub, one I wasn't sure if I was supposed to know, "leapt from the ocean like a whale"), Gandalf fell asleep against my neck.

That morning I'd been complaining to Sameer about Gandalf, and Sameer had turned quiet and kept the elevator doors closed on the ground floor. "I might have a possible solution," he said. "On next Saturday is Nishant's ninth birthday. He has been pleading for a dog that his mother's nerves simply can't permit." At the time I'd been so delighted that I could only say "Really? *Really?*" "I would not tease you when you are so distressed," he said—but now, with one soft ear tickling my cheek, giving him away seemed only a little less awful than throwing him out the window would have been.

"Quite a night," I said into his fur. "Look. If you don't like it at Sameer's, you can always come back. I promise." Before I'd even turned off the light I was asleep too. At three I woke up from a busy, fiery dream to my lamp blazing and Gandalf nibbling on my earlobe.

* * *

I was sitting in the break room on Friday afternoon, taking care not to rush through a hot tuna sandwich, when Paul told me that I had a phone call. I'd never had a phone call at work before, and I nodded, feeling professional, as I wiped my mouth and stood up. The Bronx did have a place for a rabbit after all, I was thinking. They'd ask me to bring Gandalf up and I might get to miss an entire afternoon of work.

"Henry."

"Hello?"

"Henry. I think—"

"Is this Jacob? Can you turn down the machine? I can't hear you."

I heard a click and then a long vacuum-dying noise. "Your father and I. We argued. I called Dr. K. Can you hear me?"

"Yes, you sound good. You called the doctor. Are you OK?" Paul stood just behind my chair—his chair, since the only phone was in his office.

"Not good. His heart."

"Something's wrong with your heart?"

"Sol. Your father's heart. Dr. K sent him to the hospital."

"Is Dad with you right now? Who's in the hospital?"

"Sol. Dr. K says he'll be . . . OK. I'm at home."

I felt like I'd just been pushed into a freezing lake. "Should I go to the hospital? Where is it?"

"Come get me. We'll go. The hospital's ten minutes . . . from me."

"Everything cool?" Paul said—hoping to be let into the trouble, since it wasn't his—but I ignored him and ran for the gate.

I don't remember catching a cab, don't remember the ride, don't remember pressing Jacob's doorbell. What I do remember is standing in his living room, trying David's cell phone again and again, wondering how long I had to wait before I could pick Jacob up and carry him out to the street. Before we left he had to find his keys, and before he could find his keys he had to find his glasses. In his coat and slippers, he moved like his body could only take one command at a time. Step. Step. Step. Reach. Step. Stop. Talk. "Dr. K is a very . . . very good doctor." Getting into the car—his street was full of these black noncabs—he kept saying (to the driver? to himself?), "Easy, now. Nice and slow."

"Can we hurry up, please?" I said to the driver. "My dad's in the hospital." But I don't think he heard, or maybe he didn't understand. "Don't even stop for lights, if we can make it through." But he stopped for every green light that was thinking about turning yellow, and took a few seconds to be convinced when the light turned back. Down an entire long street we were stuck behind a bus, which kept stopping right in front of us and then swinging left whenever we were about to pass it. "Here's fine!" I said as soon as I saw the red Emergency pole, but when I opened the door a truck banged by and almost took off my hand. It left a white dent on the edge of the door.

The driver—who until now had seemed so calm that I thought he might be falling asleep—jumped out to look. "Why in the fuck do you get out on the wrong side of the street?"

"I'm sorry. I didn't know it was the wrong side. This is an emergency."

"Where do you not know how to get out of a cab?" He was tall and fat and had a beard but no mustache. "This will cost five hundred dollars."

"I've only got a few dollars."

"This will cost five hundred dollars! You have ruined my entire week! You are a fuck! Write me a check!"

"I don't have checks."

"Give me your wallet! Old man, give me money for your son!" Jacob was still caught up on his side. Stand. Stand. Reach. Push. Step.

I handed the driver ten dollars and half helped, half pushed Jacob up the walk and in through the revolving door. I hadn't been in an emergency room in years. A Hispanic couple sat with pillows and blankets in their laps, looking miserable. An old woman stood frozen in front of one of the vending machines. A black boy who looked about fifteen and who had a blue snow hat pulled almost all the way over his eyes was scowling and holding his hand wrapped in a T-shirt, ignoring his mother next to him. I still thought there was a chance that Jacob was mixed-up about something.

"I'm Henry Elinsky, and I think my dad might be here? Solomon Elinsky?" The guard, a thin, gentle African man, flipped open a binder and ran his finger down the list of names.

"Elinsky. Room ten six two. Through those doors, take a left, then your second right."

"Is he OK? There's something with his heart?"

"I don't know, my friend. Go through right there and you can see him for yourself."

And finally, after pushing through heavy white doors and fast-walking down weirdly empty halls, there Dad was. And it was no mix-up. He was behind the second door in a row of rooms with glass walls, little tanks of terrible luck. Jacob came in slowly behind me, sounding like his lungs were made out of paper bags. David and Lucy were standing with a nurse on the far side of Dad's bed. The room was silent except for a beep that I guess was Dad's heart—I walked in and felt, even before I'd said a word, like I was being too loud. Dad was asleep on his back, attached to what seemed like hundreds of wires and tubes. He had a plastic mask over his nose and mouth, and he was wearing a cottony blue gown. I had to remind myself to breathe. I suddenly remembered (my brain was like a relative who's trying to be helpful but doesn't know how) that his shins had always been completely hairless.

"What happened?" I asked.

"Dad had a heart attack this afternoon," David said.

"A relatively small one," said the nurse—a tired woman in a maroon uniform—while she got behind Dad's bed and started rolling it toward the door, tubes and machines and all. For some reason I didn't want to ask where she was taking him—maybe I was afraid it was a room that meant he was going to die, or maybe I just didn't want to let David explain—so I stood and watched her push Dad's bed out of the room and around the corner like it was a shopping cart.

A doctor stepped in after a minute and said, "Dr. James Salt. Good to meet you all. Mr. Elinsky's just gone up to the catheterization lab, so let me tell you a bit real quick about what it means and also direct you up to another room, where you'll be able to settle in a bit more comfortably." He was young and red-haired and had an Australian accent, and he was chomping a piece of blue gum. He sounded like he'd been running and might take off again any second. "Now, what they're doing upstairs is they're going through an artery in the leg and performing what's called an angioplasty. That'll just open the valve, make sure the blood's getting back where it needs to go, utterly standard procedure." Every drop of fear and confusion I felt focused into hate for that piece of gum. I shivered after every smack and pop. "He's going to be here recovering for three to four days, depending, and after that he's going to have to rest up some. Diet changes, behavior changes—the nurses upstairs will go through the whole bit. He has serious blockage in one vessel and minor blockages in two, so count yourselves lucky—he was a stone's throw from something much worse. If you've got any questions, ask one of the nurses to buzz for me, otherwise let me just show you right upstairs."

David walked down the halls and even stood in the elevator like he belonged here, like every room and person and machine we passed was exactly the thing he'd been expecting to see. "Mom'll be up here in a little bit," he said, and I just nodded. I felt quiet and hollow and far away from myself. Because I wasn't sure that I could move any faster, and because I wanted to stare, I walked slowly with Jacob. There behind one half-open curtain was a woman on her back, bone-skinny and covered in red sores, attached to even more machines than Dad had been. There was a short black man who could have been dead, and a white woman standing over him holding a sleeping baby. There was a girl with sweaty hair and a bandage over her entire stomach, staring out at us so bored and hurting that I didn't want to meet her eyes. And everywhere there were doctors and nurses, shuffling in rubber shoes, passing each other folders, glancing at computers, and whispering in calm voices about pain, misery, death. Just to keep walking seemed to take more focus than I had.

Our new room was bigger than the one downstairs, but the same basic idea: a tile floor, a bed with machines at the head, a few chairs with hard cushions, a window looking out on a parking lot. A TV tilted down from the ceiling, and David, sitting on the bed, turned it on. Maybe it was just his calm that had me feeling so strange and unworried—but even then I understood that his calm could just be his way of reminding us that he was practically a doctor.

He turned on an episode of Oprah where two women in bright clothes were talking about how to stop living in fantasies. Lucy, Jacob, and I sat down in the chairs by the window. "You can only get disappointed if you've been expecting too much," said one of the women. Jacob was either sleeping or resting. "In other words," said Oprah, "it's one thing to

dream, but it's another thing to put your bills in the mail."
The crowd cheered. Lucy had a fat magazine in her lap that
smelled like perfume, and she kept opening it and then not
reading. A slow, woozy hour passed—it could have been only
twenty minutes—and the nurse from downstairs opened the
door and wheeled Dad in. We all, except for Jacob, jumped
up, like we'd been caught doing something embarrassing.

Dad was awake now, but groggy, and he said something
like, "Hey, hey," as he came through the door. The nurse,
once she'd told us that everything had gone smoothly,
watched his heart on the screen above his bed for a few seconds and then stepped out. The volume on the TV was off
now, and we all stared at Dad, even David, waiting to know
what to say. Lucy's eyes were shining. "Well," Dad finally
said, so weakly that it was hard to hear him. "Not a great day
for the home team. I don't feel too bad now, though." It was
hard to know if he was talking to us or to himself. He looked
like someone washed out by a day of food poisoning. His
eyes were closed, and wires were taped to his chest, and after
a minute—David was standing up with his hand on Dad's
shoulder—he was asleep again.

Now that he was with us, now that I could watch him not
be dead, one second after another after another, I finally felt
like I could ask what had happened. The dreaminess was
leaking out of me, and I felt it being replaced with love so
strong that it was almost terror.

Dad and Jacob had gone to the hardware store that
afternoon, it turned out, and they'd gotten into an argument
on the way home. Something small, Jacob said. Whether the

picture hooks they were buying were the right kind. Dad started to complain about feeling dizzy. When they got back he said he thought he might faint, and Jacob called a retired doctor he knew. The doctor told them to call 911, and like that Dad had been rushed down to the hospital. (I imagined the siren yelping, the cars swerving onto side streets, the people on the sidewalks saying into their cell phones, "Hold on a second, a fucking ambulance is going by.")

I looked at Dad the whole time David told me this, and I saw him the same giddy, greedy way I looked at Margaret sometimes, like I needed to memorize him. His wrinkles, his thin hair, his big, soft earlobes. His bony hands and his flat fingertips. And there, hidden but every bit as real, was his lazy, drowsy heart. A muscle as small and as brainless as an apple that holds the entire difference between this being an ordinary day and a disaster. I thought about Jacob's heart too, tucked in its skinny chest five feet away, steady as a march—had he sounded a little happy when he told me that it was Dad's heart and not his? I would have killed him right there in the hospital if it had meant Dad could soak up the life Jacob was losing, I would have snapped his neck and told the doctors that he'd slipped.

Every twenty minutes or so the nurse came in, nodded at us, and touched Dad's wires. After about an hour the need to get up leaped on me like the need to scratch an itch. (I remembered a tantrum that had started with this feeling, eight years old in the back of the white Volvo, kicking Mom's seat as hard as I could and feeling like I *had* to get out. It's something like how I imagine suffocating.) The halls were empty and bright and quiet—I kept feeling like I was somewhere I wasn't supposed to be. Every person I passed—an old man pushing his IV pole, a nurse trying not to fall asleep in front of a computer—all I saw was the heart, floating in its skeleton like a bug in a jar.

Whenever I re-realized what had happened, every cell in my body would get a burst of something cold. He'd been "a stone's throw from something much worse." From a funeral where I'd sit in front and Rabbi Tillman would pretend to have known Dad well. From knowing, when I called home, that he would never be the one to answer. From MR. ELINSKY'S EXCELLERS hanging above the door to a classroom that wouldn't be his. From Mom being left all alone with Walter (and this was the detail that made no sense, and so the one that meant he couldn't possibly have died).

I passed two men in janitor's uniforms laughing and pretending to box in front of a Snapple machine. I passed a room where a fat man was watching soccer at top volume. I passed one nurse laughing, saying to another, "We should stop. We're terrible. We are." Would Dad have felt content or disappointed or what, looking back on all those ordinary winters and Tuesdays and afternoons, and thinking he might never get any more? I let memories rise to the surface of my brain one by one. Him cleaning his saxophone on Sunday afternoons, wiping the bell with a yellow cloth, the tip of his tongue sticking out of the corner of his mouth. Him coming home with a pint of coffee ice cream in a brown bag and sneaking a spoonful from the carton. How he'd look just after Mom gave him a haircut, wet and big-eared and shirtless, a little boy again. I thought of the night when I'd knocked on his and Mom's door, how he lifted me into bed and tucked the blanket around me. This was when I'd been terrified of werewolves—I imagined claws clicking against my bed frame—and it had taken me an hour to get the nerve to run down the long hall between my room and theirs. "You don't have anything to worry about," he'd said, sounding like his eyes were closed. "I'm right here."

"What will you do?"

"If what?"

"If one comes."

"I'll . . . give 'em the old one-two."

I wouldn't have slept any easier if the U.S. Army had been guarding the door.

Each memory grew, as I watched it, like one of those gel caps we used to get on our birthdays: drop one in a bowl of water and watch it unfold into a dinosaur, a palm tree, a dad.

At seven o'clock, when I was buying a skinny hamburger down in the cafeteria, I realized with some panic how little I'd been thinking about Margaret. For the hours since Jacob had called, I'd been ignoring my job—she could have been up to anything. I called her from an alcove outside the bathroom.

"Oh, no, Henry," she said. "Is he OK? Is there anything I can do? You must want dinner. Can I bring you guys something?"

She was a pitcher of warm water poured over my head in the bath—I felt so much better that I almost had to close my eyes.

"Come find me whenever you get back," she said. "And seriously—call me if there's anything I can do. I'm so sorry. That's such an awful thing to happen. I know it's going to be OK."

"Thank you, Margaret," I said, in a voice like I was staring into her eyes. "Really. Thank you so incredibly much."

"Oh, stop," she said. "You go take care of your dad."

* * *

A couple of hours later Mom and Walter came in, looking amazingly like themselves. In the month and a half since I'd last seen them, my pictures of them had blurred—I could see each of them doing things, but I couldn't really just *see* them. But here was every single hair on Mom's head, the little white mole under her eye, and here were Walter's gray sideburns, the gap in his teeth. Mom walked right over to Dad, even before she'd hugged me and David. "Hi there," she said, and she lifted his hand very lightly.

"Hi there."

"So you've had a tough day." Mom's tears were pooling in her wrinkles. "But you're OK now," she said.

"I'm in great hands," Dad said. "David and Henry rushed from work. This is some kind of visit I've given them."

"Shh. The only thing any of us care about is getting you back on your feet."

"Oh, don't worry about me being on my feet. You didn't have to come. How did you get here?" Dad said. "Drove?"

"We flew. Walter and I raced right to the shuttle."

"Walter flew?"

"He flew. We all wanted to be here as fast as we could for you."

"I really don't hurt anymore, just a headache. It was a little scary then, though. I thought, 'Wait, not *now.*'"

"Don't talk like that. You're just fine. You're going to be better than new, and we'll get you home."

Some feeling I couldn't quite get was rising between them like water in a flooding room, almost over their heads. "Carol, I'm so sorry, my love," he said.

"It's OK," she said, and now she was crying harder, her wrinkles had spilled over. "Everything's OK. I'm sorry too."

Walter was trying to edge closer, but Dad wouldn't look away from Mom. "I'm so sorry," he kept saying. He wouldn't let go of her hand.

"Here," Mom said. "Say hi to Walter."

"Hey, little brother," Walter said. He was wearing his brown button-down shirt with the rip in the sleeve and a tight pair of pants, and since he'd walked in he'd kept his arms crossed over his chest. He was shaking, trying to smile, kicking the floor with his toe. "I thought about what it would be like to never see you again, coming here. For a few minutes I could really feel it. I don't think I could stand it."

We stood over Dad like he was a new baby while it started to get dark outside. Even Jacob stood there, leaning on the bed. It was hundreds of times less awkward than our Chinese dinner, everyone talking softly, Mom and Walter smiling and sniffling, Dad looking embarrassed and tired and pleased. When he started to fall asleep, the nurse told us that there wasn't a place for any of us to spend the night, and so we probably ought to just go on home.

Back out on the street, where it was still hot and noisy, it could have been weeks since we'd gone in, weeks since I'd raked up sheep poop that afternoon. It was hard to imagine now that I'd woken up that morning in a life without Dad's heart attack in it, that I'd pulled my tuna sandwich out of its bag and had no idea. (And why did I feel a little excited now, a little like my blood was electric?) "Too scary," Walter said, and wrapped his arm around me. "I thought for a minute I'd lost him." He seemed to be done crying, but his face kept crumpling, even while we walked. The tables along the sidewalk across the street were full of people talking and drinking, and there was salsa music, a woman laughing while she danced with her hand on her stomach, and cars were jammed together and honking at the light. Walter said he'd take Jacob home, and the rest of us got in a car back to Manhattan. We zipped over the bridge and straight up First Avenue, hitting the green lights like cups of Gatorade held out at a marathon. We were back up in the apartment when I realized that to Richie, standing waiting to help us with the door, we must have looked like we were coming from a dinner out, from a play.

We were all so polite, after being together in the hospital—so eager to seem like we'd be happy to sleep out on the street, if that would make things any easier—that it took until eleven to settle the sleeping arrangements. Mom moved into David and Lucy's room, they moved into my room, and Walter and I slept together on the living room sofa, the tops of our heads almost touching. When I called Paul the next morning to tell him that I had a family emergency, he said, "Take all the time you need," sounding like he'd known already. I felt, hanging up, that same instant eruption of freedom that I used to feel when the weatherman would get to Montgomery in the list of counties with no school.

So each morning, when I'd usually be chopping yams, I'd wake up and take the train over to Dad. There's a particular kind of dread in going into a hospital and a particular kind of joy in going out—I never failed to feel either one. Rattling over the bridge home in the afternoon, I'd have the sense that I was escaping from something, and it wasn't just the gloom of those hallways.

Mom cooked dinner each night, sometimes with my help, and we ate crowded around the table, extra chairs pulled out of the closet, one of David's jazz CDs on the stereo. Margaret happened to be over just before dinner one of those first nights, and Mom convinced her to stay. Walter told her a long, made-up-sounding story about being an usher in the movie theater at Mazza Gallerie—something about a boss with dyslexia—and then looked miserable when all the laughter didn't come. Mom asked her about her parents and her school and her town, then squinted, nodding, listening, smiling in all the right places. I'd never felt the apartment so much like a home (or was it just that I'd never felt the apartment so much like *my* home?). Right after Margaret had gone downstairs one night, Mom said, while we loaded the dishwasher, "She seems *wonderful*. And very smart. Is this serious, do you think? Are you going to see her after the summer?" I shushed her, but warmly, knowing that I was going to let her keep thinking of us as a couple.

Mom bought purple flowers and put them in a vase by the kitchen window. She mopped the floor in my room, she threw out the magazines and mail that had been stacked all over the apartment, she lined the fridge with rows of Tupperware full of Dad's favorite foods. "What I think is hardest here for Daddy," she told me, "is that all this makes him think of *his* father. He only lived to be fifty-one, you know. Hospitals have always been very, very hard for your father."

Dad and Walter's parents, Leo and Esther, had both died the year before I was born. Leo of cancer, and Esther, Dad says, of a broken heart. In pictures—which is the only way I've seen him, of course—Leo's the best-looking Elinsky I've seen. He's short, the same kind of packed-in short that I am, but he's got thick hair, a strong chin, the face of someone who knows a thousand jokes. His parents were Russian, the first relatives of mine to come to America. They bought a little house in Brooklyn a few miles from where Jacob lives now, and they turned the first floor into a bakery. Once business took off, they had two boys, first Leo and then Jacob a year later. The boys grew up and took over the bakery—Leo worked out front with the customers while Jacob, sullen even then, stayed in the kitchen. What Leo really wanted to be was an engineer, and when he was in his thirties he decided that there ought to be a machine that could cut the slits in the tops of a whole row of rolls at once. He spent five months in the attic, experimenting with different kinds of blades and motors, and finally, in the middle of shaving one morning, he thought of a design that would work. He started selling the machines to bakeries all over Brooklyn— Dad says he thinks we still have part of one down in our basement—and a company in Chicago bought the design when he was almost forty. He and Esther bought a house in Virginia, because Esther was homesick for her parents' farm, and they spent the last ten years of their lives rich. Dad says Jacob kept making his slits with a knife until the day the bakery closed.

When Dad talked about his dad's story, he turned so proud and cheery that it felt like a hint of a betrayal—I didn't entirely like picturing him so happy as part of a family that I'd never met. "Strong as an ox, kind as a puppy," he said. "If you boys end up liking me half as much as I loved my old man, well, I wouldn't be able to ask much more than that." Leo died a week after he went to the doctor to see if there was anything he could do for his headaches. Dad keeps a picture of him in a cracked frame by the bathroom mirror—he's wearing a tie and holding up a button too small to read, smiling with his eyes shut.

All this Elinsky-ness—Mom taking over every project, all the talk about Dad and his parents, Walter and I spread out on the couch like bums—was wearing on Lucy. "I'd pay for the hotel," I heard her say to David one night. Each morning she'd pour her cereal loudly enough to wake up me and Walter, and then at night, when she came back downstairs from her studio, she'd eat Mom's food without seeming really to notice it, the way people eat on airplanes. Mom's not nearly as fancy a cook as Lucy is—no crumbled goat cheese, no squiggles of sauce under fish, no fresh herbs—but Mom's is the kind of food that ruins every diet I've tried to keep. Baked macaroni and cheese in a dish as big as a snare drum. Chicken soup with real shredded chicken. Tater Tots with barbecue sauce. Even the peanut butter she bought was better than my usual peanut butter.

Dad was walking now, usually with a hand trailing along the wall, and he was starting to sound like himself again, just a little quieter. There was some basic part of what it was like to have a heart attack that he wasn't able to get across, and you could see that it was driving him nuts. "You know what it was? It was like one battering ram trying to get in and one trying to get out at the same time. Or no. Picture that a concrete wall collapsed on your chest." And then, frustrated, sounding as if I were somehow refusing to take this seriously, he'd say, "People *die* from this, you know. Die!" Circling the halls, never sure if we were coming up on our door or one just like it, we both tried to forget the strangeness of strolling through a hallway as if it were a park. "Have you noticed this poor guy? Look. I don't think I've ever walked by here when he isn't playing solitaire. Once I saw him in the lounge and asked him how he could stand to do it all day, and he just said to me, 'What *else* am I supposed to do?' Just like that, completely puzzled. What else is he supposed to do? 'Well, you could stay active,' I almost said. 'You could remind your body that you're still alive.'"

He was scheduled for an MRI on Monday afternoon, and he asked if I'd come with him. "Take me down, it'll make it easier. I had to do one of these things for my back once, and it was worse than being buried alive. You can read to me. I haven't read a thing in three days, I can feel my brain turning to mush."

The furniture in the waiting room was wrapped in plastic, and the lights were so low that I wondered at first if the office was closed. "I have a question," Dad announced to the

Jamaican woman behind the desk. "Where can I find a bath-room?"

He came back after a minute with a dark stain on the front of his pants, and when he sat down he said to her, "The sink in there splashes every which way. You're wasting hundreds of dollars every year."

"That's Maintenance, that's got nothing to do with me," she said.

"Well, it's in your office and you ought to care," he said, but too quietly for her to hear.

After a few minutes a man walked in from behind the desk and said, "Solomon Elinsky? My name's Cesar." He shook hands with both of us and stared right into our eyes. He seemed to be the sort of short person who stomps around the free-weight section of the gym looking for insults. "I'll be the technician here today, helping you with anything you need. First thing you're going to take this robe here and go change in that locker room right back there. Everything, your watch, any bracelets or jewelry, anything like that, you can leave it in the locker, and I assure you your things will be fully protected."

"I'd like my son here to come in with me, if that's OK," Dad said.

"Your son's welcome to come in with you—that's no problem—but in that case you're going to need to go to the locker room too, and take off everything metal on your person—your belt, your watch, even your glasses."

In the locker room, when Dad pulled his pants down and lifted off his shirt, I realized how long it had been since I'd seen him naked. He was saggy now—it wasn't such a surprise, seeing that body, that his heart wouldn't be in great shape. I tried to believe that I'd come out of those droopy red balls and that blank face of a penis, but I only gave myself the shivers.

"Did I tell you John Bale died?" he said, tying the belt on his robe. "I didn't tell you that? God, that poor guy, nobody saw him for a couple of days, so Roger went over, got a neighbor down the hall to let him in, found him dead in his chair."

The machine was a huge block with a tube cut out to fit a sliding plastic bed. There was a blue chair by the door for me. The machine sounded, just warming up, like the world's biggest dryer filled with sneakers. While Cesar strapped him in, Dad said, "Got your book? Start reading."

"I don't have my glasses."

"Then just talk to me," I think he said, but I could barely hear him. "Tell me something interesting."

Cesar went into a little control room behind glass, then said, over the intercom, "In ten seconds we're going to start. We have microphones in there right by your head, Mr. Elinsky. If you feel like there's any problem at all, you call for me and I'll be in just like that."

And then after much less than ten seconds he flipped a switch and Dad's body started pulling away. His legs were shaking. I felt as helpless as in a nightmare. "Keep talking!" he barked, the loudest I'd heard him in a week, but I hadn't said a word.

The room was dim and my eyes stung, so I closed them.

There was no way Dad could hear me now that he was inside, but I thought that I should talk. I crossed my legs and started.

"I haven't been playing as much as I told you," I said. "I made a fool of myself a couple of weeks ago. It was all improv, and I choked. I've never taken a worse solo in my life. I'm not sure I want to play anymore. I'm not sure when the last time was that I really wanted to play. I don't think I've ever actually been any good. I'm thinking lately that other people might have something I don't. David works so hard that he's giving himself gray hair, Margaret writes until her pen goes dry. Even Lucy somehow has all these new paintings at the end of the month, and even if they aren't any good, they're something. I've never felt anything like that. I've never worked half that hard. I don't know what I'd work that hard on. It feels so hard just to do anything."

The only way I knew that my voice was actually coming out was by the feeling in my throat. I was just watching the words march by.

"I'm happy now, though. I'm happier than I was at home. I feel like I'm onto something. It doesn't always feel hard to fill up time anymore. I never want to fast-forward with Margaret. You'll meet her. She's got a boyfriend, but even David says it's like we're dating.

"She said she loves talking to me. We go to the zoo at night and just sit in there together. She loves animals as much as I do. You should meet Newman too—he's my favorite animal there. When Margaret and I are just sitting with him, I feel like there's not a single thing I'd change. I'm just completely happy. Isn't that being in love? Do you still feel like that with Mom, ever?

"Do you remember when I walked in on you having sex? You were in the shower, it was Saturday morning, and I came in to ask Mom if I could make chocolate-chip pancakes. I had no idea you guys showered together. I came into the bathroom, I had my mouth open to ask, and then I saw . . . I went downstairs and said to David, 'Dad's got a *huge* dick.' He told me not to say stuff like that. You turned away right when you saw me, and you grunted—you were like an animal. I'd never heard you make a noise like that. I've never told anyone, not even Margaret. I thought I'd never recover."

For a second I panicked, thinking Cesar could hear me, but I opened my eyes and he was fiddling with his controls. I took a deep breath. The machine was still humming and pounding and buzzing. My throat hurt a little now, but I felt good. I felt like a dog who's been running in the park.

"I don't think David and Lucy are any good together. They don't make each other happy. I don't know what it is about her, but it's like I'm allergic. Her paintings don't *look* like anything. David says that's part of the point, but I think it's a stupid point. And the other day I think I heard her asking David when I was going to move out. I was napping, but I think she said something about the end of August. I might ask David if he wants to find an apartment with me, just stop seeing her. You can tell he wants to.

"Maybe you should think about not teaching next year. Mom thinks you should retire, start playing music again for yourself. I think she's worried about you. I don't think she thinks she could make it if you died."

By the time Cesar slid Dad out of the machine I felt all scooped out. Dad was lying down, completely still, eyes closed, not shaking anymore—my heart jumped. But then he opened his eyes and raised his eyebrows at me. "Well," he said. His hair was shooting off to the sides and his stomach was like a volleyball in his lap and his throat skin drooped.

In the locker room, naked again, he said, "I want you to finish reading to me later. I'd have been a wreck without you."

*   *   *

The night before Mom and Walter went back to D.C., I was on the couch, in the middle of the best scene yet in *Hunt for Red October*. Ramius is steering the *Red October* through a valley between mountains on the bottom of the ocean, and the Americans—just a few hundred feet behind him but afraid to crash—can't decide whether to follow. I'd stopped caring about the characters hundreds of pages ago—I usually wasn't even sure who was talking or where they were—but to think that miles under the waves there was a submarine gliding like a shark, a blue light in the middle of an ocean too big to imagine—it kept me reading at least a few pages each night. My palms were tingling when Walter said, "I'd like it if we could be totally frank." At first I thought he was talking in his sleep—he mumbled sometimes during the night, sad, low-pitched nonsense—but his voice sounded clear now. "Do you think we could, Henry?"

"OK. About what?" I laid my book down and for a few seconds I still saw a submarine dodging sharp blue cliffs. I burned the side of my finger when I turned off my lamp.

"Do you know why your father had his heart attack?"

He waited for me to answer but I didn't. My finger felt like it might burst into flames.

"I don't know how much your parents have told you, but it doesn't seem fair to treat you like a little kid. Have they talked to you about their problems?" He was talking softly, lying on his back. "I know they've talked to David. I think in some ways I almost feel like I need to step in and be a parent here. We've always had such a special connection, and I didn't want anything to hurt that. Keeping secrets seems like it could only do harm. They've been fighting so much, Henry. Just so you know how serious it's been, I even asked your father if I should move out. I really did. And now he's almost *died* for this, that's how broken up he was." He was starting to choke up.

"Died for what?" I said, fast enough that it was still like I hadn't said anything.

"I don't think your mother cares if he's happy anymore. I really don't. He's been suffering like this for over a year, but it just isn't enough. She can't cut him a break."

"Cut him a break for what?"

"She's never given one thought to what it must be like for him."

"Cut him a break for what?"

"The last thing I want is for you to be mad at me, kiddo. I'm trying to look out for you. I don't have to say anything else, but don't you just want them to both be happy, in the end? That's why I figured they were silly to keep it from you. Because they didn't realize how grown-up you'd be."

"They are happy."

"Henry. They haven't shared a bed all summer. I can see this is too much right now. I'm sorry. I was just lying here being eaten up by it. Let's go to sleep and we can talk more tomorrow. Deal?" He reached up and squeezed my shoulder.

I lay there on my back taking deep breaths, as still as if an MRI machine were looking me over, thinking how easy it would be to choke him. This sad old man who's only kissed as many girls as I have, who makes up secrets because his real life's as dull as his clothes. His skinny neck, his twiggy arms, his straight back you could break with one good punch. He was quiet for a minute, and I thought he might be about to say something else, but while I dug my fingernails into my palms, he started breathing with a click. Dogs take longer to fall asleep than Walter does. He had to be wrong. Maybe now, finally, after an entire life of falling apart slowly, he'd started to do it fast. Mom and Dad in that hospital room weren't a couple that doesn't sleep together. He's a jealous, pathetic old man. First thing in the morning I'd tell Mom something was wrong with him. Or maybe—I let my fists uncurl—I wouldn't. All she needed, on top of taking care of all of us, was to hear this. I'd go to sleep, and in the morning I'd pretend nothing had happened. Walter would tell me he'd been saying things he hadn't meant.

But thirty minutes later I was still awake, and my brain was going like a fast ride I couldn't get off. I turned my light back on and picked up *Hunt for Red October,* but I may as well have tried to read Chinese. My finger was red—I knew I should get ice but I didn't want to get up. I'd ask Dad tomorrow what was going on, and he'd nod and sigh and explain that Walter didn't know a thing about their marriage. But what if he didn't say that? What if his face went tight, he started crying—what if he said he didn't know what to do? I'd ask politely. I wouldn't accuse him of anything. I'd just tell him that Walter had said something strange, and that I needed—no, I would like—to know.

* * *

Once Dad was out of the hospital, he moved from Jacob's into our apartment. David insisted on it, and so Lucy made a demand of her own (unless she hadn't even had to say it). Walter and Mom left for D.C. as soon as Dad had settled into his—my—room.

Walter woke up solemn the morning after our talk—he gave me a look like we'd agreed on a pact—but he didn't say a word and so neither did I. Instead I watched every minute that Mom and Dad spent together. At lunch Saturday they were formal with each other—"Here you are," Dad would say, handing Mom the salad, and, "Thank you," she'd say back, each of them making some challenge that I couldn't quite untangle. When Walter and Mom were about to leave for Penn Station, she and Dad stood off in the corner of the living room talking quietly for a minute, and finally they hugged so hard and long that David, holding Mom's bag, had to clear his throat.

"So what'll it be, boys?" Dad said, once we were alone. He had an appointment with Dr. Salt in the morning, but he avoided mentioning it. His face looked drained, and David kept telling him to lie down. Dad waved him off. "Little detour, but I came here to visit you two and now here I am. Henry, I'm still dying to see the zoo."

Dad came in the next afternoon while I was doing a bird count. Passing in front of the other keepers with him I felt that same mix of pride and humiliation I used to feel when he'd come up to the middle school to give concerts. "Gorgeous zoo," he said, before we'd even seen it. "Happy kids everywhere, happy animals, fresh air. What's the name of that fat black goat with the white spots? He's enormous."

"Spanky."

"Spanky ought to be on a diet." He followed me back into the aviary, over the rubber lily pads, around the pond, and once he got the hang of what I was doing, he said, "Let's get it done in half the time. You give me page two, you keep doing page one. I'll meet you back here when I've got mine all checked off."

I don't think he looked, to Garret and Janice, like someone who'd had a heart attack six days ago—they might just have thought, instead, that I was one of those unlucky kids with stiff, grandparentish parents. He was walking slowly all around the pond and into the bushes with his sheet and his pencil, stepping over fences, holding branches aside while he ducked under them. I followed a few feet behind to make sure that nothing happened. He talked to himself while he worked, and two young moms with strollers were watching him and smiling, so he started talking a little louder. "Who's this huge sucker here? My God, you're an ugly piece of work. What's that on your bill, a hump? The Humpbeak of Central Park. Let's see, I've got two doves hiding in here, three doves—left yellow, right blue, and right black. We're looking at the bands, right? God knows if I'm right, but that's what I see. Oops, there goes black."

When Paul saw us he squared his shoulders and said, "This must be your dad. I'm Paul Marcus, director of Tisch Children's Zoo." I could see that he'd smelled the family emergency hanging over this visit—he shook Dad's hand and smiled right into his face. "Your son's done some good stuff for us. Has he introduced you to Newman? They're a riot together."

Paul was in a mode completely different from the one I saw each day—he laughed at all of Dad's jokes, rubbed the animals' necks like they were his little brothers, and spoke in a voice, I realized, that I hadn't heard since my tour. "What a beautiful animal," Dad said. "How much would a guy like this weigh?"

"Last time we weighed him he was a hundred fifty-five."

"Uh-huh, uh-huh," Dad said. "And is he a big shedder?"

"Pretty big. Not as bad as some of the rest of them, but look." Paul gave Newman's back a hard rub, and a puff of short white hairs floated and sank. "Summertime, being petted so much, it gets pretty thin."

"I see. And is he the father of all these guys?"

"No, they're actually different breeds. Those are African pygmies; he's a Nubian."

I had the itchy feeling that Dad was trying to be liked.

"It's been a pleasure and a delight to meet you," he finally said, "and I want to thank you for taking Henry on." He clapped a hand on the back of my neck. "His mother and I are thrilled with how he's ended up. He surprises me every day of his life." Paul forced a smile.

Walking Dad to the gate, I said, "What do you mean, I surprise you?"

"You really do." And I thought he was done, but his rhythm was just slowed down from all that walking. "With school and everything, people are always very impressed with David. And he's been astonishing. But, you know, you kind of take things your own way, and I admire that. And look—you're in New York, you're working, you've got your music going again. It's a hell of a thing to see."

"Dad," I said, and the words *Walter told me* were already forming in my mouth. I felt like I'd bent my knees on the high dive.

But he said, "Now, how about a nap? I think I've got the route down. Out through there and then a right at the church. Right?"

Now that Margaret and I had known each other during something important, our friendship had added a new register. If we'd written letters to each other before the heart attack, we would have signed them *Best* or *Talk soon*—now we would have written *Much love* or even just *Love*. When I'd get worried about Dad—and worry would rush over me sometimes like the need to throw up—I would go down to her apartment and after two minutes of her big eyes and bare feet my worry would vanish and I'd be free just to enjoy the conversation. She'd never really talked to me about her mom before, but now, while we sat on the Marsens' couch with our legs tucked under us and the only light in the room coming from the lamps, she seemed eager to match everything she'd learned about my family with something about her own.

Her voice wasn't quite the way it was when she told her other stories—now she'd glance up at my eyes every few seconds, nervously, and she'd say, "You don't really want to hear this, do you? I'm being such an after-school special." She told me about the day when her parents asked her and Damien to take a seat on the sofa (she was wearing her Rollerblades, she said—I imagined her long and clumsy, her wheels spinning against the floor). How she thought they were going to tell her that they were having another baby. How her mom couldn't even look at them, and how her dad kept saying, "We're keeping the house. There just isn't going to be any question about that." And how a few weeks later, after her mom told her, in the parking lot of a Sam's Club, that she was going to move to Colorado, how Margaret ran into the frozen-food section and hid. Her mom was a psychologist— she used to see patients in the sunroom off Margaret's living room, but she didn't have many patients yet in Denver. She taught three classes a week at the University of Colorado and spent her nights editing stodgy articles for a psychology journal. She lived alone in a house full of dream catchers and Japanese paintings on pieces of wood.

Margaret also told me about her first kiss—a boy named Bill Deagan. It made my smile freeze for a second, but I couldn't bear not to hear it—the driveway and how she had to pee and Bill's hand on her face greasy from popcorn. I didn't even have to ask her questions anymore, she just told and told and told.

Dad's last night he said he wanted to take us all out to dinner, including my "new pal." Jacob was sick now with the flu, but David made a reservation for the rest of us at an Italian restaurant downtown. Margaret hadn't seemed the least bit uneasy around Mom and Walter, but this dinner, for some reason, made her nervous. "I think he should probably just have some time with you two," she said.

"Lucy's coming."

"Lucy's practically David's wife. It's different. I'd feel weird."

"He'd be disappointed if you didn't come. He thinks we're together."

"I *know* he thinks we're together. That's why I don't want to come. If I go, you can't do any of your stuff—no touching, no holding doors for me. Just act normal."

"Completely normal."

"Fine."

Margaret rang the bell at seven looking so pretty that I couldn't not touch her arm. She wore a red shirt and a see-through black scarf over her shoulders, and for the first time I'd ever noticed, she was wearing makeup. "What a lovely vision," Dad said, and kissed her on both cheeks, his wrinkled lips staying out a few seconds too long. With her shoes she was taller than he was. I kept edging closer to her in the elevator to try to figure out what it was that she smelled like— the smell cut straight to some happy memory—and finally in the lobby I got it: honeysuckle. All night I mumbled the word to myself like a spell (and remembered stopping with Mom at those bright bushes along the bike path, breaking off the flowers' ends, sucking tiny drop after tiny drop until I decided to just eat an entire flower, and how it tasted like bitter planty nothing).

The restaurant was as dark as a closet—so dark that Dad almost knocked into the hostess when we walked in. But the table was in its own little cone of light, and I knew before I'd opened the menu that this was going to be the kind of restaurant where Dad pretends to faint when he sees the check. A short waiter in a white coat appeared with a wheel of cheese in his arm—everyone was always appearing here, because you couldn't see a waiter until he was right over your table—and he scooped a little hunk onto each of our plates, which another waiter came to drizzle with olive oil. A third guy came and handed us torn-off pieces of tough, white bread that had holes big enough to put your finger through.

"You must know a lot about bread," Margaret said to Dad, holding up her piece. I hadn't realized until then how nervous she really was.

"So I see Henry's put you through the whole family saga. Jacob's really the one you'd want to talk to, if we could get him out sometime. The main thing I know about bread is that you don't want to make it for a living. Bakers get up at four and don't go to bed until they've fed the sour at eleven. My father got out as soon as he could, and I've never missed anything less. If you're ever in D.C., I can teach you all you need to know about making bread in half an hour."

Margaret's real blush filled in under her fake blush.

"I remember the rolls he used to bring home," Dad said. His voice was quieter than usual, so we all had to lean toward him to hear. "Piles and piles of them in the middle of the table. We couldn't get up until we'd each had one, breakfast, lunch and dinner. My father lived in *terror* of food going bad."

At the apartment Dad had had one glass of wine, and now he'd started another, but he sounded as loose as if he'd had five. David said Dad was doing well enough that wine was OK, but he still didn't look right to me—something a little saggy about his face, his eyes like he was begging you to let him sleep. He didn't act like he'd rather be sleeping, though. At big dinners he usually likes to let whoever's sitting next to him talk and talk—afterward he'll say, "Well, I got the full biography tonight"—but here he was making a toast before the waiter had even filled everyone's glass.

"To being healthy, to having us all together, and to having my two boys be so well taken care of. At the risk of embarrassing everybody"—he seemed to be talking mostly just to Margaret—"I'll just say it's a hell of an important thing to find somebody who cares about you." He winked at me. Everyone clinked glasses and I dipped my sleeve in the olive oil.

"Tell me, Maggie," Dad said. "How many houses have you lived in during your life?"

"In my life? Well, when I was born I lived in a house about two minutes from the house where my dad lives now, but I don't really remember it. So just one, I guess."

"I've lived in eleven houses, apartments included, but each of my boys was raised in a single house, their whole childhoods under one roof. That was something their mother and

I really tried to pay attention to, and it sounds like your folks did too. What do your parents do?"

I opened my mouth to tell Dad to take it easy, but Margaret wasn't bothered. "My dad's a news photographer, and my mom's a therapist. She lives in Colorado now, so I don't see her very often. She's been thinking lately about retiring and moving closer to where I'm in school."

"My advice is not to let her give up work. You take the work out of a person and often you take the life along with it. Any sibs? I'll bet you've got brothers."

"I do! Well, just one. He'll be thirteen in September."

"He's a lucky guy—all the guys I knew who grew up with big sisters had a much easier time with girls later. Much less trouble. My wife and I always wondered about the parents who had only children. I think siblings are more important than parents, in some ways. When Henry moved into David's place, it just made my heart sing, seeing them together. As a parent you've got to keep your hands off, but when they grow up and they're still close, it's just . . . wow."

The food came, and, still talking, Dad stabbed at his pesto. Margaret had relaxed, and I don't think it was just the glass of wine. Even though David looked annoyed, and Lucy kept making a face like she was waiting for a bus, Dad had charmed Margaret. I was smiling too.

"All right," he said, smearing leftover sauce around with his bread. "One more question and then I'll be quiet and let you guys have the floor. What's the hardest thing you've ever done in your life? Something you've overcome and you're proud of. I don't want the college-essay version, I want the real story. I ask all the young people I meet, and I'm prepared to give you an answer of my own, so don't hold back."

"You go first," Margaret said.

"I go first!" Dad practically barked. "Tired of playing by my rules, you turn them around on me, I like that very much." I pushed his wineglass a few inches farther from him, but he scooped it back in without looking at me. He was flaring his nostrils with every breath. "Henry, you know this story, don't you? About David, from when I still ran the music store? It was when you were a little kid. David, you must have told him this." This is how Dad always warms up to telling a long story—by pretending to be surprised that the other people at the table haven't heard it.

"It's a funny story. Fifteen years later, soon to be a successful doctor, I'll tell." He hunched over the table now, both elbows pressed into bread crumbs.

And I had heard it, I realized as soon as he began. More than once. The store, and Caleb, the black boy they'd hired, and the twenties disappearing from the register, and David wanting his basketball card. Margaret listened with perfect polite attention, but it was effort on her face, not pleasure. As Dad wandered through the background of his story— the difficulty of selling student-quality instruments, how few businesses in D.C. would even have hired a black kid at the time, how good a worker David was—I watched her stifle a yawn behind a smile. Lucy was massaging David's palm in her lap.

"So one afternoon I pretended to have a lesson when I

didn't: I stood in the doorway at just the right angle so with the mirror on the wall I could see Caleb's hands, right into his register drawer while he's counting out. And for an hour, watching him like a hawk, I didn't see a thing."

What a bore Dad was being! Every sentence he spoke dragged along unnecessary details and unfunny asides like tin cans on a bumper. How long could he blather without noticing the expressions on our faces? For the first time in my life I felt toward Dad the simple, angerless impatience you feel toward a stranger who's got you cornered on an airplane: I wanted to be away from him. And more to the point, I wanted Margaret to be away from him. She'd started to look embarrassed now, running her finger along the edge of her water glass, clearing her throat into her napkin. How dare she!

Dad seemed to be rounding the corner into his story's last lap, and David was busy trying to get the waiter's attention, facing away from the table entirely. "So it's Sunday afternoon and I'm home looking for a pair of shoes in the back of the hall closet. And in the shoe box on the very bottom of the stack—the boys can tell you how I am, I never let anybody throw out a pair of shoes—and in the very bottom box, stuffed in a sock, two hundred and thirty-two dollars, all rolled into a ball smaller than your fist. I tell you, my heart practically falls through the floor." His forehead was turning red. To stop now would have been to admit that he should never have started, but you could see that he felt us getting away from him.

"And the whole time David won't even let me see one

inch of his face, so I know for sure he's guilty as a dog. And as a parent you feel very disappointed, but more than that you just feel sorry for the kid. I didn't lose my temper, though, did I?" But David wouldn't help him. "I made him work off every cent, extra work at the store, washing the car, and I told him that if he wanted to buy the card he was going to first have to pay the store back, then save up the old-fashioned way. And he worked his ass off, all the way through winter and into spring. I remember the day he finally came home with that card, bought with his own money, and I felt so proud I could pop."

"I never bought the card."

"Ah, don't say that. I can see the card like it's right here— you put it on your dresser."

"I didn't. I stopped wanting it as soon as you caught me. I don't know why you're telling this story."

"Maggie said she wanted to hear."

"No one but you has talked for half an hour."

Dad made his disappointed mouth and started to say something but decided against it. "To wrap things up—the hard part. Going back to Caleb. So now I needed to apologize." The feeling of the meal was ruined, and maybe the night was too, but I was so distressed at having Margaret see my family like this that I thought the entire summer had been deflated. Dad was no stranger on a plane, and every word he spoke not only bored me but surrounded me, *was* me.

No one said anything while the waiter cleared our plates. David stared at the dish of olive pits in the middle of the table and Lucy held his arm. "You haven't had too hard a life,

I guess, huh?" David said, and he sounded like he'd been thinking about saying it for a while.

"Oh, for God's sakes. I'm done. You were a kid—it was a difficult situation. I won't say another word." He made a zipper with his lips.

"Well, this has been lovely," he said, standing up. "Glad you're feeling better, Dad. I'm going home. Good night." Lucy stood up too, once she saw that David really wasn't coming back, and they disappeared into the dark. The seconds came as slowly as drips.

"Huh," Dad said. He stretched his jaw the way he does when he's embarrassed. The light felt hot with just the three of us in it. "David's always been so touchy. I forget how you've got to handle him when we haven't spent a lot of time together. If I'd been telling a story about last year, or even five years ago, but . . ." When he stopped he looked so sad, suddenly, so small, that I wanted to hug him. His eyes were begging for something again, but it wasn't sleep, I couldn't get it—he might as well have been one of the sheep for all I felt like I understood him. When the waiter came, Dad didn't even ask us if we wanted dessert. "Let's blow this joint." He whistled "Equinox" while we stood waiting for a cab—that airy way he does through his teeth—but I could tell that it was for us, it was for me. It sounded not much happier than sobbing.

*　*　*

A couple of nights after Dad left, Margaret and I were walking along Sixth eating chicken kebabs when she said, "You can see something I wrote, if you still want to." The only writing of hers that I'd ever seen, except for the stolen journal sentences, was the note thanking me for the chocolate. "But you can't talk to me about it afterward," she said. "Don't even tell me if you liked it. And you've got to promise you won't show anyone."

I lay there in bed that night holding the five pages she'd torn out of her notebook, each one covered on both sides, feeling everything Rabbi Tillman had wanted me to feel when I held the Torah. I wanted to start reading but I couldn't: I wasn't in the sort of mood that could turn this into a love letter. Everything I'd done for the past couple of days had felt sad and slow—and hardly any better when I realized that it was because Dad had gone home. The apartment felt empty again. I read the first words of Margaret's story a few times and pretended that they made me feel better. On the top left corner of the first page she'd written, *8/1/03*. I couldn't convince even a part of myself that it would be what I wanted it to be.

But I started:

The winter after my parents separated I spent Christmas with my mother in Colorado. In the afternoon she would drive me around her new town, slowing down so I could see her school, the coffee shop where she usually ate her lunch, the place where, if you craned your neck, you could get a beautiful view of the mountain. The town and my mother were in perfect harmony in the key of false cheer. We went to a movie one night (I don't know the name, but I remember an endless scene with a man's fake mustache coming loose) and she kept glancing over at me to see if I was laughing. At a barbecue restaurant that used towels instead of napkins, she ordered me what she thought was my first beer, and when even that didn't make me smile, she went to the bathroom and came back with puffy eyes.

My unhappiness that winter was so relentless, so sophisticated in its attack, that it had become an object of fascination for me. I knew that on the spectrum of suffering I could still count myself among the lucky, but I wanted to place myself more precisely. Did actually getting divorced hurt more than having your parents get divorced? How much did a friend's death hurt? How about a lost job? How about illness? How about having to make other plans? Or is it silly to think of a spectrum at all? Maybe we adjust to our suffering; maybe all pain works this way: It fills us up until it seems almost (but not quite) more than we can bear.

My grim study not only did nothing to ease my own pain; it also kept me from giving my mother the reassurance that might have eased her pain. Each day I slept into the afternoon. On Christmas I gave her nothing but a card, and stuffed the presents she gave me into my suitcase without even opening them. When we skied, I stuck to trails I knew were beyond her, and then refused to enjoy the hot chocolate she bought me at the lodge. "I know this is hard for you, sweetie," she said, and I tried not to let her see that she'd gotten through. "It's hard for me too. But six months from now will be better than today, and six months from then will be even better."

The night before I went home, we were sitting after dinner in the hot tub on her deck when it began to snow. The flakes

*disappeared as soon as they hit the water. "Tell me about home,"
she said, and she sounded so vulnerable that I couldn't bear not
to answer her. Miles away, but as clear as if it were just on the
other side of the fence, was the mountain, lit for night skiing.*

"The house feels really big now," I said.

"Is the bathroom by the back door fixed?"

"No."

*"How's the kitchen? Are you guys cooking a lot?" She was
crying without hiding it.*

"Damien's cooking. He's getting very good at pasta."

*"At pasta? That's so good. How's your bedroom? Are you
liking your new bed?"*

*"I painted the walls. Dad said I could paint them whatever
color I wanted."*

"And what did you pick?"

"Dark blue."

*"Dark blue. That sounds so beautiful. I can't wait to see it.
Oh, Margaret." She put her hand on my shoulder but didn't say
anything else. "I'm going to dry off and get some water," she
said. "Don't stay in too long." I listened to her footsteps on the
deck, the slow kiss of the freezer door, the chime of the glass, the
hiss of the tap.*

*I laid the back of my head against the lip of the tub, and
felt, as if for the first time, the web of circumstance, coincidence,
and choice that brought me exactly to this point and no other:
lying in the outdoor hot tub of a home near Vail, Colorado,
while my recently divorced mother stands in the kitchen. My entire life extended behind me (and, farther back but no less present, my parents' lives, and their parents' lives) like the tentacles*

of a jellyfish, whose simple shiny bubble of a body was me, at that moment, seeming to propel myself with nothing but the force of my own breathing.

The snow was falling so fast and thick that it seemed like it should have made a sound, but the harder it fell, the more silent it became. Snow exalts even the homeliest things: It gave every plank in the porch, every branch, the peak of every post in the fence a perfect inch of echo. As I pulled myself out of the tub, I felt all of a sudden that I might be at the end of my unhappiness, but I didn't want to move too quickly on the feeling, to startle it into disappearing. The snow squeaked underfoot. My mother's face brightened in the window when she saw me.

This moment just before I slid open the door and stepped inside, although it happened to coincide with the breaking of a months-long fever of sadness (or more likely because *it happened to coincide with the end of this fever), this was the most difficult in my life so far. I drank a cool glass of water at the window with my mother; I hugged her in the hall outside my door as long as she held tight; I sent her to bed feeling, for what must have been the first time in months, hope. And I did it all—made life once again tolerable for myself, took the first steps toward allowing my mother a new happiness—not by loving her more, but by loving her less.*

I put her pages down and my entire body felt quiet and calm, like all my organs were holding their breath. Something important had changed, I was sure of it. I wanted to go down and wake Margaret up, but I didn't know what I'd say. I imagined her in the hot tub, the mountain with lights like in a baseball stadium, the snow sticking to her hair. I felt like a tuning fork after it's been banged against a music stand, shaking with almost more feeling than I could hold.

I couldn't read *Hunt for Red October* after that, so I just turned off the light and lay there. My thinking started to get loopy, and I was most of the way to sleep when I had an idea so clear that I practically sat up in bed. Even Drew doesn't really have Margaret. She knows her stories and no one else does—kissing her wouldn't get at the important stuff in her. Not even sex would. The thought didn't seem like much when I woke up the next morning, but right then, picturing her alone on the porch in bare feet, alone in my bed with my eyes wide open, it felt like the answer I'd been looking for all summer.

ometime at the beginning of August I'd started to actually write in my notebook. I could have been desperate to have something to give Margaret, or I could just have been bored. The camps were done coming to the zoo for the summer, the rich families were all on vacation, and if anyone else was thinking about coming in, the rain kept them away. "I never seen a summer like this ever," Ramon said. "It's nice, though, you know, not too hot. I just feel bad for the animals, you can see their moods like real down. Pearl yesterday she was lying there, I swear just looking at her I got a lump in my throat."

There was so little work to do that in the afternoons I'd go and sit on the bench by the catfish—Paul hardly ever walked back there—and write down whatever came to mind. Mostly I found myself writing about being in school, people and afternoons I hadn't thought about in years, each one amazingly clear once I'd dusted it off. I wrote about Joey Strassner grinning and holding a used condom out on a stick on the path behind Somerset pool. Dad having a piece of parsley covering one tooth for an entire lesson. Waking up starving one night in seventh grade and eating an entire roast chicken with my hands. Getting lost in the Atlanta airport and being taken to use the PA system by the blond man from the hot-dog restaurant. I tried to write a couple of pages every day, and I usually ended up writing even more. Whenever Margaret came over, I'd leave my notebook on the bed and take an extra minute in the bathroom, but I don't think she ever touched it.

Sameer, though, was thrilled to hear that I was writing, and one morning he brought me an anthology of Pakistani fairy tales. "You will simply adore this," he said, "and I hope you will cherish it until you are as old as myself." I was so sure that I wouldn't adore it—so sure that I wouldn't even be able to get through a single story—that I put it in on a high shelf in my room so I wouldn't have to feel guilty every time I walked in. Giving the gift opened something up in Sameer, though, and when I came down to the lobby on Saturday morning, he was waiting by the desk, grinning, holding Gandalf's cage. "Someone has missed you and wished to say hello." It was as if Gandalf had gone through years of therapy—he stood against the bars and rubbed his nose against my finger, chittering happily. "Nishant is so grateful to you that he cannot express it. He says it is like having his own private zoo."

Later that day, caught up in the pleasure of all this giving and getting, I went to Rite Aid to get a Super Soaker for Nishant. A crowd was standing gathered outside the store on Ninth Avenue, a busy, dirty corner with a pawnshop and a Baskin-Robbins/Dunkin' Donuts. Before June, this was how I pictured all of New York—phone booths without phones and pigeons pecking at KFC drumsticks and homeless people looking dead under shredded sleeping bags. When I got closer to the crowd I saw a security guard pinning a black guy to the ground with his knee. The guy wasn't wearing a shirt, and his body was shiny with sweat. The guard was short and Hispanic. "Don't move!" he yelled, but the guy didn't seem to be moving. "Don't fucking move!" It occurred to me that they might be filming a movie.

A few feet from the guy's head was a full red backpack. "Just get me some water!" he kept saying. "Please get me some water! *Please!*" Two cops strolled over, and the security guard stood up looking worried but proud, while one of the cops handcuffed the guy. The cop yanked his arm in a chicken-wing way that made both me and the girl next to me say, "Jesus."

"My fucking eyes are burning out! Please get me some water! Please just give me some fucking water, I don't even care!" The cop, thick-necked and blank-faced, pulled the guy onto his feet and shoved him into the store. The other cop stood looking bored, leaning against a cement plant holder.

I followed them inside, along with almost everyone else

who'd been watching, and the guy, flabby and slippery and miserable, had his head back, yelling, "Water! Please, some water! Anybody! My fucking eyes are burning out!" I asked a grinning woman in line what the guy had done, and she said, "He snatched a girl's backpack and they Maced him. I hope they wring his neck." I looked at her to see if that was really what she'd meant to say, and she just kept on smiling.

While the cop pushed him down the aisle the guy pounded the refrigerator cases with his shoulder, but the cop wouldn't let him stop. The other cop, slouched and weaselly, had walked inside now too, and he leaned against the counter in front of a closed register.

"Is someone going to give him some water?" I asked. The cop didn't answer me, so I said it again.

"You giving out advice on how to treat this dude? Stick with the shopping, we'll stick with taking care of crooks. All right?" It seemed incredible that this guy, who looked like he'd be perfectly at home behind the counter at a Blockbuster, sucking Milk Duds and snickering, got to wear a gun strapped to his waist.

From the back of the store I could still hear the black guy yelling, but I couldn't make out what he said anymore, and almost everyone from outside had left. I considered buying a bottle of water and bringing it back to him, but that would mean a confrontation, shouting, maybe even getting arrested—I didn't have the courage for it. So instead, hating myself, hating the cop, I paid for the water gun and started to leave. But on the mat I turned around and said, "Someone really should give him some water."

The cop turned to the grinning woman, who had a basket full of suntan lotion, and said, "Tell Angel Teresa here he'd make a crappy cop. But have fun with your toys, huh?" She laughed and touched his arm.

This, I thought, is how a person passes from ordinary life—full of imaginary fights and stupid, bloody dreams—into the kind of story that leads the eleven-o'clock news. Just to prove that he'd been wrong to think of me as weak, I would have stormed back in and snatched his gun while he flirted, if only . . . if only just thinking about it didn't give me such satisfaction already. The moment of understanding and regret on his face before I pulled the trigger. The melony explosion, the slimy wall, the startling silence after.

Right in front of the fire hydrant where the guard had pinned the guy I saw something crumpled and white, and cautiously I unfolded it with my toe. A dirty white T-shirt. The black guy's T-shirt. It hadn't even crossed my mind how strange it was that someone would steal a bag with no shirt on, but of course he wouldn't—here it was, and it must have gotten yanked off while the guard wrestled him down. What a pleasant piece of sense! I'm not the shooting type, I realized with more relief than disappointment, and kicked the shirt out of the middle of the sidewalk.

But there was something bothering me, and bothering me more because I couldn't place it. It wasn't the cop—that flare-up was over—it wasn't anything at the apartment, nothing to do with Dad. . . . I traced the feeling back and back until I found, ridiculously enough, the BACK TO SCHOOL sign I'd passed on Fifty-second. Each one I saw—and they'd started to pop up everywhere—was a peek over a cliff into September. Every day after Margaret went back to Montana I'd matter a little bit less to her, a little less and a little less until when Drew rolled over in bed one night and asked her what my name was, she'd have to bite her lip for a minute to remember.

I don't know what I'd expected to change after I read her story about visiting her mom, but certainly something. When I saw her the next day I hugged her (even hugging me back she seemed a little embarrassed), and while we sat facing each other on her bed I said, "Thanks for giving me that. You're really a beautiful writer." She just nodded. "I loved the part about how snow piles up on everything."

"I don't really want to talk about it," she finally said. "Sorry. I hate talking about things I write." I felt like a teacher had just told me to go stand in the hall.

It wasn't just writing she didn't want to talk to me about, though. Something hard to describe in the way she acted had been different for the past week or so—as if her eyes had stopped focusing on me—but I couldn't get her to tell me what was wrong or even to admit that anything was. Conversation with her had turned so hard, so full of pauses and empty questions, that it seemed impossible that we could ever have talked easily. "Are you OK?" I'd ask her, and the first few times she just said, "I'm fine." She'd say it without a smile, without anything to suggest that she even wanted me to believe her. But when I said, "You don't seem fine. You're acting mad. What did I do?" she said, "When I'm *in* a bad mood, it makes it *much* worse when you keep *asking* me about it. OK? I'm sorry. I've just been a little depressed for some reason."

"There's nothing wrong with Drew or anything?" I wished right away that I hadn't said it.

"I want to be alone for a while," she said. (And already I understood maybe the most important thing about Margaret and me: She could make me feel better but I couldn't do the same for her.)

One night I told David how worried I was, my voice almost cracking, and afterward he said, "It sounds like she's being a girl. Girls are moody." I listened to him as carefully and nervously as if I were a patient who'd come to him with a lump on his side. That this could have nothing at all to do with me was a diagnosis I'd hardly dared to hope for.

"You're so . . . steady," she said to me once. "I don't think I've ever seen you really get mad. If somebody ran over your foot I feel like you'd just sort of say, 'That was interesting.' Are you scared of being mad?"

"I'm scared of *you* being mad."

"Why? I get mad—it doesn't mean anything. If I hadn't met your mom and dad, I'd think your parents were abusive or something. The best thing to do when I'm mad is to just let me blow it off. Then it's done."

So standing outside the Marsens' door, still holding my bag from Rite Aid, I worked to believe that her mood had nothing to do with me. And that ten days was still time for her to change my life. Dr. Marsen opened the door wearing a Yale T-shirt and a towel around his neck. His whole body glowed. "Caught me right off the treadmill. Pardon the smell.

Come in." He put his hot hand on my shoulder. "Margaret's upstairs on the phone. Make yourself at home. Want a drink? Water, Coke, beer, whiskey? I'm having a Heineken."

"I'm fine," I said, but a few seconds later he walked out of the kitchen holding two beers by their necks and carrying the little bowl of M&M's that was always next to the answering machine. "So," he said, sinking into the couch, "this isn't a bad day, huh? I left the hospital at four, already worked out, Nancy's eating with a friend tonight. You know, I see you in and out so much, but we've never really talked. What's your story, where you from?"

I told him about Somerset and what I was doing in the city, and he nodded like listening to me was a bad meal that he was determined to eat all of. To get him to talk, so I could stop, I said, "What do you do again? Margaret told me you're a doctor, but I don't remember exactly."

"That's all right. I'm a brain surgeon."

"Wow. That's like what they joke about."

"They do. And I always say, 'It's not rocket science.' You learn it just like anything else. Hardest part for me was getting comfortable cutting open skin. Med school, I always wanted to be a pediatrician. Never thought I could stand cutting somebody open." He blew out a sour burp. "But. You get used to it, same as everything."

For too long we just nodded, and after a little, both of our looks moved toward the TV, so he said, "Let's see what's on this thing." He flipped until he saw an old-looking movie on TBS with a man and woman talking on the deck of a ship. "There goes my night," Dr. Marsen said. "You've seen this?" He put his feet up.

"I'm not sure. What is it?"

"'What *is* it?' Have you heard of Cary Grant? Deborah Kerr? Oh, young people really scare me. You're missing out on a whole world. I've tried getting Margaret to watch a few movies with me, and she'll only sit through half an hour. We'll make a date and educate the two of you."

Margaret came down the stairs wearing her Big Apple Circus T-shirt and blue boxers, her hair piled on top of her head in a way that turns her neck into the best part of her body. "Hey," she said. "Giving Henry his homework?" She put her hand on Dr. Marsen's arm.

"Hopeless, hopeless, you're all hopeless. Go off and be young." He stood up, his shorts sealed to his butt, and went upstairs grumbling.

I hadn't even noticed that Matthew was in the room. He was on the floor on the other side of the couch, tapping the head of one of his plastic robots against the carpet. "Henry?" he said. "Can I tell you a joke I learned at camp today? My friend Neil Sitkin told it to me. OK. Wait. What's one plus one?"

"Two?"

"Window!" He grinned. With the tip of his finger he wrote a one in the air, touching a big plus sign, touching another one, and then an equals sign as the top and bottom. "Get it? Window!" I laughed without having to mean to—happy just to have understood him—and Margaret laughed too, not because of the joke, I don't think, but because I was laughing. Matthew looked down at his robot, not sure what to do with such incredible success.

For an hour we played three-person Mario Kart—Margaret was Koopa, and I, to her complete delight, was the princess. During a race on the beach, when Margaret knocked the controller out of my hand just before the finish line, I got this light pain in my chest that I hadn't felt in years, as if happiness made crystals grow in my heart. While we raced again I told her about the guy getting arrested at Rite Aid, and she knocked her knees against the floor and grinned and said, punching me in the leg, that she couldn't believe I hadn't called her.

"I've got an idea," she said, when Matthew ran off to eat pizza in the kitchen with Dr. Marsen. "Are you doing anything the rest of the night?"

"Nope."

"Let's go swimming."

Right away I started to think of reasons that I couldn't. Except for the day we met, she'd never seen me without a shirt.

"I'll go get my suit, meet me down at the pool in ten minutes. OK?"

She looked so excited and pretty and happy that my mouth said OK without the rest of me giving it permission.

I could wear a T-shirt. A wet T-shirt sometimes makes me look like a Ziploc bag full of raw dough, but it's better than being topless, I guess. I'd just bring one of Lucy's big towels, so I could wrap up as soon as we were out of the water. The pool was open until ten thirty on weeknights, but

I'd never seen anyone else in it after nine. Changing into my bathing suit, knowing Margaret was changing into hers downstairs, I felt closer to kissing her than I ever had. I pictured her hair all wet under my hands, her skin a little squeaky when I held her. By the time I'd finished changing I was hurrying so she wouldn't change her mind.

"A bit of evening exercise?" Sameer said, and pushed seven.

"Margaret's meeting me."

"Truly a stroke of remarkable luck."

Before the doors closed behind me, he put a hand in front of the red light and said, "May I simply say that I find your father to be an inspiring person. Before his departure, he explained to me the story of his music in such a way that I felt myself warmed by new possibilities. Please tell him that I find him an extremely hopeful individual."

"I will," I said, but I could tell that Sameer was hoping to talk more, and his mouth was open when I turned away.

Margaret was already swimming, but the pool wasn't empty. An older woman I'd never seen was treading water, wearing a white rubber shower cap. "Hell-o," the woman said and, feeling stupid, I waved. Margaret was swimming breaststroke underwater, her hair streaming. She broke the surface and said, "Come in! It's great." With her hair slicked back, her face looked big and white, and I could see every detail of her boobs through her suit. I jumped in and put on my goggles. But as soon as I came up for air, the water-treading woman said, "You aren't supposed to swim in a shirt, you know." I swallowed and cursed and peeled off my T-shirt.

While I swam just barely underwater, Margaret dove under me and swam along the bottom, upside down, looking up. Bubbles came out of one corner of her mouth, and I thought, *Margaret bubbles*. I felt more naked in those five seconds than I could remember ever feeling, my soft stomach and chest two feet from her open eyes.

"Catch," she said, and tossed me a half-deflated rubber ball. Being in the shallow end meant having my body out of the water, but Margaret wasn't even looking. She got out of the pool and made me try to throw the ball so she could catch it in midair.

The old lady left, wrapped in towels, and Margaret and I kept swimming until the wrinkles on our fingers had turned hard. "I'm leaving in a week and a half," she said.

"I know."

"You've gotta write to me."

"I could just call you."

"I know, but there's something nice about getting letters. I still have every letter anyone's ever sent me in my life."

"I don't know if I've ever really had enough letters to save. Maybe five? Ten?"

"No. Five? What about girls in middle school, friends from camp—"

"I didn't talk to girls in middle school. My mom was the only person who wrote me letters when I was at camp. She used to send one a couple of days before I left, so it would be there on my first day."

"Well, there you have it. Those are worth ten letters right

there. You've got something," she said, and moved like to wipe her nose—for a second I didn't understand her.

Panicking, I wiped at my entire face, and what came off in my hand was the worst kind of water booger, a baby yellow octopus. I didn't know what to do, so I smeared it off on the edge.

"Very nice," she said, smiling, and then with no warning she kicked off the wall and swam two fast laps, a perfect enough freestyle that I remembered her saying something once about a swim team. She breathed loudly, each breath sounding like she'd just been woken up by something scary. Swimming back to the shallow end she aimed herself at me. I didn't move, not sure what she wanted me to do, and she dove and grabbed my legs under the knees. She was trying to twist me underwater, so I went under, and she swam off, fast as a fish, and I tried to follow. I couldn't catch her, so in the deep end I pulled up to rest on the ladder, panting and happy, and she pulled up against the wall a few feet away.

"Come here," she said, and she lifted herself out of the pool. In the windows behind her I could just see dark office buildings, filling everything and blocking out the sky. She wrapped a towel around her bottom half and said again, "Come on," so I climbed out and followed her. She took my hand, and even though she'd touched me before, this felt different. The skin of my hand was puffy and papery. "Right this way," she said, and she led me into Women. My spine tingled. She didn't say anything. She flipped on the lights but then turned off all but one switch.

The women's room was just the same as the men's, except that there was a white metal tampon machine on the wall by the sinks. I could feel my pulse in my face, and I didn't want to say anything, because anything I said might disturb whatever she was thinking. "I want to do something, but no touching," she said. "OK?" I nodded. Moving like only girls can, she hooked her thumbs under her shoulder straps and peeled her suit down until she stepped out and was wearing . . . nothing. I was so shocked and nervous that I practically laughed. Great things happen fast too. She turned on the shower, smiling a little, tested the water with her hand, and, trembling, I pulled down my suit and kicked it into the corner. I'd never been completely naked in front of a girl in my life, not even Wendy, not once.

"Come in," she said, "but *don't touch*." The water was warm and hard, like little grains of rice. I felt my goose bumps melt and then rise again. She pulled the curtain closed on us, those metal rings clinking against the rod, and I kept thinking, *This is as happy as I get. This is as happy as I get.* Our shower smelled like bleach, until she squeezed white foamy soap from the wall dispenser into her hand, then it smelled like lemons. The ground was as rough as sidewalk. There was a metal dish on the wall. I stood as far back from her as I could, which was only about three feet, and even in the almost-dark I could see: her breasts with their brown nipples, her wide, white stomach, her strong legs, her big black triangle of hair, her long feet, her girl knees, her arms. And when she turned around to wash her hair, her bright white butt, completely bare. Foam washed out of the tips of her hair and onto her back, ran off between her legs. She had a mole the size of a dime on her right hip.

She stepped past to let me get to the water, and her body just barely touched mine. Warmer and smoother than anything I've ever felt, her entire back tickled my entire front. I pretended to wash my hair but really just stood there watching. "I really want to touch you," I said.

"No."

"I would never tell anyone. You'd never tell anyone—it would be like it never happened. We wouldn't even talk about it with each other."

"No."

"Definitely not?"

"Definitely not. Just this. So we'd have this one thing to remember."

I realized, after a few seconds, that she was looking at my body the same way that I was looking at hers. "Don't suck in," she said, so I sucked in a little less. "You've got very nice arms." I just let the water run all over me and didn't say anything.

"Put down your goggles."

I hadn't even realized that I was still holding my goggles. I put them on the soap dish and instantly forgot them.

"Your legs are funny," she said.

"They curve in."

"I like them."

"Walter says I'll have back problems."

"You have such a little waist."

"Not really that little."

"I mean under there, you can see your hip bones."

My legs were shaking, even in the hot water. I had less of a boner than you'd think, it was like my penis didn't want to end this either.

"Let me rinse off again, then I'm getting out," she said. My stomach sank, but I still didn't say anything. While she rinsed her hair she closed her eyes and let her mouth hang open, and water ran off her lips. I wanted so much to kiss her that I had to squeeze my arm not to.

When she got out, I stayed in, with the curtain open, and watched her dry off. I thought, *She gets to see herself like this every day.*

"You getting out?" she said. "Don't forget your T-shirt." She pulled shorts out of a cubby.

"I'll get it tomorrow," I said. I pulled back on my bathing suit, freezing now, and together, in towels, we walked into the bright hallway.

"Hi, Sameer," Margaret said, like we'd just come back from renting a movie, and he nodded and smiled but seemed to want to leave us alone. When the doors opened on twelve, she said, "I'll talk to you tomorrow. Good night, Sameer. Good night, Henry." It felt absurd, but five minutes after we'd been naked together she was gone. If this was her acting like it had never happened, she was too good at it.

"I trust you had an enjoyable swim," Sameer said, once the doors had closed.

"Incredibly."

"If it doesn't feel very mundane," he said, "tomorrow I

am bringing cupcakes to honor Janek's birthday. We'll be playing Ping-Pong from five until six. I am sure he would have further things to say about Margaret then."

I nodded and said I'd be there, but I had no real idea what he'd said—no real idea what anyone said—for the entire rest of the night.

* * *

"I want to be sure I understand. You are taking a shower with a girl and you still end up in your bed alone," Janek said.

"Perhaps the mere fact of being in one another's company outdid the importance of sexuality."

"Were you naked in the shower?"

"The details of Mr. Henry's sexual dealings ought to be fodder for him and for Ms. Margaret, and that is where it should begin and that is where it should end."

Janek was trying a new forehand that sent two out of three shots off the table, and I was lying on my back on the row of chairs. The game room was hot and smelled like cake frosting and dryer sheets.

"But there was no sex! There's nothing not to talk about! Whenever I'm in the shower with a girl, you can bet that if I don't screw, something's the matter with her. Have you showered with a girl, Sameer?"

"An utterly foolish question."

"You either have or haven't. I've showered with two girls. One is my wife, but only a few times, and another is Nadja, who lived downstairs in my apartment in Prague. Now you."

"My wife and I have enjoyed great, great intimacy."

"What's that? You've talked about a dream? You rub her feet after work?"

"We have enjoyed sexual intimacy that someone of your tastes could not begin to appreciate nor to imagine."

"No. I can't imagine it. Henry, do you think Sameer's having sex we can't imagine?"

I sat up and my head swam. "I have no idea."

"The truth of my sexual life is not a matter to be judged by the two of you. It is fact, and it as indisputable as a piece of rock."

"A piece of rock! Steamy!" Janek grinned yellow at me.

"I am miserable!" For a second I thought Sameer had meant to say something else. Janek and I stared. "I am in grief that the highest point of my day is playing a child's game with a man whose intelligence I do not respect, having my sexuality put under inquisition, listening to the stories and details of others' romances as if they were of greater interest to me than my own. I am horrified! I cannot accept it."

Janek looked at me and raised his eyebrows, but his smile was nearly all panic. "We were joking."

"And I was not." Sameer stormed out, and if there had been a door to the room, he would have slammed it. For almost an entire game Janek and I were too uncomfortable to talk.

Finally, he said, "To be serious, I have only showered with one woman, and that is my wife. And we do nothing these days except wash. Just to shower, I think, is more than enough."

*   *   *

I didn't see Margaret for the rest of the week. After work on Friday, Dr. Marsen told me that she was taking a nap and then closed the door before I could ask to see her. Her cell phone was off—I must have listened two hundred times to her message, memorizing every pause and note. I asked Georgi if he'd seen her, and he said, "Yesterday she came out looking very upset. Is everything not all right?"

Was I supposed to touch her in the shower? Had I screwed that up? Or should I not even have said that I wanted to touch her? Maybe I should have said no to the whole thing, maybe she was feeling guilty, maybe she'd told Drew and now they were breaking up. This seemed so likely that for a while I was almost certain. I paced the apartment and bit my knuckles, but time wouldn't pass. On Saturday I decided to walk all the way to Ninety-sixth Street, just so I wouldn't sit in the apartment and call her every five minutes, but I walked without noticing anything and called her from my cell phone every three minutes. What sort of thing is that to want, to shower but not to touch? To look at me? Why? So I could look at her? Does she really want to be looked at that much? Sunday afternoon I talked to Mom and Dad, and when Mom, before she handed the phone over, said, "Your father's being a pest," I thought, *If their having problems will make Margaret call, then let them be getting a divorce.*

On Monday, before I left for work, I wrote a note and put it under the Marsens' door:

Margaret,

When you read this, please come find me right away. I'm very worried.

Henry

All day at the zoo I kicked pebbles and hid from kids. Was there something a little pathetic that she could tell me to just *look* at her and I'd act like we were in second grade and she'd picked me for her team? I'd seen naked girls before. And Wendy's body was probably better than Margaret's. Her boobs weren't as big, and yes, from certain angles she could look a little like an eleven-year-old boy, but there were other times when you'd see her and think, *Wow, now that's exactly what a naked girl's supposed to look like.*

Doing Change I got tired of talking to myself, so I walked over to Ramon, who was leaning against Othello's pen. Usually he'll give you advice until you can't remember what the problem was, but today he wasn't interested.

"My son's coming home on Saturday. I tell you, my mother-in-law's invited so many people I think we're going to have to put a tent in the backyard. I say to her, 'This kid's coming home from the desert, first time he's setting foot in the U.S.A. for twelve months, you're going to overwhelm him. You can't go from being a soldier, riding in a tank, sleeping four hours a night, storming right into Baghdad—

you take a guy who's been doing that and give him thirty aunts and a plate of barbecue wings and he's going to turn right back around.' I'm excited, though. I haven't seen him in . . . let's see, the last time I saw him was on September sixteenth, JFK, I sat there at the security gate until his plane boarded. Watched all the way until takeoff. Longest time I haven't seen my son since he was born. His mother, man, his mother can't believe it. He sent us a picture, all strong now, all tan. He's always been a strong guy, been arm-wrestling me since he was ten, but now you see him and you just say, 'My *God*.' Like cantaloupes. He's going to give us some grandchildren soon, he says. He's got the most beautiful girlfriend, this girl makes me glad for my son but sad for me, you know? Beautiful, beautiful girl, hasn't seen my son in a year, but every week she's coming by the house to check up on us, making sure we're doing OK, comparing letters. They're going to have some children you're not going to believe."

Garret wandered over, and pretty soon Ramon was telling him about the pie his mother-in-law was bringing. I went to talk to Newman. He'd been calmer since the camp groups had stopped coming, maybe even a little depressed. Yesterday a little girl had stood at the fence with a handful of food, reaching into the pen, calling, "*New*-man, *New*-man," but he just lay there five feet away, not looking up. He was lying on the ground now in front of the shed, and I sat down on the stump facing him. He turned his eyes up to me without moving. "I'm going insane," I said. "I thought the shower was the start of something, but now I think it was the end. I just can't come up with anything I did wrong. Anything. And even if I did—why can't she just *call*? Why would she not just take two minutes to call?" Newman sat up for a second and then lay back down, hitting the ground as hard as a full bag of trash.

"What's going on with you?" I said. He wasn't asleep, and he didn't even look especially tired—it was just that the only part of him moving was his eyes. "What do you have to be upset about? The weather? Do you want some peanut butter?"

Newman stood up with lots of slow stretching. He spun around twice and then lay back down with his head in my lap, as casually as if it were an accident. I was so grateful that I choked up. "Oh, you're one good boy," I told him. "If you ever need to talk, just come find me, we'll figure out what to do. I come to you, you come to me. Deal? Nothing too big, nothing too small." I scratched him hard on his lower back, and he lifted his head and bent it way over backward, smiling with his lower teeth pushed out.

Sunday morning when I woke up there was an envelope with my name on it inside the door:

Dear Henry,

I'm sorry to have been so scarce. My grandmother passed away on Thursday morning, and I've been a bit of a mess. I promise I'll come find you as soon as I'm feeling up to facing the world.

Yours,
Margaret

I felt drunk. Before going to bed each of these nights I'd said to God, *Make this not my fault and I'll do whatever you ask.* And He hadn't just made it not my fault—He'd made it His fault! I needed to go for a walk to keep from calling her. I decided, with the click of settling on something exactly right, that I ought to go find her a present.

"I saw your friend," Georgi said, "and she seems to be very upset."

"Her grandmother died." Suddenly Georgi's face looked ten times sadder than it had even occurred to me to feel.

"It is so, so sad, burying a grandparent," he said. "I have four times, and it only becomes more hard. My grandfather's funeral, I don't even like remembering it."

The word *funeral* was a dark, clanging bell. Margaret was probably going to leave for her grandmother's. Was there any way she'd come back to New York for just three days? Was this really all I could manage to feel when a friend was grieving? Taking in this new truth about myself, I felt the way I had when I first noticed hair in one of my armpits: disgusted, excited, a little bit strange to myself. If this ugly, blind neediness is loving someone, then I'm not sure I want anyone to love me. But how was I supposed to think about anything but what this meant for me? How did Georgi manage to feel sad when for all he knew ten minutes before, Margaret's grandmother had been dead for twenty years? Even I would never have known that she existed if I hadn't asked her who that woman was in the picture on her dresser.

I pulled out my phone and called her—the silences

between the rings took so long that during each one I thought I'd been disconnected. She softly said hello.

"Margaret!" I said, sounding a little too bouncy. "I just wanted to say I'm sorry. About your grandmother. That's terrible."

A crane as tall as a building swung slowly in front of the sun.

"It is. Thank you for calling." She blew her nose. I pictured her in bed in a pile of Kleenex with the shades down and the lights off.

"When I was worrying about my dad dying, I remember I kept thinking how strange it would be to never hear his voice again. Are you—"

"Henry, I'm sorry. I don't really feel like talking on the phone."

"That's OK. Do you feel like walking? It could be good just to get some fresh air and move a little. I'm on my way to Columbus Circle, I could come back and get you."

"I think I'll pass. Bye, Henry."

"Bye," I said, hoping to sound hurt.

"Bye."

I hung up and made a face that said (to who?) that I was embarrassed but not too worried. But I was. She really was a wreck—and I really didn't know anything to do about it. I walked into the flower shop on Fifty-eighth. It was as small as David and Lucy's bathroom, and the only person in it was an old man on a stool with a game-show-host face and glasses. "Question," he said, and at first I thought he was talking to someone behind me. "Do you know Elizabeth Burtrell?"

"I don't think so."

"She could go by Lizzy. Black hair, quite short, *very* striking."

"Sorry."

"I ask because she used to work for the Wildlife Conservation Society—I saw your shirt. She was at the aquarium. We used to go watch the jellyfish some afternoons."

"I work at the Central Park Zoo."

He smiled, but now it was a shopkeeper smile. "Can I help you with anything today?"

"I just wanted to buy some flowers."

"Who for?"

"My girlfriend."

"Does she like lilies? I've got some callas, we could put them in with a little baby's breath. Or roses, if you wanted to be more traditional."

"Can I mix the roses?"

"You can do anything you want, so long as you're paying. And that's not flowers, that's life."

I chose three red, three white, three yellow, and three peach. I'd only meant to get a few when I came in, but realizing just how little I could help Margaret had changed my mind. The man wrapped them in heavy paper and swiped my card with a flourish.

No one answered at the Marsens', so I left the flowers leaning against the door. Their mail was piled on the doormat, and on the blank side of a magazine subscription card I wrote, *For Margaret, Love, Henry.*

At six I hadn't heard from her, so I went around the

apartment making sure that all the phones were hung up. Still nothing at seven, and I was too distracted to eat dinner, so I went out for another walk. I started down Fifth, past the NBA store, past a garden, past buses beeping while they let old people on, and I tried not to think about anything except what I could see and hear and feel right then. One of the classes I took in my half semester at American was PE, and the stumpy, jolly woman who came in to teach yoga made us go for heightened-body-awareness walks around campus. She called it meditation on the hoof, and the few times I did it, I was surprised to find myself feeling calm and glowy for the rest of the morning. So. A dull short pain in my right shin. A breeze making the sweat under my arms cool. The smell of roasting nuts. A gray sky. Far-off church bells. The feeling of wanting to snap a pencil.

I thought (*a helicopter whapping, a dog's cold nose almost touching my knee, a cell phone playing a classical song I half know*) about life without Margaret. How had my happiness come to depend on her, instead of on any of these hundreds of women walking past? They're not any less pretty—some of them are much prettier—and their lives aren't any less interesting or strange. Why (*a bright white seagull almost sideways*) could I just as well be looking at mannequins? And why, if I did have to let one person control my happiness (*a sour taste in the back of my mouth*), did it have to be a person who doesn't love me? But of course she didn't! We'd only known each other for three months! So how long did it take, then? Who really could love you (*wind chimes, incense*) except for your family? And how could you settle for that?

Dad (*a man sneezing and really saying* ah-choo!), I can't have you be the person in the world whose death would make me the saddest. You chose Mom, you loved your parents less (*a loose page of newspaper doing cartwheels, a billboard of a model laughing in just her underwear*), when can I? When have you lived enough that it starts to count? How do you get over knowing (*a squirrel too scared to move, an ambulance speeding, an old black woman taking a picture of herself*) that the person doesn't have to love you no matter what? And that you don't have to love them?

On the way back up Fifth I walked on the other side of the street and decided so suddenly to go into the church on Fiftieth that I must have looked like I was trying to shake off someone following me. I'd never been in before, but Margaret talked about how beautiful it was every time we walked past. It looked from the outside like a castle, all these stone peaks and two wooden doors that could have let in an elephant. Inside it was giant and stone and quiet.

By the guestbook was a white marble bowl of water on a table, and I watched a Hispanic man touch the water and cross himself, leaving wet spots on his shirt. Hundreds of red candles sparkled in the dark on tables all up and down the walls. The benches were old and wooden, with maybe fifty people sitting on them, but there was so much space here that every person got to be alone, got to feel like it was just him and God. It would be hard to think little thoughts here, under this ceiling, in this building as solid as a mountain, with that gold cross glowing in the front. I sat on an empty bench near the middle and picked up a copy of *Celebrating the Eucharist*.

Behind the cross was a bright white room with a hundred-color stained-glass window, and I stared straight ahead, waiting to feel something. A man a few benches behind me had a juicy cough. *I think I'm in love,* I thought so hard that I almost said it. *I think she could love me back, but I need help. I want my life to start. I'm sorry her grandmother died, but this is my last chance. I've never felt like this before.* Slowly, after maybe ten minutes, maybe twenty, I stood up and walked down the aisle, trying to feel changed, trying to imagine what sort of trouble everyone else here was in. At the door I dipped my fingers in the water, but a bald man in a robe was watching me, so I wiped them on my shorts. I walked back out onto the street, and once those doors closed behind me I might as well never have come.

There was no note under my door, no message, no Margaret waiting in tears of joy. "When did you leave the flowers?" Lucy asked. She and David sat a few feet apart on the couch, each with a glass of white wine.

"Five o'clock."

"She really should have said something by now," she said. "Maybe she's out of town?"

"I don't think so."

"Don't make him worry," David said. "She's probably a little overwhelmed. Girls are very weird about flowers."

"*Girls?*"

"You. Women. Jesus, stop it. Look. She's probably out to dinner. Give her till tomorrow. If you don't hear from her, call her and ask her what she's doing."

"When I get roses," Lucy said, in a voice like she was talking to herself, "I don't wait till the morning."

"Henry. Could you excuse us for just a minute?"

So I went into my room, and at nine I couldn't wait anymore.

When Mrs. Marsen saw that it was me, she stepped out into the hall and pulled the door almost shut behind her. "Henry," she said. "Those were lovely flowers." She touched my wrist. "I'm afraid Margaret's really not in good shape for a visit right now. Did she tell you there's been a death in her family?" She was whispering.

"She told me."

"I'll let her know you stopped by."

"Can I go in for a second?"

"I really don't think you'd better."

And I was looking at a locked door.

I was thinking about ringing the bell again when the elevator opened down the hall. A guy about my age, in jeans and boots and carrying a Blockbuster bag, said, "Excuse me," and let himself into the Marsens' apartment. I didn't realize who he was until he'd closed the door behind him.

I rang the bell and, once it had faded, rang it again. I could hear through the door how annoying it sounded, but this was my heart's siren, I couldn't have stopped even if I'd wanted to. Drew answered and said, "Did I lock you out?"

"Are you Drew?" My eyes were wide, my heart was pounding, the muscles in my neck were tight enough to rip.

"I am. What's your name? You all right?" He was as tall as

Margaret, and seemed like the sort of gentle, strong person who doesn't curse. It wasn't hard to imagine him chopping down a tree.

"I'm Henry."

"Henry! My bad. All right. Margie told me about you. How you doing? I'm sorry about that." He shook my hand, and even then I had to try not to think about all the things that hand had done.

"I was coming to talk to Margaret."

"I'm sorry, man. She's actually having a pretty rough time right now. I think maybe it would be better if you came back like tomorrow or something? Is that cool?"

I heard Mrs. Marsen call from the kitchen, so I nodded and rushed back down the hall.

Upstairs I paced around the apartment trying to think of a reason that this might not be the end. Maybe he'd flown here because she'd told him that she was breaking up with him. Maybe her grandmother dying had made her realize what a mistake it would be to spend her life with this bear. But he hadn't sounded like someone fighting to keep the girl he loved—he'd sounded like a plain, happy dad who gets through life without ever having to think about how. Oh, Margaret, you lied to me. I don't know about what, exactly, I can't tell you how and when. But one day we're showering and then four days later your boyfriend's answering the door—you shouldn't ever have given me any hope. The first day we met, you shouldn't have asked me to watch Matthew, you should have waited to pee until you were back in your apartment, you should have stayed a girl who I'd see maybe once or twice in the elevator and smile at and that's *it*. I really hated you right then, Margaret. I couldn't have gotten through the night otherwise. I turned every second we'd spent together into a reason, and by the time I woke up on Monday morning, I was like a house burned down to pipes and bricks and black.

* * *

So that afternoon, when she walked up behind me on the rocks while I was feeding the turtles, for a second *I* didn't even know what I felt. "Hi," she said, and then nothing. She stood with her left leg crossed over her right, the way she did when she wanted to be small. "Sorry I haven't been around. I've been a wreck."

"That's OK," I said quietly, and I wasn't, I realized, all the way burned down.

"I'm sorry if it was weird to meet Drew like that. He said you seemed really upset. I wish I could have planned that better. Those were such beautiful flowers you gave me. It's just been so hard. . . ." And for the first time I saw her cry. It wasn't pretty crying, it was real crying with a wrinkled chin and red eyes and a runny nose. "I'm sorry," she finally said. I handed her a few pellets and one by one she tossed them into the water. A pointy black turtle mouth popped up wherever a pellet landed, it was like the world's easiest video game.

"I was thinking today about when Nana used to pick me up from school," she said. "I feel so terrible about it. I used to be embarrassed to walk with her, for some reason, so I'd wait inside, watching her until she gave up and went back home. It's so sad thinking about her standing out there waiting."

Watching her cry I felt something sore in me pulled toward her.

Paul pushed through the plastic flaps in the tree and said, "Henry, did you strip Sheep?" He looked at Margaret, and she turned so he wouldn't see her face. "I don't want to have to talk to you again about visitors during work hours. Finish up turtle, then strip."

Margaret hugged me before she left, and I knew I smelled like the zoo but I also knew that it didn't matter. When she pulled away she laughed at herself for having wet eyes again.

While I stripped Sheep I felt sad in the happiest way there is to feel sad—I couldn't imagine hating Margaret any more than I could imagine hating Newman. My problems were as ancient and as beautiful as icebergs. I imagined Margaret's grandmother on her back in a coffin, her mouth open, her forehead cold. This woman who'd stopped on walks to tie Margaret's shoe, who'd fallen in love and fought and bought a house and washed dishes: She'd rot the same as a fallen tree. Under every footstep on the planet is someone who once thought, *Not me! They'll never forget about me!*

Each year on his father's birthday, Dad drives out to the graveyard in Virginia and spends the day there, sitting and thinking above all that dirt and bone. Afterward he comes home and hugs Walter, and they retell the same stories and shake their heads and talk about their dad as if he were living happily in Florida. Margaret once said that she wanted to be cremated—maybe they'd cremate her grandmother. Every-one seems to think about cremation as if it just meant press-ing a button and turning into a pile of ash—so much less gruesome than slithering, fat pink worms—but no one ever talks about the fire. Your chest popping and folding and turning black like a Coke bottle in a bonfire. All that cooking meat.

And suddenly the idea of *Margaret* dying took all the hap-piness out of my sadness. Nineteen years old, not even sick, but it felt as close as if she'd been ninety-five: That body in an oven, that hair and those cheeks and that voice burning up into pebbles—it made my heart hurt. I wouldn't be able to stand it, I didn't think, even if I just read about her death in the newspaper sixty years from now. And it didn't have to be in sixty years, it could be next month, it happened every day in every neighborhood in the city to people who'd meant to get old. All the taxis that don't stop for red lights, all the thousands of ways a body fails, all the lunatics on subway platforms—how does anyone who's in love ever relax for a minute?

Ramon was leaning on the fence watching me. I had no idea whether he'd been there for fifteen minutes or fifteen seconds. "You look like you got something eating you," he said.

"Margaret's grandmother just died."

"You serious? Man, I'm sorry to hear that. There's noth-ing sadder than death, even the old folks, I say rest in peace and I'm praying for you." Dudley jumped up on the fence and started chewing on Ramon's sleeve, but he didn't seem to notice. "My mother died four years ago, toughest woman on the planet. Doctor says he's never seen anybody that tough—he says he's seen forty-year-olds not like her. Death comes, though, that's the truest thing anybody ever said. Death does come."

When I was in high school, I ate lunch occasionally with a peppy, nerdy gymnast in the grade below me named Rod Chang. He'd drive us, holding the wheel carefully, in his mom's car—it had a little computer screen on the dashboard that showed a map of the few blocks around you. This was a year or two before this kind of thing became common, so, trying to prove that it was necessary, Rod would type in an address practically every time we got in the car, even if we were just going to the same Subway that we'd gone to the week before.

Reading the first fifty pages of *Hunt for Red October*, once I'd stopped stumbling on the names, I'd felt like I was driving Rod's car around Chevy Chase, each street clear and bright. I knew exactly where I was, where I'd just been, where I was about to be. But around page two hundred, when the story started to cut between all the different submarines and ships that were out looking for the *Red October,* I started to feel like I was driving out in Virginia by Dad's parents' farm, maybe—I'd go down whole streets without being exactly sure where they pointed, I'd realize I was in a new town but that I didn't even remember leaving the last one. And now, reading on the couch, almost at page four hundred, I may as well have been driving in the Sahara—I'd go for fifteen pages and realize that I didn't know where I was, what direction I was headed, a single thing I'd just seen. I kept forgetting, as I read, that the *Red October* actually wanted to get somewhere: The ocean, with its mountains and valleys and storms, seemed like a complete world, and it was hard to imagine Ramius and the rest of them wanting to walk down an American sidewalk. I was turning pages now just so I could say that I'd finished, to myself as much as to Margaret. And because reading, unlike TV, could keep me from thinking about her and Drew for minutes at a time. They'd eaten dinner the night before at a French restaurant, and shards of the dinner kept flashing at me—the bottle of wine on the table, Margaret's bare foot resting on Drew's knee, the waiter setting down a piece of chocolate cake.

David walked in holding a bag of groceries. "What part are you at?" he said. "Did you get to the shoot-out with the cook? How slow are you reading?"

We'd hardly crossed paths for the past few days, and while I told him about Drew coming to town he sat, completely undistracted, listening. "The boyfriend cometh," he said. "She's some kind of tease, huh? I mean, all these months she's going for walks with you, spending all this time with you, coming out to dinner with Dad and everything. Does Drew know about all that stuff?"

"He doesn't care. I really don't think she meant anything by it." I was talking into the pillow.

"You know what, then? Fuck it. She thinks she's happy with this guy, you don't need her. If she's the type who needs two guys all over her, the best thing you can do is just disappear. Don't call her, don't go downstairs, nothing. Just let her think she's lost you."

"And then what?"

"And then nothing. And then when she goes back home, she's learned she can't just fuck with people."

"I don't think she's fucking with me."

"You don't think she's fucking with you? You think she hasn't noticed that you're in love with her? Girls like her seriously drive me nuts."

"Girls like what?"

"Girls who . . . whose whole thing is seeing how many guys they can wreck. You've got to feel bad for the boyfriend of a girl like that, because he's never gonna be enough."

When, exactly, had David learned all this? Who were all these girls that drove him nuts? How do girlfriends and hookups and scandals happen to everyone else the way canker sores happen to me?

I hadn't thought I would, but I said, "It wasn't just talking. We took a shower together once."

"Ho-ly shit. Are you serious?"

I nodded.

"You're serious? Here?"

"Down at the pool."

"So you hooked up?"

"She said we couldn't touch."

"Seriously?" He looked so thrilled, so worked up, so something, that I thought he might pound through the table. "She is *terrible*. She's fucking torturing you. You've got to tell Drew about the shower. Neither one of you should ever talk to her again."

"What about Mona?"

"Who?" But I watched him realize who I meant.

"Mona. Why's that any different?"

"Are you fucking serious?" He talked quietly now, even though Lucy wasn't home. "They're completely different. Mona *e-mails* me. That's it. She tells me where she went for dinner and asks me what classes she should take. We're not fucking taking showers. Don't ever complain again that I don't tell you anything."

Hearing about Mona's e-mails spilled a glass of cold water in my stomach, but I didn't say anything.

"Do whatever the hell you want," David said, standing up. "If I were you, I'd tell him."

But on Tuesday morning, when Margaret called and asked if I wanted to come out to lunch, I almost sounded honest to myself when I said that lunch sounded good, no, it wouldn't be awkward, I was actually eager to get to know Drew. I put on a pair of David's fancy pants and black shoes and went downstairs with our shower tucked in my pocket like a grenade.

We ate at the corner table of a deli on Fifty-eighth, a place I'd sometimes gone to get chicken soup on the rainiest days in June. "I can't get over how much everything here looks like a movie," Drew said. "This morning we walked past the *Seinfeld* restaurant and Margie didn't even want me to take a picture." While he talked—even while he didn't talk—Margaret looked at him, and I tried not to realize that she'd never looked at me like that. He had a dimple on one cheek that you could stick a match in.

My sandwich came first, and when I started eating a fry, Drew gave me a look. So I waited for everyone to be served, and Drew, sounding only a little shy, said, "You guys mind if I bless the food real quick?"

The guys at the next table were listening while Drew looked down at his lap and started in. "Thank you, O Lord, for the food and for bringing us together and for giving us this beautiful day. Bless our new friendships and bless this conversation. Amen."

"Amen," I barely said, and to keep the surprise off my face I imagined Drew and Margaret in bed, but that was awful, so instead I imagined that first moment of seeing Dad in his hospital bed.

Margaret and Drew looked up and tucked in their napkins and picked up their sandwiches like this was any other unblessed food and conversation—this was just the way meals started. The idea was for me to "meet Drew the right way," so all through lunch Margaret asked him questions to get him to talk. It was a radio interview, and Drew was the guest.

About being a ranger: "Well, I guess most of what I do is just walk around making sure nobody's in any trouble. I probably cover, I don't know, ten, fifteen miles a day. You survey whatever wildlife you see, check the water levels on the river, write down how many campers are in each site, make sure everybody's got the right permit. You see a grizzly every now and then, that's pretty cool. Couple of weeks ago, I was telling Margie, I came back to the cabin for lunch one afternoon and a big female—eight-fifty, nine hundred—is just lying on the porch, snoozing right in front of the door. I shot out of there rocket-fast. Pretty solitary job, though, most of the time, but it really is a beautiful spot. For my tastes it sure beats going to an office every day and sitting in front of a screen."

His music: "That's just a silly thing my friends and I do. I'll send you one of our tapes sometime, if you feel like laughing. Do you like Johnny Cash? He was my big hero growing up, so I made my mom get me a guitar, and started just writing songs. I was ten years old, down in my basement singing how my wife left me and everything, because that's just what I thought songs were about. But now my friends Allan and Pete and I get together sometimes and mess around. Pete's got a four-track, so we can dub stuff in, make it sound like there's a whole chorus of us with all these harmonies going."

His flight: "The pilot said, 'Passengers sitting on the right side will have a beautiful view of Manhattan,' and I was on the left, so I was crawling all over this lady doing her crossword puzzle, apologizing and everything. But I swear, if I lived here I'd just sit at the window all day and look down at everything. The tallest building in Great Falls's eight stories. And there's nothing even to look down on once you're up there. You guys are living the life. I don't know how anybody ever goes home after New York."

Everything he said made Margaret smile, or laugh, and she would shoot me looks that seemed to dare me not to be charmed by him. I almost said to her, "You don't seem too upset anymore," but instead I sat through lunch very calmly, very quietly, sad in a cold, broad way completely different from the dramatic suffering I'd expected. I almost forgot about the grenade. I'd loved her so much that my stomach ached, I'd been so mad at her that I'd thought I'd need to breathe into a paper bag, but right then everything I'd felt seemed like scratchings on a beach. This tall, smiling girl with long hair and a square jaw, sitting next to this slow-talking Montana park ranger—who were they? How did I get to be sitting at a table with them? I felt like a balloon that someone's accidentally let go.

After lunch, they walked holding hands down to Times Square to see if they could get tickets to a play, and I told them that I was going home to read. I didn't know whether loving Margaret was the dream and realizing she was a stranger was waking up, or if it was the other way around, but everything I saw seemed to have been polished down to its strangest core. Every woman I passed, even the old ones and ugly ones, I thought, *Somewhere there's a guy who thinks about no one but you.*

Instead of going home, I walked up Sixth and into the park. It had started to drizzle, so almost no one was at the zoo. Garret and Janice were the only keepers on duty, and they both wore green zoo ponchos. Janice raked Goat while Garret leaned against the shed playing a game on his cell phone. "Hey, Henry," Janice said. "You just can't get enough, huh? It's a crummy day, though, crummy, crummy, crummy. We've only had five people all afternoon. Paul says we can close at four thirty if no one else comes. How are you doing?"

"I'm actually having kind of a bad day," I said.

"Ooh—I'm so sorry. Coming here can sometimes be just what it takes. Do you want to talk about it, or do you just want to be left alone? I can go do Sheep if you want to hang out with Newman."

"It's just . . . it's just something with a girl."

"Say no more. I've been divorced twice, never going down that road again. For every one person I know who's happy in a relationship, I know ten who aren't. Such a tough, tough road."

"You were married twice?"

"Both very bad marriages, once when I was much too young to this very dashing older man who worked in newspapers, and once five years ago to a very *not* dashing man who turned out to love to make me feel terrible about myself. I used to be a very, very needy sort of person, and now I'm finally starting to learn how to make myself happy. Better late than never, I guess. But here I am giving you my whole history, and you're the one with the bad day. I'm sorry. Go on."

But I didn't want to go on. So instead I said, "*Could* I finish Goat?"

"It's almost done, but you can finish clearing the shed. You're sure you want to do it in your nice clothes? It's really yucky in there."

"It's fine," I said. The inside of the shed smelled like pee and mud, and before I'd even started my socks were wet. David's socks were wet. It felt good to work my muscles, though. Each time I scooped the shovel under and tossed a square of wet bedding over my shoulder, I grunted. The hay was my summer so far, and I was ripping it apart. Margaret was right then listening to him and smiling, kissing him without having to lean down, flipping through restaurants she'd marked in her guidebook—and it didn't have to matter to me. Didn't have to. I had a vision of myself at forty years old, a half stranger to my teenage self, standing in front of a mirror in my future bedroom with a head full of new memories and names and worries. The house would have an address—those numbers would eventually sound as natural to me as the numbers on Mom and Dad's door do now—and a kitchen with a sink that I'd be able to use in the dark, and a staircase whose creaks I'd come to expect. For as long as I kept my head down, piling the soggy bedding into a trash bag, I felt carried off by this vision, held above the confusion and muck of the summer like a meal on a waiter's tray.

* * *

But then Thursday afternoon happened. I hadn't seen Margaret and Drew since that lunch, and a part of me thought that I wouldn't, that we'd pretend to regret that we hadn't said good-bye and then never talk again. She'd called a few times, to tell me where they were going—the top of the Empire State Building, Ground Zero, the Brooklyn Bridge—and I'd listened without suggesting that we get together, hoping to sound like I didn't quite know why she was telling me all this. Wednesday night I stayed home and finished *Hunt for Red October*. The cook turned out to be a traitor (to Russia? to America?), and Jack shot him in the boiler room. I closed the book feeling exhausted but satisfied, as if I'd just made it to the bottom of a tub of ice cream. Thursday was going to be the first day of my new swimming routine, of living in New York without Margaret.

All that afternoon at work I'd been on Change, standing by Goat, trying not to listen to Garret tell me about his new video game.

"The thing is, you're Frankenstein and you're trying to kill the guy who made you. But people keep coming after you with burning sticks, and the whole time your body's falling apart, so—"

At four thirty, when he'd run out of things to say and we were just hanging over the fence watching the goats, Ramon came out of the staff gate and said, "Power went out—goddamn stereo went out right in the middle of my game." A minute later he came back and said, "Power's out in the main zoo too. What the hell is this? Either of your cell phones working?" My phone wasn't getting service, but it never did there. "This fucking stereo, I plan my entire day so

I take lunch during the seventh, eighth, and ninth, and now the goddamn power goes out."

I thought it was just a zoo problem until I left Children's at five. The path was much more crowded than usual, and the circle at Fifty-ninth was completely clogged with cars. A woman walking a white Great Dane said, "Excuse me, do you know what's going on?" I shook my head and followed her over to a group of high-school kids sitting around a radio on a bench. One of them said, "There's a blackout. All of New York. Whole East Coast, too, and all the way over to Detroit and Cleveland."

Fifth Avenue was a parking lot, and so were all the streets coming onto it—the traffic lights and walk signs were completely dead. The sidewalk was like Times Square just after a show gets out, except no one was in a hurry, everyone was scanning the street, moving at sleepwalking speed. An old man stood leaning on a walker by a fire hydrant, shaking his head at the street.

"You understand what's going on here?" he said as I came near him. His dentures seemed to be too big for his mouth. "They shut off the power, they can do whatever they *want*. They shut off the power, nothing we got defense-wise does any good. Go ask any cop what's happening here. Osama first does the planes, then waits a couple years, works on the power grid, and once it's out, it doesn't have to just be buildings, whole country's gonna burn."

I kept walking.

But seeing the expressions on everyone else's faces—and

seeing Fifth Avenue, all these thousands of cars blocked and honking—I wondered how I could have passed by dread so easily. Half of the country all of a sudden had no alarms, no lights, no God-knows-what sorts of weapons that need computers. And my cell phone still wasn't working. I felt the cold flush I get in my face when something important is going wrong. A woman in spandex shoved me in the back and rushed past me. It was the news about Cleveland and Detroit, I realized, that really should have tipped me off. The zoo, the city, the country—the afternoon had the spreading, clammy shape of a disaster movie. Real fear, I realized, had dried up completely in my memory. September 11 memorials and speeches and TV specials, none of it had anything at all to do with the feeling—we were like people who take hundreds of cell-phone pictures of their nights out as they happen, trying to rush them off into the past. But terror, the real thing, is as private and as miserable as nausea.

The first plane had hit while I was in first-period English with Mr. Dulac. One minute I was trying to sleep with one eye closed, and the next minute Mrs. Lam knocked on the door to make the announcement. How scared *she* looked was the scariest part. After forty-five minutes of listening to Mr. Dulac whisper and chuckle about *A Midsummer Night's Dream,* terrorists! "There's another plane missing too," said Vince Fraser, who'd been able to get through to his mom. The men they kept showing in military uniforms in front of blue curtains, the people reading the news, the teachers sitting right there with us on the floor in the lounge—they all had the look of dogs whose owners are leaving. Lisa

Gabardine was crying so hard that I thought she must know someone.

Sameer stood outside the revolving door frowning. "I woke up this morning with a terrible feeling. I have an ability to sense inside what will occur on the day arriving, and this morning I said to Nishant that he must be unusually careful because something very awful may well come. Thank God only that I am not one of those suspended in the elevator, in full darkness, to stay for no one can know how many hours. Janek is between the seventeenth and eighteenth floors, and my prayers for he and his wife are sincere." The lobby was humid and dark. For some reason Georgi was pouring water from one big jug into lots of little buckets.

"Hello, Henry," he said, not even trying to smile. "Are you going up to your apartment?"

"I think so," I said.

"Have Svetlana take you up—she has a light. The stairs can be very brutal. Take a rest when you need one."

It hadn't occurred to me that I'd have to take the stairs. Even with lights those staircases unsettled me, as dirty and empty as the hallways where people get stabbed and left for days. And now they were completely, completely dark. Even with the door open I could have been at the edge of a pit. Svetlana's light was the kind of squeeze-light that hotels give away, and its glow only lit up itself. Across the lobby the skinny old jogging man and his wrinkly wife were waiting at the other staircase, so I said to Svetlana, "My watch has a light. You should take them up."

"You're all right?"

"I'm all right."

"Let me go with you for the first half, then I come down and take Mr. and Mrs. Sinowitz."

So we started. It was worse than any exercise machine. These were the steepest stairs I'd ever been on, and since I could never see how far I had to go, they felt as endless as a treadmill. By the eighth floor I thought that my legs might give out, by twelve I thought I might have torn one of my lungs. Svetlana, square and blond, was hardly even panting. "Is all right if I go back to lobby? You go up to your floor? The light is bright enough?"

"Very bright. No problem." And she was gone. I sat down on the stairs to rest, and my legs rooted themselves to the floor. I'd never felt so trapped, so much like I was being punished just by having a body. The staircase felt suddenly as if it were collapsing around me, and in the rubble I imagined Margaret, Sameer, David, Dad, Mom, Walter, Olive, Newman—bodies twisted, faces pale and bashed. Was this what they called a panic attack? Or was it just being out of shape and going up twelve flights of stairs?

I stood up again, thinking mostly of escape, and something close to terror pushed me to the top of that next flight and onto the next one too. By fifteen I was moving, and I hardly even had to use my watch. I knew exactly when to turn, when to stamp on the next big landing. Much faster than I'd climbed from the lobby to twelve, I got from twelve to twenty-three. I came out into the hallway so winded and glowy that I almost forgot to be afraid.

Someone had set up flashlights like lanterns outside each

of the doors, and inside our apartment I found it almost as light as it was outside. The buildings and streets through the living room windows looked basically the way they always did, except that the lights on the Citibank sign were out, and the streets were even more crowded than they'd been when I left work.

"Hello? Hello?" Lucy came out of the bedroom in her painting clothes, and for once she didn't look disappointed to see me. "Henry! You're home! What's going on out there? Did you just come up the stairs? Have some soda. It's *boiling* in here. We have to save water—Georgi said the water we've got in the tank right now is all we're going to have until they turn the power back on. I didn't even know water had anything to do with the electricity." We sat down together on the couch in the living room, facing those windows, and I realized that this was the first time that we'd ever put ourselves alone in a room together on purpose. I imagined a neighbor pounding on the door to tell us that the building was coming down. Would we have sex? Would we jump?

"Has David called?" I said.

"No one's called. I can't get through to anyone. The landline's still working, but no one's picking up. I'm hoping he just left the hospital and walked home, but can you imagine if he's on the subway? What are they going to do with those people stuck on the subway? I would *kill* myself. Can you imagine? It must be so dark, and no one has any flashlights—I'm freaking out just talking about it. I can't even get through to my parents. I've just been here for an hour going crazy."

And she really had. I'd never seen before how fragile all that order was, how much panic lay just underneath her personality. She seemed, right then, stripped of all her bossiness and moodiness, tucking her hair behind her ears over and over, like a terrified little kid. I could care about her, I realized. She could be my sister-in-law.

I stood up to call my parents, but once I was holding the phone, I decided—like an ex-smoker who lets himself have a cigarette during a crisis—to call Margaret instead.

She wasn't picking up, and her answering machine wasn't working—it was just ringing and ringing and ringing. I called home.

"Hello?"

"Dad?"

"Henry? How are things? You're back from work?"

"Are you guys OK?"

"Of course we're OK. I feel great. I walked all the way into Georgetown today, didn't stop once."

"Is your power out?"

"Let's see—nope. Power's on. You're giving me the creeps. What's doing with you?"

"The power's out, Dad." My voice was cracking. "The power's out all over New York and all the way to Cleveland. The power's OK in Maryland?"

"Power's A-OK. Hold on. *Carol!* Is the power working in the kitchen? I don't *know* what's happening. Henry says all the power's out in New York. Here, wait a minute, I'm going to go look." I heard Mom in the background saying something, then Dad saying, "I don't know. That's exactly what I'm doing."

One night when I was a junior, Dad, who still did his report cards with a typewriter, came home from Safeway with a free AOL disk. "What do you look so surprised about? Now show me what's what." When he used the computer he balanced his glasses on the very tip of his nose, and I had to work to keep from tearing the mouse out of his hand. I showed him the Web site for the *Washington Post* and how to check basketball scores, and he said, "This is what's going to change the world? Baloney." I'd hardly seen him use the Internet since, but I guess he'd kept up, because after two minutes he came back and said, sounding bored, "CNN-dot-com says there's a blown circuit in Michigan, routing problems all through the East Coast, electric companies working like mad to fix things up. You'll be back in business by morning."

Mom had picked up a phone now too, and she said, "What's happening? Are you all OK?"

"Everyone's fine," Dad said. "A screwup at the power company."

"Have you got bottled water?" Mom said. "Why don't you go out to the store and buy some—everyone in the city'll be buying it."

"Listen to your mother. Everything else OK there? Do you have food? Go out to a restaurant. Restaurants are going to be giving the stuff away—no power means everything's got to go."

Lucy was in the kitchen with me now, emptying out the

fridge and trying to listen. When I hung up and told her that there was nothing to worry about, she let out a fluttery noise and put her hand on her heart, and I could almost watch the panic leave her.

"Oh, thank God," she said. "Now let's just get David home." She started to move to hug me, but the ordinary distance between us was filling in already, and I saw her decide, just before she would have had to lift her arms, to go back into the living room instead.

Margaret still wasn't picking up (since I was having one cigarette, I figured I might as well finish the pack), and no one was answering at the Marsens'. David walked in just before seven, his face dripping, and he shook my hand and said, "Good as hell to see you." While he told Lucy the story of his trip home, I grabbed a flashlight from the pantry, a forehead-strap light of David's, and ran down all those stairs and out onto the street. I didn't know if I wanted to say something crushing and final to Margaret, or something loving and weepy, but I needed to work up the courage to find out. It was her last night.

As the sun set and all these windows and stores and signs didn't light up, the blackout settled down on the city like a storm. By now everyone must have heard that this wasn't a crisis, because the whole street had turned into the parking lot outside a concert. A group of construction men leaned against a glass building drinking cans of Budweiser with a whole case ripped open at their feet. A bald man without a shirt stood on the corner of Fifty-third and Sixth with a guitar, playing "Drive My Car" and throwing back his head to sing. Outside the Sheraton stood hundreds and hundreds of confused-looking people, families and couples and businessmen, all crowded onto the sidewalk. A man on a bike asked a little girl what they were all doing.

"The card keys don't work for our rooms," she said. "We're all locked out."

The air could have been coming from a vegetable steamer. I felt like I'd wandered into the middle of a holiday in a foreign city, full of firecrackers and men on stilts and shouting.

My entire body twinged when I saw the sign for Ray's—I was starving and hadn't even realized it. Inside, it was dim and so hot that I had to keep pulling at my shirt to keep it from sticking to my stomach. A short Middle Eastern man a few people ahead of me had taken off his shirt, and he still may as well have been wearing a black sweater.

The men behind the counter, either caught up in the emergency or just feeling ignored in the dark, were shouting. These were the same three grouchy, leering guys I knew from regular nights, but now—because some manager had decided that they should stay open—they seemed as brave as firefighters or cops. The fat one at the ovens would say,

"Light!" and the tall one at the counter, who'd been using the flashlight to count money, would shine it on the ovens, and the oven guy would slide out a huge droopy pie on one of his wooden trays. "How many plains?" the stubby, serious one at the cash register yelled. "How many plains? No slices tonight! Whole pies only!" And all around the room hands shot up, mine included, and somehow after only twenty minutes I walked out with a hot box of pizza.

I sat down to eat on the edge of the Citibank fountain, regretting already that I was going to eat the whole pizza and that I was going to find Margaret. But this was regret as a kind of license: *Since I'm already guilty, I might as well go ahead and earn it.* I'd eaten four slices, the springy bread and sweet sauce and cheese so hot that I had to make a little O with my mouth, when a homeless woman stumbled up and asked if she could get something to eat. I felt so embarrassed about how little I wanted to give her a slice that I gave her the biggest one I had left. "Thank you, my brother," she said. "That'd be some piggy shit, eating eight slices when a woman is starving right here. I mean that."

The fancy grocery store on Fifty-sixth was open too, and I went in more to see it transformed than because I wanted anything in particular. A happy-looking woman stood next to the ice-cream freezers waving a flashlight over all the choices— I decided that she'd probably moved to New York a few months before, and couldn't wait to tell her friends at home that she'd been part of this. "Half-price ice cream," she kept saying. "Pints, quarts, pops. Ben and Jerry's, Breyers, Häagen-Dazs. Everything half-price." I bought two Häagen-Dazs bars for a dollar each, and—because they were already turn-ing soft, because I didn't want to think—I broke into a run headed back to the apartment.

Sameer was still standing by the revolving door, and when he saw me he said, "I feel a relief that comes from all over my heart. Janek is safely recovered, and I have just heard on the radio that riders are walking out of the subway and that there has not been a single mortality, praise to God."

And there, after I ran up the twelve flights to the Marsens' front door, my legs burning, my mouth hanging open, was Margaret in her Cardinals T-shirt. She held the door open just enough for me to see that she was wearing boxers. Hope, even hope you imagine that you don't espe-cially depend on, dies so hard. "Hi!" she said. "Sorry. We were just . . ." And peeking past her I saw Drew, wearing a towel, and on the table next to him a short candle and a glass of wine. He was trying to hear who she was talking to. Margaret wasn't wearing a bra, and her legs were wet. "I thought you were the Marsens," she said. "Sorry. Isn't this insane? We were just sitting here and *boom*—every light in the apartment went out. David and Lucy are OK and everything?"

"I'll come back." My heart was pounding to get out.

"OK! That would be great. We should definitely see each other, though. I really want to talk—I'm leaving in the morning."

"I brought you ice cream."

"Thank you!" She took it like a dirty sock. "Great. Thank you. Definitely come back."

I waited a minute and rang the bell again, and when she

answered this time a towel was wrapped around her waist too. She wasn't holding the ice cream.

"I love you, Margaret," I whispered. I wanted so badly for it to be true that I practically felt it. She stepped out into the hall and shut the door behind her.

"Stop. We'll talk later, OK? This is a bad time."

"I *love* you." I'd never stared harder at anyone. I was frantic. I put my hands on her waist, and the only thing between my skin and hers was a towel.

"Don't touch me," she said, and I lifted my hands away.

"I love you."

"Stop saying that. Go away, Henry, OK? I really want you to go away."

"I love you." I don't know what I thought would happen.

"You don't know me."

"I love you, Margaret."

"Please, please go away."

So I did. Before her apartment door had even clicked shut, I was all the way to the stairwell, alone again. I threw my melted ice cream into what could as well have been outer space, sat down, and for the first time in what must have been years, I really cried. I wasn't sure—even as I was choking, gasping, moaning—exactly what I was crying for, or even if I could have stopped. My heart hurt, the actual muscle—it felt like it was being squeezed by a metal hand. I pounded the wall and laid my head on my knees and wailed. And the door didn't open.

As I sat whimpering, I felt hate spark somewhere in me—and then, with a whoosh, it caught. I hated Dad for his babbling and lying and Mom for her self-pity and David for his ridiculous life. And Margaret—her most of all, for her dramatic faces and her trembly writing and her donkey laugh. I blew my nose loudly into the dark, and stood up, sore from crying, glowing with bitterness, and started back down to the street.

The only lights on Fifth now were a couple of cars pushing slowly uptown. The crowds had all disappeared. A few people slept on the benches by the park entrance, and on the grass along the path a few couples lay on blankets, looking straight up at the sky. I sat down on a bench and looked up too, and there, like spilled glitter, were the stars. I felt small, staring up, trapped in my skin. The tear paths on my cheeks had turned dry and salty, and humiliation crept its way up my body like ivy. When my head had hung back so long that my neck had gone numb, I stood up and started deeper into the park.

At the zoo I had to turn on my light to see that Ramon wasn't at his guard station. I yanked the supply gates open the way Paul had taught me, and then clicked them shut behind me. I pushed through the plastic flaps, the same way I'd walked hundreds of times each week all summer, and I came out in the aviary, by the rabbit pens. Except for whatever the light on my forehead shone on, all I could see was my watch. Nine seventeen. I let myself into Goat—the spare key behind the shed flashed in my light—and there was Newman, curled up in his corner. I knelt down to rub him and he lifted his head.

"How are you?" I said, whispering for some reason. "I'm

alone. I'm completely alone. It's just me and you." I scratched along his jaw and he stretched his legs out straight, all four hooves off the ground at once. "You're so good," I said. He shook his head and his ears flapped. "You are. Come here." I stood up, and by pretending to have a treat I got him to stand up too. He'd never looked so simple, so plain and unconcerned and animal. This could have been because he'd just been sleeping, or it could have been because I'd never wanted so much for him to be the opposite. Suzie was the only other goat awake, and she scratched the spot between her horns on the edge of a stump. "You've got to act very calm about this," I said. "If we see anyone, stand completely still and don't make any noise."

I creaked open the gate, and with only a little nudge Newman took his first steps outside the pen. "That's not scary, is it?" I locked the gate, leaving Suzie staring, and Newman and I walked down the path, past the hay shed, back out the supply gate, and into the park. We walked slowly down to the main path, and Newman stayed right beside me, stopping every few steps to sniff the air, heeling like a show dog. I twisted my light's beam as wide as it would go, so that I'd see him even when I was looking ahead. We walked away from Fifth and from everyone who was looking at stars, deeper into the park. It seems strange, now, that it didn't occur to me that I might be mugged or worse. "These are the rocks," I said. "Sometimes I eat lunch up on those flat ones over there. Up here is where a guy always sells pretzels. The main path's out that way, but we'll go up here. I'll show you the tunnel." Even with my light, it was hard to believe just how dark it was once we were in the middle of the park. The buildings along the avenues had disappeared completely. Newman stopped to nibble grass, and I said, "Is fresh grass good? Go right ahead. Enjoy it." He seemed as much at home here as he did in the shed—nothing in his face or body said that he was the least bit surprised to find that the world included all this.

"Here. This is the tunnel. Listen. *Henry and Newman!*" I called, and the tunnel called back. For the second that my light blinked off, the dark was even deeper than it had been in the stairs at the apartment. *"Henry the Masai! Out walking his goat."* He cocked his head and moved his ears like he was hoping to hear better. We started walking again, now with my hand on his back. All I had to do to steer him was to lean my palm one way or the other. "These are my favorite benches in the park. I'm going to sit down for a minute— you can climb up if you want." He just stood at my knees while I sat, breathing in all the air he could, looking over at me every few seconds to see if I was ready to move yet. "Thanks for coming out. This is the best I've felt all night." We walked silently for a few minutes, past the statue of a dog, down a hill, onto a path where the bricks were red instead of gray. "I should really bring you to see these trees during the day sometime," I said. "They're like something out of a—" And that's when something cracked on the ground in front of us. It was probably just one of the hard, wrinkled nuts that I sometimes liked to toss at tree trunks, but in all that quiet and dark it sounded like a clap. I jumped back, and

Newman darted to the right. He hopped over the low chain between the path and the grass.

I walked after him, down the hill, and it took a few seconds for me to realize that he might actually not stop for me. He was starting to run, his barrel of a body bouncing with each step. *"Newman,"* I said, "stop. Stop right now." He was slower than I was, but it was hard to run while keeping my light on him. For a second, at the bottom of the hill, I was close enough that I could have grabbed a handful of his hair if I'd lunged. But instead I slipped on a stretch of mud and twisted my foot. A short, hot pain flashed in my knee, but I kept running. The bushes rustled as he squeezed through them. "Hey! Newman! Come here *right now*!" I couldn't see him anymore. I clapped and I screamed. I ran around the bushes, still with no sight of him, and then back to the path, as if it all might have been a trick. I limped, yelling his name, down the hill, into the woods and back out, all over a field with a soccer goal, onto a part of the path that I'd never seen. I knew every step could just as easily be taking me farther from him as closer, but I kept going. All the blood in my body was in my knee. And Newman was nowhere. Over and over I yelled his name as loud as I could, and let myself hope, before I walked on, that this time I'd hear those answering clops.

I must have walked more that night, even with my knee, than I'd walked altogether the entire summer. I saw miles of paths that seemed, no matter what I did, to lead me to Fifth Avenue, I saw ponds the size of lakes, a hundred jungle gyms, fences, one huge building with a wall made completely of windows, fields and fields and fields, mountains of rocks, statues I'd never seen, fountains all without water, hundreds of fences. Once I heard something move behind a tree, and when I ran over I saw two men who I'm pretty sure were having sex. Later, or maybe earlier, I sprinted into a bush after what was probably a squirrel or a rat and scratched up my arms. A few hours after I started, when my flashlight was already starting to die, I saw a scooter just lying in the path, and for a while I rode it, paddling the ground with my leg that was now less sore than numb.

I'd forgotten how this felt, the cold, sweaty dread of looking for a lost animal. For my old dog, Tucker, I'd spent hours all over Chevy Chase when I was a kid, driving slowly with Dad up all the streets we'd been over ten times before, certain that he was gone forever. But then, after we'd both be considering giving up, we would turn up some street and there he'd be, wagging while he nosed through a trash bag, or standing guiltily while some little girl in a bathing suit held him by the collar. Once (the time before he didn't), he even made it across River Road, all the way to the Pancake House, and when we finally picked him up, I was so grateful that I stuffed my entire allowance in their tip jar.

So even knowing that I wasn't going to find Newman didn't stop me from looking. My watch said three twelve when I first sat down to rest. (*Dad said he'd go up Cumberland, and I'd go down.*) My throat hurt. If I could just have Newman back, I wouldn't mind, anymore, feeling like my life was empty—empty was better than full of crushed glass and battery acid. (*I turned on Dorset and saw something gold on the median strip on Little Falls. Tucker! He was sitting, panting, traffic rushing in front of him and behind him.*) For another hour, with no scooter, I walked without even saying his name. (*Don't move. Don't see me. Please don't move.*) When my flashlight died, just as the sun was coming up, I realized that I was only a few feet from the zoo. (*But he did see me. And he ran for me, the same jump into running as when I'd clap for him in the park, and I was looking away when the car hit him, but I couldn't keep from hearing.*) I was so tired that I could have thrown up, and a few minutes after five I finally walked out of the park feeling like I really understood suicide now, the perfect clean escape of it. (*I faced away from the street while I pressed my walkie-talkie. The only thing I could say was, "Dad. Dad. Dad."*)

A few people were out now, a fat man with sunglasses and a denim jacket, a Hispanic woman pushing along a shopping cart full of black garbage bags. I saw that there were lights on in a few windows before I understood what they meant. My knee was better now—with only a little dip I could walk at something like normal speed. Georgi stood behind his desk, resting his head on his fist and looking like he'd been dragged out of a Dumpster. "Good morning, Henry," he said. "We are back in power."

"Good to hear," I said, and my throat croaked. They were the first words I'd said all night to anyone but Newman.

Upstairs, after giving the door a few light knocks, I went into David and Lucy's room. David shot up in bed looking exactly the way he's always looked when you wake him up too suddenly. "Where the hell have you been? We were freaking out."

"Sorry. I was in the park."

"What the hell were you doing in the park?"

"Walking. When did the power come back?"

"Three in the morning. I even called your damn girl-friend. She said you might have done something stupid."

"I did," I said, but David was already back down.

I sat with a glass of orange juice on the couch in the living room, looking out at the city, wondering how a night that felt so much like a dream could actually count for so much. Every cell in my body begged me to lie down and close my eyes, but for some reason I didn't want to give in, so instead I took a shower. And standing under the water, shutting my eyes while shampoo ran over my face, was when that strange moment came when what happened last night broke off from the morning and turned into the past. It made New-man seem really gone. Once I was clean and changed out of yesterday's clothes, I called Margaret's cell phone. It was quarter to six—she picked up after a few rings.

"The power's back," I said.

"Are you calling to tell me that?" I couldn't tell if she'd really been asleep or if she was trying too hard to sound like she'd really been asleep.

"No. Aren't you leaving soon? I wanted to say bye."

"Where were you last night? I came looking for you. Did David find you?"

"I was in the park. I did something dumb."

"What?"

"It was really dumb."

"What was it? Tell me."

"Can I come downstairs?" I said. "I don't want to tell you on the phone."

"Don't ring the bell. I'll open the door."

Her suitcases were laid out in the Marsens' front hall, packed to go. She wore the same red T-shirt she'd been wearing the night before, and the same pair of boxers, and she really had been asleep. Creases were pressed into her cheek, and when I reached to hug her, her skin was still hot from her bed.

We sat on the couch in the living room, the blue couch that smells like cat pee, the same couch we'd sat on dozens of nights that summer. The sun was coming up in the window over the dining room table. Drew was asleep upstairs, but somehow I didn't feel sick about it.

"So what happened last night?" she said. She had morning breath, musty, and it's weird but it made some old ash glow in the way I felt about her. I wanted to smell it again.

"I lost Newman."

"The goat?"

"The goat." And I explained. About no one being at the zoo, about going in to be with him, about how it had seemed like a good night to show him the park. About the moment when he ran, and how many hours I'd spent looking for him. She was awake now, but her feet were still tucked up under her.

"Are you going to tell anyone?" she said.

"No. I'll go back and look for him in a couple of hours."

"But you'll get in trouble. Is letting out an animal illegal? You should tell Paul. Say you came in to check on him, because you figured that nobody would be there during the blackout, and when you were leaving you accidentally let him run out."

"Really?"

"It'll be much better if they don't find out themselves."

"But shouldn't I at least wait to see if I can find him?"

"Just tell him. Really, I think it'll only get worse if you don't."

And finally having told someone, and not having had her sob or scream or call the police, right away I needed to be asleep. I yanked off my shoes and curled my head into her lap and closed my eyes. Lying in her lap meant something completely different than it would have a month ago—there was no hope in it, no giddy scheming, just a warm, sad settling at the end of an achy summer. This, and not the shower, was the memory I wanted to keep. She sighed, assuming, I guess, that I'd still think she was giving in to something, and laid her head against my back. Until eight, when Margaret jumped up cursing that she'd overslept, when I realized that I was still stuck with everything that had happened the night before, we dreamed curled up on each other like I'd been right all long, like we were meant to be husband and wife.

* * *

At eleven, while I was struggling to stay awake over a bowl of Raisin Bran, Paul called the apartment. I only realized how much I'd been dreading it now that the phone was ringing. "I'm in here alone," he said, "and we've got a problem. Do you know anything about it?"

"About what?" I said, and that quickly I was locked in my lie.

"Newman's gone. The pen's closed, everybody else is there, no Newman. You don't know anything?"

"I have no idea. Did somebody take him?"

"I don't know. You live near enough to walk, right? I need you to come in and help."

So I walked into work and sat with Paul in the break room while he pulled on his fishy lower lip and stared at the phone. Margaret was at the airport now, and I kept half dreaming, half remembering our good-bye. She was wearing shorts and her backpack, smiling at something that didn't have to do with me, and Drew was already in the cab. "Stop acting so sad," she said. "I'll call you when I get home." I opened my mouth to say that she didn't have to, and she said, "I will. I promise."

Paul told me—and everyone else he talked to—that his roommate and two of his friends were out looking for Newman, and that someone would be staying in the office in case anyone brought him in. He kept repeating this plan, and each time I nodded like now it was sure to bring him back. "This can't happen," he said. "This absolutely can't happen. I don't care if the guards need to walk in, they *needed* to be here. I live on Fourteenth and I managed to get here. I'll bet you twenty bucks Ramon's in bed right now." Every few minutes he'd try to call another one of the keepers, or Ramon, but no one was answering. "We've never lost a single mammal here, not one. This is going to be a fucking disaster. This is going to be front-page news, this is going to completely fuck everything up." I felt, while I listened, closer to Paul than I ever had—he was so miserable that he didn't have the energy to treat me like a lazy, new keeper. I felt like I was watching his thoughts.

Of course, I should have been nothing but nerves and guilt, I should have been as jumpy as a murderer who hears sirens. But instead—thanks, probably, to being so tired that my brain seemed to be wrapped in cotton—I felt puzzled about what could have happened to Newman. What sort of a thief would swoop down on a goat? And for what? If Paul had looked up from the phone he would have seen real confusion on my face. And that, I decided, was going to be the key to getting away with this—to convince myself that I wasn't getting away with anything.

"Could you go do feed-out?" Paul said. "Give Lily a few extra few pieces of apple. And hey." He finally turned to me. "Thanks for coming in." The zoo was as peaceful, as empty and sunny and quiet, as a farm. In the daylight it seemed impossible that Newman could be gone forever. He'd wake up on some warm hill, eat a little grass, and find his way back to the zoo by the afternoon.

Just after one, Janice came rushing in, looking frazzled and dirty. "I'm so, so sorry, guys! I had to spend the whole morning at the vet, and my usual vet wasn't open, so I had to go forty blocks away and the wait there was just a nightmare. I got your message. What's happening? Have we found him? How can I help?" Paul told her just to wait with us for now, and once she'd settled down she started to tell me her blackout story. She seemed still to be living it—I wondered if she'd slept. "Did you see me run out of here yesterday? I'm sorry if I made anyone worry, but all of a sudden I realized I'd left the windows closed in the morning, and I just thought about my cats baking in there with no AC. And then the traffic home was completely stopped, and I thought I should just get out and walk, but I couldn't, because I didn't have a light, and what if I got caught in the dark? So I asked this man stuck next to me in the traffic jam, this complete saint, and he gave me an extra flashlight in his glove compartment. And so finally I got home and they were both OK, except Gwen seemed a little slow, like maybe something had happened, you know, so just to make sure I had to take her into the vet this morning, and when I left we still didn't have electricity back. And then this. I can't believe I wasn't here. You must have rushed right in. Oh, poor Newman!"

I had that drunk, sleepy feeling of being able to see into the truest parts of people, and once I'd escaped Janice's babble, I realized that she misunderstood something about me. She thought—and why shouldn't she?—that I was a keeper because I thought it might be part of what I wanted to do with my life. All her panic, her frantic work, her apologizing— it was real. She'd quit her job (at a TV station, was it?), come to the zoo, she stayed late and volunteered for the worst assignments—she really wanted to move up. And in a few months she'd probably be transferred to the main zoo— Penguin was her dream—and from there maybe to Brooklyn, and from there to the Bronx: For her this sounded like a life. A few weeks earlier I would have talked about Margaret and sounded no less convinced, no less bursting, but now I felt cut loose, drifting toward some island that I couldn't see.

"Henry? Have you seen the spare key from the shed?"

"Hmm?" I was raking together a pile of poop in Goat, and I hadn't even heard Janice coming.

"The key from the hook. It's missing. I'm going to go tell Paul."

And that was when I did start to feel like a murderer. Paul rushed out looking furious, with Janice just behind him. Still holding my rake I went over to look too—the key really was gone. *Idiot, idiot, idiot.* "I'm going to call my cop buddy and I'm going to get a lie detector machine," Paul said. "Every single staff member is going to have to tell me where they were last night."

"Wouldn't non–zoo people look for a key there too?" I said. "It's kind of an obvious place."

"In the pitch-black? On the one night nobody was here? It was somebody who knew." The key felt as big as a dinner plate in my pocket. "Come inside and help me call people. We're getting everybody in here."

* * *

It didn't take a lie detector. The other keepers started to show up around three, even the volunteers, and with all of us waiting and looking at each other in the break room, I became too aware of my body, my face. Ramon came in at three thirty, and after he'd talked to Paul for a few minutes, he told me he had something to show me. He walked me into the aviary, and while we stood on the bridge he said, "You do this thing?"

I didn't say anything.

"That's all I needed. I don't know what sort of shit you got going, I don't know what happened, but you took Newman out of here—I can't have my job in danger here in any way. First thing you do, you go in there and you pull Paul aside, real quiet, you tell him you need to have a private talk." He didn't look at me, and I understood now how it would be to have Ramon for a dad. "You tell him everything—I don't care what it is, you say it. And once you do that, you beg and plead for him to go easy on you. I don't know if you've got him in your apartment, I don't know if you've got him as your pet, I don't know if you killed him and ate him for dinner, but you tell Paul exactly what went down and just maybe he won't call the police. And you better not mention to him that I've been letting you in here at night. You mention that, I don't know what I'll do, but so help me God I won't forgive you as long as I live. You work here one summer, have a cute time with the animals, make some play money to show Mommy and Daddy, I've worked here fourteen years and I'm not about to go looking for something new. Not one word."

Shaking, I did just what Ramon told me. Paul's office seemed to be running out of air.

"I've got something bad to tell you."

He just stared at me, mean as a hawk.

"I did a really dumb thing. Last night I realized that no

one would be here to come in because of the blackout, so I decided to come check on everybody. I came in and I went into Goat, and I must have left the gate unlocked, because when I turned around to leave—Newman wasn't there." I hadn't felt like this, so scared that it was work to talk, since elementary school, staying in at recess with Mrs. Walters. "By the time I noticed, he must have gone out the front exit, because—"

"How could he have gone out the exit." Not a question, very steady, like a Paul robot.

"I . . . must have left that open too."

"What keys did you use to open the front gate. Did you take your keys home yesterday."

"No, I turned my keys in. It must have been . . . I must have . . . I know, what I did was I came in through the supply gate, and you know how you can just get that open with your hands? That's what I did, and I must have left it open. And when I realized he was gone, I looked all over the park, I was out all night, I couldn't find him. I looked until this morning."

"What time did you last see him."

"Probably around ten last night. But I'm pretty sure he'll turn up, because I really don't think he went that far. I'll go look for him. I really feel so terrible about this."

Paul called the apartment that night. He said, "Tom and I have made a decision about what needs to happen." Tom's the tall, shaggy director of the main zoo. My heart jumped up into the middle of my face. "You're going to leave the zoo, and you're never going to come back. Not even as a visitor. You're going to turn in your uniform tomorrow morning, and that's the last time we want you making contact with any Central Park Zoo staff."

"What about Newman? No one called?"

"We haven't heard anything, and if we do, we won't be letting you know. And we won't press charges, so long as you don't mention to anyone—*anyone*—how Newman got out. Tom's going to make a statement tonight calling this a probable theft. If any reporters or anyone else gets in touch with you, don't say anything except, 'No comment.' If you say anything else, we'll come after you hard as we can. Understood?"

"Understood."

I was alone in the apartment, and even though the sun was almost down, I hadn't turned on any lights. I walked over to the living room window, rested my forehead on the glass, and tried to shake off Paul's voice, tried to make my heart slow down. I looked at the street twenty-three stories down, cars and people moving and waiting, and wondered if Newman was somewhere I could see. Such a simple problem, and so impossible to solve. Wherever he was, it was only one place, he only had one body. I'd find him. Even if it took months—hikes through the park in the snow, taxis out to Queens, boats, helicopters—I wouldn't let him disappear. I couldn't.

But first I needed some sleep.

* * *

First thing every morning for the next week I woke up and turned on NY1 to see if they'd found him. On Monday they interviewed Paul, standing out in front of the main entrance, and looking right at the camera, he said, "Newman brings joy to thousands of children every year. We are asking for anyone who has any knowledge of his whereabouts to remember that." There was a little article about him in the paper, but I don't think David or Lucy saw it—I wouldn't have if I hadn't been looking. At dinner one night, trying to sound casual, I told them that I'd decided to quit the zoo to try to find a job to do with music. I'd only wanted to work at the zoo for a summer anyway, I started to explain, but I could tell from their faces that I didn't need to bother.

As long as the sun stayed up each day, I searched for him. I didn't go near the zoo, but I must have walked every square foot of the park, and eventually every street in Manhattan. At night I'd ride the subway, and whenever I could, I'd stand in the very front of the train. Pounding through those tunnels, seeing only the tracks and flashes of graffiti, I felt as close to finding him as I ever felt aboveground. By the time I'd looked for a few days, I would have been just as surprised to find a woolly mammoth as to find Newman.

New York without Margaret, without a job, was as lonely as a permanent Saturday afternoon—I'd talk so long to Sameer whenever I saw him that he'd started making the same hurried, nervous faces around me that I once made around Ramon. Friday night, after I'd walked all along the West Side Highway, I rented *The Hunt for Red October*.

David and Lucy were out to dinner with Lucy's parents, at an expensive Japanese restaurant a few blocks from the apartment. I'd thought I was coming to dinner too, but when Lucy saw me changing into my dress shoes, she said, "We were actually thinking this would be just a me-and-David thing. OK?"

The movie was long and dark and not much less confusing than the book. It made being in a submarine, which I'd thought of as clean, powerful work, seem hellish, like being trapped under the kitchen sink. The ocean looked terrifyingly huge and empty.

I'd just finished the movie and a burrito, and I was lying in their bed too full and sad to move while the credits ran all the way down to the costume advisers. I could hear David and Lucy arguing as they walked from the elevator, Lucy saying, "That *is* my point. That's *exactly* my point."

David came in and sat next to me on the bed. He untied his tie and undid his top button. He looked like he wanted something. Lucy came and sat on the arm of the chair by the window and started scraping at a stain on her dress. She flipped the light on. "Well," David said. "Tonight seems like as good a night as any to talk about this." I was sure—sickly sure, suddenly—that he meant Newman. "Were you thinking about looking for your own place?"

"My own place in New York?" I sat up.

"Summer's over, you're done with the zoo—I think you should start doing your own thing. Wouldn't you like not living in somebody else's house?"

"Home wasn't anyone else's house."

"Look. I'm not kicking you out. We're not. But what if we

say in the next week or so you'll start looking? I can help. We'll find a studio somewhere, get you all set up, you'll probably just be twenty minutes away." He was trying to make this a light talk, a little piece of business to take care of before he went to sleep.

"This is what you want?" I was only looking at David.

"There's no reason to get like that. This should be what *you* want."

"Is this what you want or is this what Lucy wants?"

"Don't do that. There's no distinction. We've been very generous to you—much more generous than you'd have any right to expect. You should be pretty damn grateful that Lucy invited you here in the first place."

"So this was her decision." I felt reckless, cornered, a little crazy.

"This was our decision. It's nobody's *decision*—it's what should happen. Knock it off."

"Who brought it up first? All I want to know is who decided it was time for me to go."

Now Lucy stood up from her chair, and when David reached to hold her arm she smacked his hand away. "You listen for a second. When we decided to invite you here, we said it would be for the summer, and summer's over this week." I'd never heard her talk so loud. Her face was red, and both hands were balled into fists. "We said you could find a job, but now you're just lying around all the time, putting your shoes up on our bed—"

"I always take my shoes off."

"I've *seen* you with your shoes on the bed! It doesn't matter! Your hosts want you gone! They invited you, now they're saying the visit's over! Doesn't that mean anything? Doesn't that seem like enough? Stop looking at me like that!"

"Why did you even ask me to move in?"

"Look, why don't we just—" David said, but Lucy didn't stop.

"It was a favor to David. And I'm not—"

"So you never wanted me?"

"What does it matter? I invited you to come live in my apartment!"

"Your parents' apartment," I said.

"Fuck you! You're telling me about being a self-made man? You couldn't even finish *freshman year* of *college*. You're a *child*! As far as you're concerned, this is *my* apartment, and I don't have to defend it! And if letting you live here doesn't seem nice enough to you—then you're even dumber than I thought." And she turned and walked into the bathroom.

David looked down at the comforter between his knees. "Look," he said. He gritted his teeth and flared his nostrils. If there was a moment to change sides, to get away from his life with Lucy, this was it. "In a day or two we'll start looking for what we can find. Tonight let's just go to bed."

In my room, tingling all over, I started to pack. They wanted me out in a week, I'd be out in a day. I'd leave before they even woke up. I still had most of my zoo money in my account, and I could stay in a hotel until I found a place. Maybe I could go live with Sameer for a while in Brooklyn.

But with my duffel bag in one hand and my saxophone case in the other, the idea of this new, lonely life hit me so hard that I sat back down on the bed. I did finally leave that night—I was out of the apartment by midnight—but I left for the only place where I knew they'd never send me away.

Virginia

I'd only been home for a few weeks when Mom proposed that we come out here. "Otherwise I just don't think your father will stop fretting about school. He's going to get sick again for these kids. I think trying this would be a big favor for him." And for her. For as long as I'd been home she'd been going to bed at eight, and always seeming on the verge of coming down with something, although she never made it clear just what. "No, I don't want to do that," she'd say, if Dad asked about a walk along the canal or a movie. "No, you should go ahead without me."

And when she did venture out, to the pharmacy or even just to mail a letter, she'd come back bristling with reasons why she wouldn't be making that mistake again soon. There was the man who sat in his silver BMW reading the paper while she waited for a space ("And he had one of those *awful* little beards"). The woman on Dorset who let her sprinkler run all over the sidewalk ("Look!" she said, holding up her damp shirt, eyes blazing. "Just look!"). When she came back from the grocery store one afternoon, she told me that she'd seen Wendy and her dad in the parking lot. "He gave me the nastiest look when I said hello. Did that not end well?" I shrugged, but I felt stabbed, thinking of the night I'd run from her house. I'd hurt Wendy as lightly as if I'd been canceling a Blockbuster membership, and the thought of seeing her made my entire body itch. Suddenly an escape to the country sounded like just the thing.

The farm in Virginia, where Dad's parents spent the last few years of their lives, is a few miles from the Blue Ridge Mountains, a wide wooden house on thirty acres that I remembered as being covered in wildflowers and tall, stinging grass. My parents have owned the house since I was born, but we'd never used it for more than a week or two at a time in summer, or sometimes for a few days during Christmas break to see the river frozen over. For a couple of years when I was little they rented it to an old man named Cliff who I only ever knew from his raspy, formal voice on the machine. Cliff wanted to plant hay in the meadow and build a shed to raise pigs and ducks. Dad talked about selling him the house, sometimes, but Mom wouldn't hear of it. She loved the property, the woodpeckers and creeks and pine trees, but more important for her, I think, was the plain, amazing fact of owning such a place. It was like a great-grandfather's watch, something you were obliged to keep even if you couldn't be bothered to use it.

We drove out on a Saturday morning, with Olive sleeping and stinking in the back of the Volvo. Our mail would go to the post office in Warrenton, so Mom wouldn't miss her magazines, and the Lippetts, next door on Cumberland, would water our plants. Dad's classes would go to Mr. Sally, the sub with the eye patch, and Dad promised not to "zip back" more than once every couple of weeks. Shut in the car with Mom and Dad and Walter, I felt for the first time since I'd come back the old craving to leave. Being home again had seemed like a kind of miracle at first, a Swiss mountain resort that could cure you with just its air. I picked right back up the bottle of Pert Plus that I'd left on the rim of the tub three months before, fell asleep in my bed without setting an alarm, took walks in the afternoons along streets whose sidewalk squares and tar stripes seemed as dependable as the sun. But now, without even the radio on in the car (Dad always insists that we not play music until we're on the highway, for some reason), I kept thinking, *These are the people whose love I've fallen back on?*

When I first got home from the train station, Walter didn't even stand up from the couch. "Glad to see you home," he said. "I don't think you'll find a lot of surprises." He seemed to have settled into the role of acting perpetually disgusted with how Dad was treated. He wanted me to play some part in this too—every few days he'd try to corner me into a conversation about Mom's latest cruelty—but I'd started to avoid him.

Dad had looked better when I first got home than he had in New York—or maybe it was just that I was used to seeing him in Chevy Chase, and so didn't look at him so closely. He'd come on my walks with Olive after dinner, and he'd spend the whole time clearing his throat—he had a rattly, wax-paper cough—and telling me the names of musicians I ought to talk to in D.C. "I don't want to play sax anymore, Dad," I finally said one night, and I'm not sure what I expected him to say, but it wasn't, "Yeah? Well. You had a hell of a run, anyway." He acted hurt for the rest of our walk, but he didn't mention it afterward. He and Mom were sleeping in the same bed—one night I pretended to need the Tylenol from their bathroom—but all their conversations were short and sharp, full of quiet looks. I asked Mom once, while she skimmed the fat from a tall pot of chicken stock, if she and Dad were mad at each other, and she said, "I think we're both just a little disappointed." It was easier now to imagine her being cruel, and to imagine Dad doing something to deserve it, but I hoped we could all just live with their problems the way you live with a bad back or a bald spot.

As we set our bags down in the dusty front hall in Virginia, it seemed like each of us was trying not to be the one to say that this was a mistake. Walter opened a cabinet to get a glass, and a mouse jumped out and disappeared under the couch. I went to wash my hands and found a cricket as long as my pinkie sitting in the sink in the first-floor bathroom. In the fridge was a block of cheddar cheese turned completely green, and a bottle of orange juice expired in 2001.

But the next morning—our first morning there—I woke

up when the sun was just coming up, and this bedroom where I'd once spent weekends sulking and playing Game Boy suddenly seemed like just the place to figure out what I ought to do next. I went out for a walk with Olive, in my clothes from the day before. The air was cold and stung to breathe, and the mountains looked like someone had traced their edges with a pink highlighter. We walked down the hill in front of the house to the creek, the grass turning my sneakers dark, and then we went back through the trees along a path that was covered in pine needles. Olive would run up ahead, huffing and happy, and then come crashing back to show me a branch. We stayed out for more than an hour. Back at the house I made a cup of hot tea, even though I don't really like hot tea, and I sat out on the porch for the rest of the morning looking at all these hills and trees, taking little sips.

That night Mom and I went out to the car after dinner to bring in Olive's food, and as soon as we stepped onto the porch we both gasped. The stars were out. It was the feeling of turning around at an outdoor concert and seeing for the first time what an infinity of people are behind you. Each star was a lighter held up, and I was floating over a crowd that was endless in every direction.

At the car Mom put her arm around me—her touches are rare and painfully thought-out. "I *am* proud of you," she said. "I know how hard it can sometimes be." I felt, for the couple of minutes that we stayed out there together, as if she understood more about me than even I did—certainly more than Dad did. She can seem sometimes as if family is as much a chore for her as remembering to separate the recycling, but there's some sympathy I get peeks at sometimes, some understanding so strong that she'd crack if she always showed it.

Walter glares at her whenever he thinks no one's looking—he sits inside each day by the fire, reading and underlining in a book about the Civil War. He pets Olive, who sleeps next to him, like he's kneading a loaf of bread, and sometimes he'll say things like, "Listen to this: Five thousand boys died, your age and younger, ten miles from here," and then seem disappointed however I react.

Being out here really does seem to be good for Dad. Even when Mom tells him not to, he carries in wood, and with his cheeks all red he'll fiddle with the fire until it crackles. "If there's anything better than being with your family by a good fire on a cold day," he'll say, "I'd like somebody to tell me." Each of us can think of a hundred things better, of course, but we just sit there, and all our quiet goes up the chimney like smoke. I look at him sometimes and I'm able to connect him, in a way I couldn't used to, with the Dad he was when I was little. I remember him flexing his right arm for me and Evan Feller, how proud I was of the bulge. I remember standing in front of him in the living room, telling him the hardest math problems I could think of, and how happy I'd be when he'd make me sit down next to him to solve them. "First you always write it out. You write down everything you know." This Dad's a grayer cousin of that one, less sure, less quick to leap into a conversation, but only at night, sometimes, when he starts to fall asleep in his chair, do I have that feeling around him like I'm watching the last bit of sand rush out of the timer in Pictionary.

During the day Mom keeps busy with work on the house—the upstairs bathroom needs to be repainted, the back porch needs to have the wasp nest cleared away—and then in the afternoon she goes for walks down to the river. Sometimes I go with her, and while she sits on the bench swing reading a magazine, I'll walk down to the bank and skip rocks. In an entire walk between the river and the house—she walks slowly, always pulling needles and leaves off the trees as she goes—Mom and I sometimes don't say more than a couple of words. We're no more awkward together than a pair of deer.

I was sitting upstairs one night a couple of weeks ago before dinner, reading on my bed, when I heard Dad crying. I thought at first that someone was choking, and I rushed out of my room, but stopped at the banister when I saw him, lying on the couch with his face in Mom's lap. "I don't know how," I heard her say to him. "I just don't see how I could, again." I knew right away, little as I wanted to—the knowledge felt like a hammer blow to a block of ice.

Mom told me the next day while we walked back to the house from the river. "Daddy and I are going to try living apart for a while," she said. "We'll stay here until you go, but after that I think I'm going to find a place of my own. This is something we just need to try." I nodded, harder and harder as I became less and less able to speak, and finally she said, "I'm so sorry we can't just . . . stay a certain way. For all of us. I really am."

In the feverish night or two afterward, I talked for hours

on the phone to David, both of us stopping every few minutes to say, with a shiver, "It's just so *weird*." Other things that this would mean—separate vacations, both of them dating, a new house for Mom—kept falling on me, one after another. The acceptance letter from University of Arizona came that week (I'd practically forgotten that I'd applied), but I hardly had the energy to read it, let alone to think about what it meant. I was a monk of misery, and this house, with its dried-up wasps on the windowsills, its freezing bathroom floor, Mom and Dad floating past each other like ghosts, was my temple. I thought time might stop completely.

But then a letter came from Margaret, the only one I ever got, and, strangely enough, it set life in motion again. Mom handed me the envelope, and I wanted to know what was inside, and even that—just wanting something—may have been the beginning of the thaw. It began without even a "Dear Henry":

After Newman Ran

A few weeks after disappearing, Newman wandered aboard a ship bound for a stretch of ocean where the world's most delicious fish were said to flourish. His only duty, the captain explained once they had set sail, would be to listen for the sound of the trawling net tearing. For days and weeks, as Newman stood upon the deck, he could hardly sleep for the excitement of his new life. Just thinking of the immensity of this water (for he had been studying the captain's atlas, and he felt certain that all the world's oceans were really one ocean) made his eyes grow wide and his ears stand erect. Eventually, when land was far behind, he did sleep, but he dreamed only of the ocean. When he woke up his imagination began at precisely the point where his dream left off, and when he fell asleep he began to dream at precisely the point where his imagination left off.

The weeks passed, and Newman's skin, beneath his coat, grew dark, and his body grew tough, for he couldn't stand to eat more than a few bites of the fish that his crew hauled aboard each evening. It tasted strange to him, salty and slick. He began to forget that he'd ever done anything at all but stare at the ocean, and as he went to fewer and fewer meals, he began to feel deeply lonely. Even the kind captain, who early in the voyage had made a point of sitting with Newman for a few minutes every afternoon, could, after all, take only so much silence.

Newman began to dream, and to imagine, that the ocean called out to him continuously: This week we are feeling irritable, Newman. Expect a great tantrum. *And soon enough, to the surprise of everyone on board except the silent goat, the boat would be heaved about by waves as tall as buildings, and dropped in troughs as deep as canyons.* We are calm today, Newman. Life seems to us, in spite of it all, like a quite beautiful thing. *And the sea would be a deep blue pool, extending to the horizon in all directions.*

One day, while the rest of the crew enjoyed their lunch, Newman heard the ocean say, Join us. Why be a bit of debris on our surface, Newman, when you could come live inside us? There is no loneliness underwater.

And so Newman, moving more quickly than he had moved in months, rushed to the edge of the ship, and without even a glance back at his shipmates, leaped overboard. The water was colder than he had expected, but calmer too, and just beneath the surface was a silence unlike any he had ever known. His ears fluttered along open in the water, and when he had descended ten feet, the ocean spoke again. Louder now than it had sounded from the ship, and clearer, the voice seemed actually to be composed of the voices of thousands of fish, millions of fish, all speaking quietly and together. Such an elegant swimmer! Surely you have done this before? *Their mouths opened and shut in precise unison. Newman felt the sound against his entire body. And he did find swimming to be surprisingly easy, like walking in three dimensions. He even found that he could do somersaults; he was as graceful as a ballerina. He learned to breathe underwater by watching the other fish; he learned how to ride the current, how to expend no energy and yet to stay afloat.*

By his second day underwater, Newman felt his rear hooves growing together; he felt a long, ridged fin rising from the skin on his back. His hairs drew into his body, slowly but steadily, and he felt his skin hardening, smoothing. You are beautiful, Newman. We have never seen such a fish! *And that was when he realized that a fish was indeed what he was becoming. His front hooves melded into a fin under his belly, his bones lightened, his muscles quickened, his neck disappeared into his face, his eyes sharpened and lost their lashes. All that remained of the land-Newman were his ears, which still flapped in the current, white and veined and lightly furred.*

He bobbed below the waves, nibbling at passing bits of seaweed, and passed the rest of his life without thinking of his time on land again.

That night I skipped dinner—Mom and Dad had been talking more since the announcement, as if knowing they would be apart soon had loosened their collars—and I sat down at the desk in my room with my notebook.

I decided to start out by fixing Margaret's story. Newman doesn't float off and nibble seaweed and live happily ever after. I felt utterly certain about this. He enjoys being a fish, sure, the freedom of it, but one day he's swimming along when he feels a strange tug and suddenly a net is lifting him. He's caught with thousands of his friends, all struck silent, and they're heaped onto a deck, where Newman blacks out from panic. And when he wakes up, he's in a small tank with a face staring in at him that he hardly recognizes at first: the captain. He's on a shelf in the captain's study. The entire crew comes in, over the course of the next few days, and they all marvel at this long-eared whitefish, they tap the glass and smile and lift his tank to look at him in the light. Newman cries invisibly into the water, left alone there in the dark, and he loses all sense of time—but then slowly, as the months pass, he learns to stand it. He stops missing the ocean, stops missing the land, learns to give up missing entirely. He lives and he lives, peace tucked inside him like an extra organ, until years later, on a different voyage, the captain comes in one morning and finds him gently floating, dead.

I blurted all this onto the page, my hand working so fast that it started to burn, and when I sat back in my chair I was in the world again. The pain I'd accumulated that summer, the guilt and the shame, started to seem, over the next few days, like a kind of private wealth, a secret hoard I could lose myself in. I locked myself in my room and wrote for a couple of hours each morning, describing the summer as well as I could remember it, and those hours managed somehow to radiate out, making everything that I hadn't been able to bear before tolerable. My notebook started to look like it belonged to a crazy person—scribbled into the margins was a paragraph about a white blimp that had appeared out the window one night, moving behind the buildings as slow as a whale, and another about sitting up in bed a few nights after Margaret and I first went out for ice cream, the blankets around my waist, thinking that the hard part of life was finally over.

I've been writing and writing, as if paradise were waiting on the last page, because that, I've realized, is the secret to getting anything done: pretending that it matters. "I hope you're going easy on us in there," Mom said the other day, appearing over my shoulder. I told her to knock it off. We're all going back to Chevy Chase in a few days, and I'll only have a week to pack before Arizona. My roommate, apparently, is going to be someone from Shanghai named Wen Li. On the "Getting to Know You" form, under "Favorite Music" he wrote, *Dance,* and under "Interests" he wrote, *Making/breaking computers.*

"I would be so nervous," Mom says. "You seem as if you move across the country by yourself all the time." And I am nervous, but not as much as I would have expected. Lately I've been watching Mom daydream while she stands waiting for the coffee machine or while she goes slowly up the stairs at night, and I think I've begun to understand the slow accident of her life better, how she got married and started a family and even how she decided to move out, but how she never meant for any of it to become quite so *final*. And I find strange comfort in that, the way a life will happen without your hovering over it. I feel as if Arizona, and the entire rest of my life, really, has already happened, somewhere just out of view, and all I've got to do now is live it.

I'm coming to the end now, but before I stop I want to write about something that happened a few weeks ago, the night after I got Margaret's letter. Walter and Dad had gotten into a screaming fight during dinner, because Walter had told Mom that she was hopeless, and just to get out of the house I took a flashlight and started down toward the river. There were no stars or moon, and it was as dark on the meadow as anything I'd seen during the blackout. Before I even got close to the water, though, I heard barking. Olive was asleep up at the house, but even if she hadn't been, this was much higher than her bark. It made no sense, of course, but for a second I imagined Newman, tall and white, walking out of the woods. I could smell him. So I started to run, pushing through the dark that felt like curtains, and the barking got louder and louder. It was coming from the other side of the river, but close by. On our side there's a field and then the riverbank, just a slope of mud, but on the other side is a hill too steep for walking, covered in thin brown trees.

I could hear just where the barking was coming from, but I couldn't find it in my light. I stood there scanning and scanning. It was easy, in the dark, to imagine the water alive with yellow crocodile eyes, monkeys rustling in the trees, lions pushing through the tall grass. I thought I heard a splash in the river, and when I followed the sound with my light, there the dog was, just across the river in a hollowed-out cave of mud. The river was high and brown and fast, and the little dog—*BARK! BARK! BARK!*—stood under a mud lip, too tired and cold to move. I kicked off my shoes and socks and peeled off my clothes until I was shivering in just my boxers.

"I'm coming," I said. "Relax." And that first step into the water made my insides shrink, but I took another step, and another, and another, and even when my foot sank into the muddy, leafy booby-trap stuff along the bottom, I just pulled my foot out and kept walking. The river smelled like cold dirt. I'm not sure if it was the hardest thing I've ever done, but it was close. Every part of my body except my brain was shrieking for me not to take another step.

At its deepest the river came up to my chest, and I kept my arms up, swinging over the water, the whole time murmuring, "Here I come, here I come, here I come." I wasn't even sure if I was cold anymore. She stopped barking once I got a few feet away, and now she stared at me, growling softly and trembling. "Don't worry," I said. But when I reached out for her she gave a different kind of bark and got as far away from me as she could. She must only have weighed fifteen pounds. I reached out for her again, keeping the light on her, and she pressed against the roots at the back of her mud-cave and shook. There was something pink and round hanging from her stomach. "You're not helping me," I said, and finally, with one arm under and one arm over, I got her, and I pressed her tightly against me.

"I'm here," I said into her head. "I'm right here." At first she was calm, but after a few seconds, once she understood that I was taking her, she tried to jump out of my arms into the water. She was so muddy that I could barely hold on to her, and she kept squirming up to my face, most of the way out, before I could wrestle her back down. I could have been wearing a space suit, I could have been completely naked. "We're almost there, we're almost there, we're almost there." I ended up carrying her all the way back to the house, my whole body still frozen, and when I got there Mom called the police, who acted like they got calls like this all the time. While Walter made tea for me, the dog, who had a collar but no tags, scampered around the living room, sniffing under furniture while Olive walked after her. And when the policeman came, he made a face and told us that that was a tumor on her stomach, that someone must not have wanted her anymore. He picked her up and locked her in a plastic crate and drove away, and for the whole rest of the night I sat by the fire with my itchy blanket wrapped around me, feeling too stirred up—too awake—to talk.

But what I keep remembering is a moment just before all that, when I was still carrying the dog across the water, alone and freezing and whispering with mud smeared all over my face, and how happy I felt, how simply and suddenly happy. What a strange place for a life to start, I remember thinking, and my flashlight flickered on the water.

ACKNOWLEDGMENTS

Thanks to John Burghardt, Sara Crowe, Josh F., Arthur G., Scott, Josh H., Ruth and Bill Holmberg, Adam, Nishant, Jennifer Jackson, Rosemary Meskiel, Dina, Ben Solomon, and Annabel Wright.

P.S.

Ideas,
interviews
& features . . .

About the author

About the book

Read on

Q and A with Ben Dolnick

Henry made his journey to adulthood in New York. What does the city teach him? What do you love most about it?

The thing I like most about New York – and the thing that most affected Henry, I think – is the way it both turns you absolutely anonymous and invades your privacy. It's surprisingly easy to go entire eight-hour days without saying a word to anyone, or even meeting anyone's eyes, but you're also so physically close to so many people that you inevitably witness the strangest and most intimate parts of people's lives: fights, confessions, grand delusions.

Is Henry's work at the zoo based on your own experience?

The physical details of his work certainly are. Everything he does on a typical day – the raking, the shovelling, the scrubbing – is something I did that summer, and all the animals are real too (I go back to visit occasionally, but they're less interested in me than I apparently am in them). But once I started writing about his work, I found I had to bend it in various ways to make it do what I needed it to do in the book. That's a fairly common experience for me – however intently I set out to depict the reality of something or someone, the fiction has demands of its own.

The book is filled with humour: who are your comic influences?

The books I find the funniest tend, for reasons I don't understand, to be ones in which the jokes are quite difficult to explain or even to locate. I think Alice Munro is hilarious, and Penelope Fitzgerald too, but whenever people ask what exactly is so funny about them, I can't explain – there's something incredibly funny about seeing a character act precisely like him or herself, if that makes any sense. I get a similar feeling from watching Ricky Gervais in *The Office* – David Brent is so helplessly himself, I could just watch him all day.

There is a wide variety of characters in the book - from young children to the eccentric men who work at David's apartment block or at the zoo. How did you recreate their different speech patterns?

When I was little, I was always being scolded for mimicking people – the teacher who coughed before he answered, the waiter with the lisp. Trying to capture and reproduce the specifics of someone's voice is something I've always found myself doing semi-compulsively on my own, so writing fiction is just a way to keep it up and to call it a 'job'.

Who is your favourite character?

I like Ramon – I love people who talk too much. And I like the homeless woman who ▶

Copyright Jerry Bauer

LIFE
at a Glance

BORN

Boston, 1982. Lived outside Washington, DC, from age three to eighteen.

EDUCATION

Columbia University, NY.

CAREER

Worked (though never for very long) as a tutor, a zookeeper, a research assistant in an immunology laboratory and a bookseller. Now writes full time.

FAMILY

Engaged to be married.

LIVES

Brooklyn, NY with fiancée and pit bull mutt. ∎

3

Q and A with Ben Dolnick
(continued)

◄ comes up to Henry when he's eating pizza during the blackout. She only has one line, I think, but it might be the sentence in the book I'm proudest of.

There are three generations of brothers in Henry's family: do you think there's something special in this sibling relationship?

I'm always incredibly interested in siblings, in fiction and in life. I find the physical similarities and differences fascinating, like hearing a piece of music interpreted by two different artists. And I love all the different ways they relate as adults – it's so strange, to have known someone so well for so long; you always see the child behind the presentable grown-up face.

So many characters in the book have driving passions – Margaret's writing, Lucy's art, Solomon's music. Do you think this is a help or a hindrance in life?

It's certainly helpful in giving a shape to a life, I think, and (on a smaller scale) a shape to a day. For instance I don't know how I would have made it through school if I hadn't always had the notion in the back of my mind that this was all worthwhile because it would help me become a writer eventually. Having such strong desires does make disappointment inevitable, of course – professional disappointment and personal disappointment both, since the work is

❝ The thing I like most about New York – and the thing that most affected Henry, I think – is the way it both turns you absolutely anonymous and invades your privacy. ❞

never quite what you'd hoped. But I can't convince myself that a life of pure Buddhist detachment would be preferable, although it's often tempting.

Are you musical?

I've got considerably more musical enthusiasm than talent. I did play the saxophone in high school, along with a little piano. And I still play the guitar about like a seventh grader (mostly Weezer and Nirvana – I'm a human time capsule). If I could snap my fingers and acquire any one skill in the world, I think I'd become a great cellist. Music seems to have such an advantage over every other medium – a so-so book doesn't make me feel very much, a mediocre movie is a chore to sit through, but even the corniest song can sometimes give me a neck shiver like only a handful of novels can do.

Is Henry's love for Margaret a result of his age? Or is idealism a necessary part of romantic love?

I do think all romantic love probably involves a bit, or more than a bit, of idealism, but there's something particular about late-teenage love that I wanted to get in the book. I think there's a little window in that period when it seems that all of your life's difficulties might be solved just by joining up with a single person. And you half know it's hopeless, so you cling and struggle all the more. ▶

❛ I'm always incredibly interested in siblings, in fiction and in life. I find the physical similarities and differences fascinating, like hearing a piece of music interpreted by two different artists. ❜

Q and A with Ben Dolnick
(continued)

◀ **What is Henry really setting free when he lets Newman escape? Did you want Newman to have symbolic value?**

I'm always wary of symbols that are too well thought out, too clearly mapped onto some set of meanings, but Newman did come to be more to Henry than just a goat. When I was writing the book I honestly didn't think about it – I just had a feeling that this was something that had to happen. But thinking of it now, I can see that Henry probably had the half-cruel, half-generous wish to rip Newman from the confines of his life and give him the world, good and bad.

Are you working on another novel?

I am, in the same fitful and frustrating manner that I wrote *Zoology* (I had naively hoped that this one would somehow come easier, or that I would discover in myself a well of discipline and superhuman organization). It's about a family over the course of twenty or so years, but it's still such early days that I'm hesitant to say very much about it. ■

6 I'm always wary of symbols that are too well thought out, too clearly mapped onto some set of meanings, but Newman did come to be more to Henry than just a goat. 9

Top Ten Favourite Books

ALL OF ALICE MUNRO's books of short stories
I love these books immoderately. Each of her
stories is a technical marvel, but usually it
isn't until the second or third reading that I'm
able to notice just how she's managed this or
that effect, since I'm too caught up in her
characters and their lives.

U & I
Nicholson Baker
This is, by a large margin, the best and most
honest book about writing I've ever read.
And, like all of Baker's books, it's a musical,
funny and surreally precise piece of prose.

The Ghost Writer
Philip Roth
I love this book's self-containment – a
handful of characters, a short stretch of time,
a single house. And yet you really feel the
broadness of life in it, these characters'
connections and longings and
disappointments. I love his more expansive
books too – *American Pastoral, Sabbath's
Theater* – but something about this one keeps
me coming back. It works almost like a short
story, in that nothing could be cut.

Innocence
Penelope Fitzgerald
This novel is shockingly efficient – thirty
pages of her prose is like a hundred of most
other writers'. But somehow – depth of
research? brilliance of word choice? – she's
able to make a scene march off the page and
into your mind. ▶

Top Ten Favourite Books
(*continued*)

◀ *Time Will Darken It*
William Maxwell

This is an old-fashioned novel (maybe timeless is a better word), but it's also as wise and as vivid – about the feeling of an empty house in the middle of the day, or of a cocktail party that's gone on too long – as anything I've ever read. *Time* is the sort of book about which people say 'nothing much happens', but I couldn't put it down.

Infinite Jest
David Foster Wallace

When I was in college this was my favourite book – and in fact it seemed likely to be the only book I'd ever need. I couldn't believe its range of voices, its insightfulness, its bizarre and baroque architecture. I wanted to live inside it. My fever for the book has cooled a bit since then – it could hardly have warmed – but the novel still seems extraordinary to me. It's terribly sad in lots of places, and full of nearly perfect prose.

The War against Cliché
Martin Amis

I've had this book for years, and seem to be reading it constantly, and yet I *still* don't think I've read every essay in it. It's very rare that a book makes me laugh out loud, and rarer still that a book of literary criticism does – here I laugh out loud at things I've read tens of times before. Just a model of what reviews could be.

Top Ten Favourite Books
(continued)

Swann's Way
Marcel Proust

I keep bogging down in Volume III of Proust, but this first one, particularly the 'Swann in Love' section, is as perfect a book as I've ever read. Comparing him to other writers is like comparing a cheetah to a jogger. I read him and rush back to my keyboard – where I find myself futilely typing out woozy, endless sentences, longing for some bit of his lucidity.

The Collected Stories
William Trevor

I've lately been in the habit of reading one story of his a day, and I'm always amazed – as with Penelope Fitzgerald – at how quickly he's able to sketch a scene, a life, and how mercilessly he's willing to subject his characters to their miserable fates. Strange that such a depressing writer could leave you so elated.

The Last Samurai
Helen DeWitt

The more I reread this book, the more I love it. At first glance it seems messy and even hysterical (it's full of untranslated Greek and Japanese and obscure literary and historical allusions) but after a hundred or so pages you find yourself following it with no trouble, and you find too that it's graceful and funny and even moving. Hardly ever have I seen the action of a mind so faithfully presented. ■

A Day in the Life of Ben Dolnick

SINCE *ZOOLOGY* WAS published, two things in my life have changed: I've stopped tutoring, and I've adopted a dog. Any time freed up by the first of these developments has been more than filled by the second. On a typical day now I wake up and spend an hour or so in the park, throwing the ball for Bonnie and hoping she doesn't get into anything disgusting (the other morning she ate a dead pigeon). Then I make myself coffee, and write and edit and stare out the window until lunch. I'm working on a second novel now, and this is fitful, frustrating, addictive work.

In the afternoon I usually read for a bit (a short story or a few pages of a novel) and then work for a bit longer on my own stuff before heading out to shop for dinner. Next thing I know it's evening and Bonnie's pinballing around the apartment, letting my girlfriend and me know that she wouldn't mind another trip to the park. And then to bed. All of this, I should add, is punctuated by bouts of email checking, and trying to remember when my library books are due, and rearranging the clutter on my desk. ∎

How I Wrote *Zoology*

by Ben Dolnick

WRITING, LIKE TIDYING the apartment, is an activity that I seem capable of doing only in little gasps, and with the promise of a peanut-butter and Nutella sandwich afterwards. Occasionally I read interviews with writers who describe sitting at their desks for eight hours at a stretch, typing until the letters on their keyboards wear away, and I feel a guilty little drop in my stomach and haul out my Daily Planner. *If I start setting the alarm for seven, and editing yesterday's work while I eat breakfast, and …* Creating such a plan, I've discovered, can be so satisfying that I forget entirely about executing it.

I wrote *Zoology* over the course of about two years, mostly in hours stolen from one thing or another. I was working as a tutor in the evenings then, so the days had a countdown quality – I'd type for a bit, then flip open an old notebook or a Philip Roth novel, and notice that the clock had leapt a half-hour closer to four o'clock, when I needed to go out and be presentable. Sometimes on the train (most of my appointments were about an hour away) I'd have a crucial-seeming idea for a scene or a character and I'd scribble a page or two in the notebook I carried in my pocket, and then spend much of the following morning trying to decipher my own shaky scratchings. After lunch I'd write for an hour or so, only to realize just before I left the apartment that what I'd been writing was all wrong and would have to be thrown out, and so all during tutoring that night I'd be too despondent to remember the quadratic equation. The next day I'd resolve to work ▶

How I Wrote *Zoology*
(continued)

◀ steadily until I was *certain* I'd written something that would stay in the book, only to realize just as I was settling in that I was twenty minutes late for a dentist's appointment.

It seems hard to believe, describing it, that a book could ever come out of such a process, but somehow it did, it does – and this seems to be my method, if it can be called that. Writing a novel feels to me like swimming across a stretch of ocean, and having no 'stroke' at your disposal other than treading water. There isn't much to do except hold your head up and hope the tide is favourable.

And yet I hope to spend my entire working life at this, and in fact feel happier and less aware of time when I'm writing – when it's going well, when I'm deeply into a character or a paragraph – than at almost any other point in the day. A kind of fog seems to clear away, a mental soupiness evaporates, and I'm left feeling like I *could* do this for eight hours a day, I *could* wear my keyboard down to nubbins. The tide is carrying me along.

These periods of clarity and purpose, I've noticed, tend to follow a certain type of experience. The characters and incidents in *Zoology* don't come from my own life (though many of the settings do) but one thing in the book did happen to me, and it was just the sort of experience I'm referring to. I was biking one night between a bookstore and the house where I grew up – this was a summer when I was home from college – and suddenly, out of perfect darkness, fireflies began to light up, hundreds of them, and it was such a beautiful and unusual effect that I laughed

6 Writing, like tidying the apartment, is an activity that I seem capable of doing only in little gasps, and with the promise of a peanut-butter and Nutella sandwich afterwards. 9

out loud. I gave this experience to Margaret in the book, but I wanted to get it in there mostly as a way of honouring it, setting it apart, seeing if I could do justice to a particular moment at which the world seemed to show itself to me as being especially worth loving. I sped home from the bookstore and wrote down what had happened, and this impulse – to try to catch a piece of life in words – is why I suspect I'll be writing for the rest of my life. For all of its difficulties, all the days on which I find myself checking and rechecking the expiration dates in the fridge, it's the thing that – when I'm at my most alive – I feel compelled to do. ■

6 It seems hard to believe, describing it, that a book could ever come out of such a process, but somehow it did, it does – and this seems to be my method, if it can be called that. 9

Behind the Scenes

by Ben Dolnick

Scenes in *Zoology* with autobiographical significance

Somerset: Henry's elementary school is a real school, and it really is just a three-minute walk from my parents' front door. I've hardly been back since my fifth-grade graduation, and the school has recently been transformed into a massive, modern mall/fortress sort of place, but describing Somerset as it used to exist was one of my favourite parts of writing the book. In the first drafts of the book Henry's dad ran a bakery, but this never felt quite right. The whole time I was writing *Zoology* I worked as a tutor, and one afternoon I was working with a kid at his school and afterwards I went to the bathroom down the hall. The moment I walked in and saw those brown paper towel dispensers and the low urinals, and when I felt the terrible cold and smelled the dust rising from the radiator, I knew I had to get a school into the book, and I realized that the father's job was a way to do it. I felt like an internal traffic jam had just cleared.

Rio Grande: This is the Mexican restaurant in Bethesda where Henry picks up dinner for his parents and Walter when he's living at home. This was my favourite restaurant growing up – the one that I always clamoured for my parents to take us too – and I was thrilled to find a home for it in the book. I didn't get to describe it at all, not the strange pipe-covered ceiling nor the decorative sacks of rice nor the tortilla-making Rube Goldberg contraption, but that all comes to mind as soon as I hear the name. I knew that hardly anyone who read the book would know of the restaurant, but it felt important to me that when the Elinskys went out to dinner it was to a place I could smell, see and hear.

The pool: I'm not sure that any Manhattan apartments actually have swimming pools – I've certainly never seen one. But I wanted one in the book – I liked the idea of Henry ploughing anxiously through the water like one of *Hunt for Red October*'s submarines – and so I put a pool in David and Lucy's building. I wrote a few pages about it, and they felt OK but not quite as alive as I would have liked, so I went ahead and worked on other scenes. Then one day I was doing laundry and I added bleach to the machine (I have a gift for turning my white clothes pink), and as soon as I smelled the bleach I knew I could write about the pool the way I wanted to. The bleach transported me immediately to being seven years old, standing waiting for my dad to change clothes, listening to the showers running. When you get deeply into working on a book, I've found, the world really does seem to become a scavenger hunt of sensory clues – everything you encounter points the way towards something you've been writing about.

The subway and the homeless man: When Margaret and Henry are riding to Henry's first gig, a homeless man with a duffel bag full of sandwiches comes onto the train and asks for everyone's attention. This man still appears occasionally on the Lexington Avenue line, and his voice is one of the most remarkable instruments I've ever heard. It is genuinely ▶

15

Behind the Scenes
(continued)

◄ impossible to talk – or even to think – while his voice is booming. I could have devoted a whole chapter to it. The copy-editor at first changed his lines to ordinary type, but I insisted that they be put back in all caps. It still doesn't quite convey the power of his voice, but it gets closer.

The blackout: New York City did in fact have a blackout in the summer of 2003, but my experience of it was much less exciting than Henry's. I spent most of it sitting in my apartment, sweating, reading by flashlight and occasionally calling my parents in DC to see if there was any news about what was going on. At one point I did go out onto the street in search of food, and I found an atmosphere not unlike the cheery chaos I tried to describe in the book. I took notes on it as it was happening, but I didn't realize until many months later that this might be a nice backdrop for the book's climax. I wanted a spur, other than Margaret's leaving, for Henry to have a feeling of urgency and high stakes, and this intense, unusual night seemed to fit the bill.

Henry's search for Newman: One of the less pleasant features of working as a tutor was the travel. I was perpetually having to cross from one side of Manhattan to the other. I'd have a kid on the East Side followed by one on the West Side, and rather than wait for the crosstown bus, which tends to travel not much faster than a leisurely crawl, I'd walk. This was almost always an easy walk, but occasionally I'd manage to get lost on one of the paths and find myself popping back out on the same side from which I'd entered half an hour earlier. My sense of direction has always been horrendous – I used to need a map to get to the town basketball courts – but this experience seemed to have something to do with the park itself, how loopily it had been laid out. I knew that it would be a maddening place to look for a lost animal on a dark night – which, for my purposes, was all to the good. ■

Ben and 'Newman' in the zoo

If You Loved This, You Might Like ...

Extremely Loud and Incredibly Close
Jonathan Safran Foer

When his father is killed in the September 11 attacks on the World Trade Center, nine-year-old Oskar Schell sets out to search for the lock to fit the key he discovers in his father's cupboard. His journey to come to terms with his loss is beautifully interlaced with his grandparents' story, from their harrowing beginnings in Second World War Dresden to their experiences as immigrants in New York. A poignant and sensitive novel written in pyrotechnic prose.

....

Life of Pi
Yann Martel

This fantastical Man Booker Prize-winning novel is told in the voice of Pi, a sixteen-year-old Indian boy. It begins in Pondicherry, India, where his father runs the local zoo, but Pi's true adventures start when he is shipwrecked on a lifeboat – with only a crew of animals from the zoo for company. A dazzling work of imagination, hilarious and utterly original.

....

A Heartbreaking Work of Staggering Genius
Dave Eggers

A deeply moving and emotional account of the relationship between Dave Eggers and his seven-year-old brother after both their parents die within months of each other. Far from sentimental, this is a memoir infused with an incredible wit and energy which marks Eggers out as one of the great new voices of the twenty-first century.

The Rachel Papers
Martin Amis

Martin Amis's first novel, written in 1973, this is the story of Charles Highway, a highly intelligent, sex-driven teenager who is determined to have sex with an older woman before he reaches the age of twenty, by any means possible . . . A funny and light satire.

The Catcher in the Rye
J. D. Salinger

Salinger captures brilliantly what it means to be an alienated adolescent through the caustic voice of his sixteen-year-old narrator Holden Caulfield as he roams the streets of Manhattan over the course of a couple of days. A cult classic since its publication in 1951.

Breakfast at Tiffany's
Truman Capote

The adventures of a strong but vulnerable woman in New York in the 1940s as she tries to find happiness while running away from a difficult past. Audrey Hepburn made Holly Golightly an iconic figure in the film but it is the rich and lyrical prose in this short novel which makes it hard to forget. ∎